TESTIMONY OF AN

IRISH SLAVE GIRL

TESTIMONY OF AN
IRISH SLAVE GIRL

> *I was born Cot Daley, in the city of Galway, in the nation of Ireland. That would have been some time before the massacre of the Protestants, for I was above ten years of age when I was stolen for Barbados. . . .*

KATE McCAFFERTY

VIKING

VIKING

Published by the Penguin Group

Penguin Putnam Inc., 375 Hudson Street, New York, New York 10014, U.S.A.

Penguin Books Ltd, 80 Strand, London WC2R 0RL, England

Penguin Books Australia Ltd, 250 Camberwell Road, Camberwell, Victoria 3124, Australia

Penguin Books Canada Ltd, 10 Alcorn Avenue, Toronto, Ontario, Canada M4V 3B2

Penguin Books India (P) Ltd, 11 Community Centre, Panchsheel Park,
New Delhi - 110 017, India

Penguin Books (N.Z.) Ltd, Cnr Rosedale and Airborne Roads, Albany, Auckland, New Zealand

Penguin Books (South Africa) (Pty) Ltd, 24 Sturdee Avenue, Rosebank,
Johannesburg 2196, South Africa

Penguin Books Ltd, Registered Offices: Harmondsworth, Middlesex, England

First published in 2002 by Viking Penguin, a member of Penguin Putnam Inc.

1   3   5   7   9   10   8   6   4   2

LIBRARY OF CONGRESS CATALOGING-IN-PUBLICATION DATA

McCafferty, Kate.

Testimony of an Irish slave girl / Kate McCafferty.

p.   cm.

ISBN 0-670-03065-1

1. Barbados—Fiction.   2. Young women—Fiction.   3. Irish—Barbados—Fiction.
4. Indentured servants—Fiction.   5. Slave insurrections—Fiction.   I. Title.

PS3613.C33 T47 2001

813'.6—dc21   2001045604

This book is printed on acid-free paper. ∞

Printed in the United States of America
Set in Centaur MT
Designed by Nancy Resnick

For Patrick, Peter, and Suzanne

PREFACE

Between the reign of Elizabeth I of England (1558–1603) and the restoration of the monarchy with Charles II in 1660, an estimated 50,000 to 80,000 Irish men, women, and children were shipped to Barbados as indentured servants. Under Elizabeth, the British Empire expanded its labor market through a statute which called for the conscription of "tinkers, jugglers, peddlers, wanderers, idle laborers, loiterers, beggars, and such as could not give a good account of themselves."[1] After the Battle of Drogheda in 1649, The Lord Protector, Oliver Cromwell, stepped up the forced indenture of Irish political foes to the Crown, Roman Catholic priests, peasants whose farms had been appropriated as plantations and war spoils, and the unemployed or "dissolute" of the towns. During the 1650s, Peter Stubber, Governor of Galway, held as "usual practice . . . to take people out of their beds at night and sell them for slaves to the Indies."[2] In 1656, Lord Henry Cromwell, when requested to send "1,000 Irish Wenches," responded that "while we must use force in taking them up . . . you may have such a number of them as you shall think fit to make use upon this account," and added that 1,500 to 2,000 Irish boys aged twelve to fourteen could also be captured and sent.[3]

Obtaining the labor urgently needed to clear the rain forests of the colony of Barbados for plantation crops such as indigo, tobacco, and cotton had posed a serious problem since its foundation in 1627. The typical colonial method of enslaving aboriginal peoples was not practicable in Barbados. The Arawaks, native to the island, had abandoned it almost two centuries before for reasons still not understood by scholars. However, after the Battle of Drogheda the requisite labor force was available at £3 to £5 a head, payable to the mercantile companies whose ships transported the kidnapped, trepanned, or exiled slaves.

And slaves they were. The usual initial indenture was for a period of seven years, after sale in Barbados. During this period of time, the indentured's master determined the amount of food to be given, when and if medical attention would be called for, and what sort of corporal punishment would be meted out. Not until the Act for Ordaining the Rights Between Masters and Servants (1661) were bodies of dead servants ordered to be investigated with an eye toward the master's culpability.[4] While scholars have argued that the bodies of slaves belonged to their master while only the labor of indentured servants was his, noted authority on global slavery Orlando Patterson insists that this distinction "makes no sense whatsoever in real human terms."[5]

For indeed, masters sold and traded their servants (thus lengthening their terms), gambled them away, flogged them occasionally unto death, and in other ways demonstrated the ownership of their bodies. Irish indentured servants were referred to as "stock," were matched for forced breeding—indeed were designated as a subhuman species. In an example of this, historian Hillary Beckles chronicles a woman who was traded at market for a pig: she was weighed and valued at sixpence a pound, the pig at less per unit.[6]

Before the Restoration the planters of Barbados found indentured labor cheaper than African labor, although from the 1650s the latter was on the rise.[7] Until the 1660s the sanction which authorized African slavery was that the enslaved were pagans. Along that same line, Christians, it was held, should not technically enslave fellow Christians though this was never scrupulously followed. In line with this rationale, Africans were stolen to become bondsmen in perpetuity, while Europeans were stolen to be indentured for a finite period. However, legal acts and proclamations were easily enforced which extended the indenture of the bondservant for one, two, or three years, or which doubled her/his bondage. One escaped servant, Esquemeling, "had known many who had served thus for fifteen or twenty years."[8]

The same source, in 1664, informed the world that during indenture, "white servants" were treated as inferior chattel. Because they were cheaper and easy to obtain, "the toil imposed upon them [is] much harder than what they enjoined the Negroes, their slaves, for these they endeavor to preserve, being their perpetual bondsmen, but these white servants they care not whether they live or die, seeing they are to serve them no longer than seven years."[9]

History has proven that the Irish were not docile bondsmen, whether at home or abroad. The novel which follows is the story of a fictional Irishwoman trepanned to the island of Barbados in the year 1650 and sold into bondage; and of her imagined participation in one of the historically verifiable plans, undertaken jointly between Irish and African slaves, to overthrow the plantocracy of the island. The Irish perspective is important to the history of resistance to colonialism. It is also important because involuntary indentured servants "laid the foundation for African chattel slavery in Barbados."[10] But perhaps it is most important, at the beginning of the twenty-first century, as part of a little-known history of affiliation, across race and ethnicity, between groups conventionally defined as incompatible.

ACKNOWLEDGMENTS

A passing comment by Nate Mackey, writer, musician, and professor at UC Santa Cruz, impelled the first footstep, in 1989. I found another hint in the poetry of Edward Brathwaite, of the University of the West Indies. Pondering year after year what Harry Berger Jr. has to say about ascribed and achieved difference helped me examine expectations of both "race" and affiliation in a manner that seems more authentic. Gus Claffey of Creevagh, Clonmacnoise, taught me about generations of St. Kieran's pattern-day celebrations. My neighbors in the Kerry *gaeltacht* were great about translating the odd word or phrase into Gaelic for the text. And when I lost half the original manuscript from my hard drive during a gale, my good friend and neighbor Alice Hannafin saw that it was like losing a person I loved, and stood by me. A wandering Korean professor seeking shelter from another rainstorm encouraged me to rewrite, citing Tom Payne's experience, and insisting that the second take would be even better. I listened to him. Mary Reynolds of Malin Head was so matter-of-fact about the book's relevance that I had to believe it myself. While teaching at Dar Al Hekma College in Jeddah, Saudi Arabia, my colleagues Omarine Rafie, Dr. Aladin, and Suhair Al Qurashi taught me wonderful viewpoints on women, Islam, and history, which are lamentably still not available to the Western world. I was able to clarify the import of verifiable history to this fictional work through presenting a portion at a conference organized by my friend and colleague Dr. Maher Bahloul of the American University of Sharjah.

I want to thank my energetic and knowledgeable agent, Barbara Braun, who match-made my relationship with Kathryn Court of Viking Penguin. Kathryn, my editor, restores faith in postmodern publishing by harmonizing business acumen with visionary aesthetic sensibility. I am also indebted to Viking Penguin editors Alicia Bothwell and Sarah Manges.

There have been many whose critical appreciation has inspired the development of my work: among these, John Chandler, Marti Ainsworth, Lucille Clifton, Joy Harjo, Scott Momaday, Larry Evers, Betsy Breault, Laurie Voeltz, D. Coryat, and Andy Lynch, Bonnie Bassett and Greg Steltenpohl. The image is of guide ropes beside a swinging bridge. I most often cross that bridge, trying to both enter and question alternative worlds, with Judith Neva Johnson. To all of these, and you, I tell Cot's story.

TESTIMONY OF AN

IRISH SLAVE GIRL

I

When he has finished attending the select sick of Speightstown Gaol, Peter Coote retires to his office to wash his hands. The slave named Lucy holds a basin of tepid water as he rubs his long fingers with soap, then rinses them. He raises his wet hands as she bends to set the pan on the fieldstones of the floor. Water trickles down his fingers and over his pulse, soaking the thickness of rolled-back linen and lace cuffs, as he waits. The pan scrapes on the floor. The water feels unclean; she moves too slowly, but he tries never to show impatience before an African.

Behind Coote the shutters stand open for any breeze from the garden of fruit trees. His back is to the light coming through the window, so that as Lucy straightens she cannot see his features, only a dark shape of head and body with a thin aura of light around the head. She cannot mark him staring at her hands, pink on the palm, earth-brown and tough from labor on top, as she takes the blue-and-white towel from her shoulder and offers it. She waits in silence as he wipes his hands in the cloth. Then from the dark shape that is his face his thin but pleasant voice says, "Lucy, when we are done, fetch the white woman to me."

"Cot Quashey," Lucy says.

"I believe the only white female on the prisoners' roster is named

Cot Daley," Peter corrects cheerfully. He rolls his clammy shirt cuffs down. Lucy tosses the towel over her shoulder once again and bends to lift the basin of soiled water, humming softly. "Before you leave," Coote instructs her, "close the jalousies. No damn use to wait for a breeze. Even the parrots desist their squawking in this heat. Listen . . ."

The slavewoman holds the basin motionlessly. With no reaction at all to his instruction, she stares at the wall to the left of his shoulder and continues to hum. Filtered sunlight limns the soft curve of her young cheek. He feels the usual twinge of irritation at a lack or slowness of response, but turns the feeling into evidence for his hypothesis. Coote is conducting a firsthand inquiry to advise his merchants' group in Bristol, concerning which of the lower races brought to bondage have the ability to focus, concentrate, think, obey, multiply, perform brute rote activity, etc.—and to what degree. Would it not be sound business to know which type of servant to purchase for which sort of work? Near fatal mistakes have been made in the past. He waves toward the window.

Lucy perches the pan on her hip and rolls the wooden slats almost closed with her free hand. When she has left the room, he goes to the escritoire and notes his observations of her "docile slowness" in the margins of the Apothecary's Journal. Then he takes down another ledger which contains the treatments given the sick at Speightstown Gaol and tallies the expenses for the medicaments dispensed this morning. Finished, he puts the ledgers back upon their shelf and pours himself tea before setting out the materials for the upcoming testimony. A batch of parchment. A small pot of squid ink. A wooden box of quills. A tray of white sand.

As he organizes himself he hears the water from the basin being hurled onto the hard-packed clay of the yard. It makes an oval slop, the sound of the shape of its shadow. The sudden action in the sleepy garden disturbs the dozing parrots. They craw and rustle for a moment. The sound their wings make flapping is the sound of something much larger than Peter Coote knows parrot wings to be.

When he is ready he steeples his hands, which emerge from their cuffs of flower-patterned Irish lace, on the thin sheaf of paper. His elbows lean lightly on the arms of a fruitwood chair. When the slave and the prisoner come to the door he says, "Lucy, you may take the tea things." To the other he says gravely, "You may sit down." He has removed a small velvet-backed chair from its place facing the escritoire because he knows the Irishwoman's back is at a stage of suppuration, despite his washes of comfrey and alum. Silk velvet stains easily—he has placed a low backless stool in its place. The prisoner slumps upon it now.

Lucy gathers his tea things onto a tray. Without a word she moves into the shadow of the fieldstone hall. Peter Coote watches her go, marveling at why her buttocks, beneath the rough-spun indigo-dyed petticoat, seem to swell immediately below her waist, perhaps six inches above the position of his own or those of the white woman seated now before him. He has noted this formation in African men as well as women, and postulates that it denotes, or perhaps leads to, a deformation of sensuality.

"Now," he says to the white woman. "You are wise to come forward under the circumstances. The flogging is over and done with, but the exile is yet ahead . . . as it says here, 'in the Caribbe islands, according to the Governor's *pleasure.*'" He looks up at the woman. He sees nothing; nothing memorable. An aged face and slight body, clad in a gray Osnabruck petticoat bedraggled at the hem. A rough wool shawl draped across the festering shoulders. Skinned-back hair under an unbleached cap makes her cheekbones jut like a red Indian's. The eyebrows are a faded cinnamon, eyelashes so blond they're almost albino. A few snaggled teeth, large pale eyes. To this nothingness he finishes, "And you will want to incur the Governor's pleasure when it comes to selecting your future home. A civilized place like Jamaica, perhaps, where a woman like yourself can earn a living from small barters . . ."

Peter Coote smoothes the lace of his cuffs back from his wrists. He uncaps the jar of ink, positioning it to the upper right of the stack of parchment, and intones, "So then, biddy. Kindly begin your testimony concerning the plot which our Governor has foiled. In which the Irish and the Africans together on this island"—he is writing his own words—"planned to rise up against the masters which God gave you in this life." From the hallway through the open door comes a slight rattle of silver against china. "Lucy! Go away from there," he calls sternly. Bare feet recede down the corridor until their slap diminishes entirely.

"I care not which rock I end my days on," the woman before Peter Coote says suddenly. "But I will tell my story, for my own purposes."

Coote chuckles dryly. "You are hardly in a position to further your own . . . purposes," he remarks after a pause.

The haggard prisoner before him insists, "I am indeed."

"Well what then?" asks Coote, choosing the path to amusement over that to annoyance.

"I will tell the Governor, Colonel Stede—or you as his man—I will give you testimony on one condition."

"And that, pray tell?"

"That it be *full* testimony. That you record everything I say, not simply what you seek."

"That is the trade?"

"If I'm to sing I must be given your word."

"But . . . what if I don't want to give it?" smiles Coote, lifting his powdered eyebrows toward her quizzically.

"I am ill, sir, who knows that better than yourself? I may have a hard time in the remembering of details," replies the woman curtly.

Everyone knows the transparent craftiness of the Irish. Coote refuses, now, to let his future fall into her hands. The task he's taken on is to serve the Governor by obtaining revelations from the captives who were involved in the latest plot.

"All right. Let us begin," he shrugs, dunking and wiping his quill, "at the beginning. Tell your full name and how came you here, unto this island."

"They call me Cot Quashey now, or Quashey's Cot, but I was born Cot Daley, in the city of Galway, in the nation of Ireland. That would have been some time before the massacre of the Protestants, for I was above ten years of age when I was stolen for Barbados.

"The Daleys were a tribe for journeying. In the times of kings in Ireland"—here Peter Coote raises his eyes and smiles indulgently, as if at a child's fable—"the Daleys were *seanachies*, what you call bards. They traveled the world in all its strangeness and brought back its songs, its tales and poetry and wisdom. There are Daleys, I have heard, in Galicia in Spain, in France, in Egypt—wherever there were people who valued the stories of the world. But by my time, or my grandfather's time, those who sat on their fine rumps in Ireland's courts no longer marveled at the stories told by those they deemed of lesser worth. And so, like everyone else, the Daleys learned to hold their tongues.

"My father's name was Mihawl, my mother's name was Moya, and I had one older brother, Martin, who had gone as apprentice to the quarries near Athlone. I had a sister Breed who married to Killcorrig before I was born, for I was the last sparkle in my father's eye, as they say.

"My father was a saddler and my mother kept a stall, selling viands in the market in Nun's Island there in Galway City. I remember so little of her. But on market days the farmers came to our house to sell her meat while the morning star still hung in the sky. Ours was a narrow house, double-storied above the workshop where my father had his saddlery, and I would wake sometimes, the cold steaming over my pallet, as my mother bent out the open window hauling up a haunch or side she had just purchased, with a rope. She was strong and sturdy, right up to her death. The license to sell victuals had been in my mother's family for a long time, and was handed down to her.

"My mother took me with her to market and sat me underneath an upturned cart. This was her stall. I squatted on a hessian sack with extra cuts of meat around me. Sometimes the market cats would crawl under with me, too. They kept the rats away but I must swat them when they tried to gnaw more than the scraps I fed them. The meat smelled like cold clean flesh and blood, only dead. The cats smelled nervous, dirty, and alive. I recall my mother's voice above me as she weighed and sold the meat. She spoke in Irish with our own sort of people, rich and poor. She spoke in English with the soldiers of the Sassenach.

"When I faced the street from below that stall, peeking through the loose weave of hessian sacks she hung to protect me from the weather, I saw the white hose and satin petticoats of the wealthy, the muddy boots of the militia, the bare feet and raw brogues of townspeople and farmers. The horses shat as they clipped by; the dogs lifted their legs to claim the smell of raw meat with a spray of urination.

"Away from the street I faced the boundary of my mother's skirts. They were brown and plain, except on holy days when she donned a scarlet overskirt. When I sidled close, the heat of her came through the cloth. And every now and again, even whilst she might be talking with a customer, her hand would slip beneath the cart's edge and seek my face. Her hand was coarse and thick and often cold; and it seemed very large, for it could cup my entire jaw from ear to ear. I still remember the scratchy gentleness of her fingers on my cheek. Through contrast, her hands taught me my own young smoothness. The smell of mortal meat was always on her hands; in summer they were oilier and darkened.

"As a wee'n my whole world revolved between our alley in Galway, the market of the victualers, and an annual pilgrimage of thanks and merrymaking which my parents always brought me to. This feast happened on Saint Kieran's Day, September ninth, down in Clonmacnoise; and its being close to Athlone there were times when my brother Martin got leave to join us. We made the pattern to Saint Kieran, spiraling his well as the bashful cattle stared from the margins of the field. People dunked their hands into the black scummed water to banish warts and carbuncles. Along the roadside, tinkers lined their orange and yellow painted carts, selling potatoes, boiled eggs, fortunes, relics, and the like. Our own cart we parked in a field beside the Shannon, where I collected swan feathers in the morning fog, when the tide breathed out. Close by the banks where our cart sat was a midden where my father liked to fish, saying that the old ones knew the deepest pools where the biggest fish had made their cities from time untold.

"We went to Clonmacnoise to keep a vow: my mother had been barren for six years after her wedding, till a neighbor brought her to Saint Kieran's pattern day. They took her to a holy stone at midnight, where she hiked her skirts, sat on the rock, and prayed." Cot Quashey snaps her fingers once. "Like that, the children came— first Breed, then Martin. And twenty years later, Saint Kieran still kept them in mind: for when the field seemed dried up, I sprouted into their lives.

"My old ones would attend the Masses and the rosaries, while I scrambled up the midden. This was the place where the old forest dwellers, who wore skins and roamed together, came to catch their fish, dig mollusks from the mud, and trap the unsuspecting deer. There, in the mound we call the *fulachta fiadh,* they roasted their catches and their kills, and feasted all together. I played there, poking sticks into the mound, piling the Shannon's slick gray stones and shells around its base, pretending I was mother of a tribe, a-feasting. 'Twas there I basked inside the child's wordless, humming confidence that the sun, the river and the breeze, the folk, the fish, the bawling cows—all would provide for me.

"But then my mother died when I was six or so, of brain fever, and I was left to the care of my father. I cannot tell you much of him either. He bade me eat and be quiet, and sit by the hearth to fetch him this and that. My father was renowned for his harnesses and especially for the collars that he made. A collar must fit close so as not to rub; yet not too tight, for a horse's neck swells beneath a heavy load. They said he made a bit that sat in a horse's mouth like a sugar-teat in the mouth of a teething child, so that the horse would come to take the pressure as helpful in its travail, and not treat the bit as an enemy. It was like this too with the harnesses he made. They were systems for guidance, not prisons for the head. You wit that I learned something of horses from my sire.

"He was a man uncommon thin, who mostly sat in the corner stitching leathers, pounding nails, while firelight and brown shadows played over his bones. I would watch him. He was so frail I was often frightened that he would follow where my mother'd gone, and leave me all alone.

"He liked a drop or two as well, and I remember that he used to squeeze my hand and nod and wink, when he was at the jar. I used to feel confused, for I never knew what the nod agreed to, or what bargain the squeeze was meant to seal.

"Two autumns after my mother died, my father sent me to the convent to learn from the sisters there. I returned home every Sunday and every holy day and cooked a meal for him. He loved his stirabout and a fine lump of meat, and praised my cooking. The nuns taught me English, and to read and write and cipher to a degree. I remember that the abbey kitchen smelled like cabbage. The chapel smelled like cold ashes and doused fire. But my father's house smelled like bacon, and leather scraped and twisted. Leather smells like animal sweat: the scent of the animal partly wakens once again under the heat of human hands."

"It seems you lived by your nostrils when you were young," Coote remarks dryly. "Pray get on with it."

"The nuns were like old aunts to me, because I had no Mam. I did shy duty by my sire and he by me. We went no more to Clonmacnoise, but he took me to two horse fairs up the country, for he needed help with the young colts along the way. And the fifth summer after my mother's death—my last in his keeping—he took me to Cruach Padriag, where I scrambled barefoot up the scree to ask peace for her soul. But I was glad to return to my Galway convent, and the waiting nuns with their female smells and softnesses.

"And so my small years passed, until the Yuletide when I was about eleven years of age. That year some women in our street prevailed upon my father that I should go a-wrenning on Saint Stephen's Day with their children—children who had been my playmates before my mother died, though I knew them only by sight since I had gone to live at the convent. Do you know the Lá Droilean, sir, and the custom of the wren? In the countryside the bands of people might go off into the bushes, and catch the wren, and break its pretty neck. For the wren it was who led the Roman soldiers to the bush where Christ knelt hidden, and betrayed him, and did the same to poor Saint Stephen. But in the city streets and alleyways we children only donned the masks of animals and wilder sprites, and danced along the streets, seeking charity in the name of the Lord.

"My father made my mask. He wove it of thick straw, a square sort of cage like the spirit of a byre in winter, come alive. It had slitty-slanty holes which my own eyes stared through. Over my woolen petticoat and bodice I wore a surcoat of my father's. I remember it was gray, and the skirt of it was tied into a knot behind me like a tail. My hair hung down all goldy-red in the mirror in the winter's light, and like a lion, mane and all, my father said I looked. He stood in the half-door as I joined the neighbor children. I did not know them really anymore, for since my mother died my time was spent with nuns, or in the saddlery. I was not allowed out of the house on my own. Once, when I was eight, my father had sent me off to buy some eggs at market, but I made my way to the laneway of the victualers. I thought I saw her there, hefting the dark joints of beef and hams above her cart. A cat came to wind and purr about my legs. I was afraid to cross the lane and come closer, in case, because of my approach, she turned into a stranger. But I was also afraid to go away, in case this time she'd leave forever. So I stood in the gutter in the rain while the cat whinged round my ankles.

"When they came to find me they told me I'd been lost. I said nothing, thinking how I'd go back again soon as I might, and even if it were her *phuca*—her ghost, you'd say—I'd be with her. But after that my father kept me in with him on holy days and Sundays, and I forgot the looks and ways of the streets which I had moved in safety through with my mother, for she was like the queen of the market folk, I think.

"When I set out a-wrenning that Saint Stephen's Day, my father, Mihawl Daley, tucked my mother's brass ha'penny whistle into the pocket of the big gray coat I wore, that I might play a tune for charity. 'Do you recall your old mother playing a jig on that for you when you was small?' he asked. But I didn't. Later, on the boat and in my early years on this infernal island, I tried and tried to imagine those same thick stiff fingers that sought my face in the dim storage space beneath the stall, curling around the shaft of golden metal. Lifting, curved; tapping down again so neatly on the close-set holes. Music, my mother, abandonment, betrayal, more—all wound into a druid's knot within my mind.

"Disembodied: in the dark—floating detached from her sturdy arms and her warm skirts—that was the only way I could summon up my mother's hands, or imagine them playing a tune to comfort me."

· · ·

"First we wrenned for my father. There were several of us, I among the largest, and we milled in circles in the dance as someone behind a wolf's mask beat a drum. Another played the pipes. But always at the corner of my memory, most vividly, is the swirl of a girl's striped cotton petticoat. It was pink and gray, though once it may have been red and white; and it flared from her bare legs and the brogues tied to her feet as she twirled. The drummer thrust a broken cup out to my father. "Ah, may God bless us all," Father said, morose and tender. He put a coin into the cup. Then we ran on down the narrow street with voices shrill and thumping feet; with sticks clacking and two tunes played at once on different whistles. One by one or all together we cried out, 'The wren is the king of all the birds!' and 'Give us a penny to bury the wren.' We swooped to the doors of market vendors, the midwife, a joiner and his apprentices out sawing planks before their shop in the crisp air. The wife of a seaman lived where the lane swung off in two directions: she gave us a penny and a great chunk of brack for our hunger. And so we danced along. There was . . . was it Nell, whose Mam was a fowler . . . ?"

The Irishwoman's voice fades. Her eyes search the dim sepia corners of the Apothecary's office. "Was that her name? Sure, I can't remember now. Their faces were all masked in straw or motley, or as goats and bears and horses and the like . . . The street was runneled thick with mud from the winter rains, laden carts, and horses' treading. There must have been peat smoke in the air on a cold afternoon like that, and the rich smells of Christmas meats a-roasting. But no. I try to clutch onto those last moments in the place that I was born to, but I was so busy *living* them! How was I to know I'd have to capture everything I ever wanted to remember of Eire for the rest of my life?

"Then the afternoon was growing dimmer. Some children turned toward home again after the seaman's woman's house. But those of us still singing, jumping, clanking coins against the cup, turned down a lane I had not seen before. Dusk came upon us suddenly in that narrow street, its sky blocked out by overhanging balconies. But fire glow shone through open shutters and half-doors beneath a row of signs a-swing. I looked up and saw a donkey and a tankard, blue and gold, on the sign whose door we ran toward next.

"There was a woman standing in it, fine and big, just like a mother. Her rough strong fists were bunched at her waist on either side of her red skirt. 'Come in, ye little wrens, come in to us,' she laughed. The chins of two men leaned over her shoulders, making round eyes at us and jesting.

"At this point the little drummer ran away. Perhaps it was good luck, or else his saints were with him, but he shrieked with laughter and was gone, cloak swirling round his dirty feet. The girl with the striped petticoat was with us still. She and I locked elbows and swung high as someone tootled on the pipes. That girl wore a mask like mine, a mask of the field: the mystery of both harvest's bounty and winter's death, and the dry silent seed that lies behind everything. When our tune ended the little drummer with the broken cup had not returned, so the men behind the woman at the door reached pennies down into our upcurled palms.

"Then the woman moved to stand aside. A fireplace blazed in the stone wall to the left of the door. Her skirt was taffeta and caught the orange and purple flutters of the flames. She bent a little forward from the waist and held her tankard down. Her bodice was unlaced, her breast powdered and sweaty, and her teeth tiny and even. In the firelight her eyes, dark eyes, sparkled with mirth. She found my own eyes underneath the mask and held them.

"'Will ye not come in for a cup of punch, my dears?' she smiled as we shuffled in the street. There was a smaller lad in front of me as we pressed past her: I recall his head, masked as a goat, jutting ahead as he peered around the room. I crept close to that safe, gay skirt and taking out my brass whistle made as though to play it. But only squeaks and squawks came out. The woman set her drink quickly on a bench. Her hands dipped suddenly like heavy birds. She raised my mask as one hand swept under and behind my hair, lifting it to drape over the shimmering green stuff of her sleeve. 'Ah, yes,' she cried. Of the publican she commanded, 'You Baldy, mix up your finest Yuletide posset for this child.'

The little lad who had entered the tavern before me was taken up onto the knee of an old seam-faced seaman with one leg, who sat at a sort of low bench. I remember the brownness of that man's face. Even on that cold winter's eve he wore a waistcoat with no sleeves; his iron arms were covered with wavery blue-scrolled designs. He was tickling the boy who began to squirm away, when suddenly he lifted him into the air by the scruff of the neck, as if weighing a sack of goods. While the merry din went on around me the lad dangled, goat mask askew, face purpling, from the seaman's fist. 'Somewhat too small, this one, for work,' the seaman mused. 'Pity though. He's a beauty, ain't he?'

"The woman saw me watching this. From outside the voice of the girl in the striped petticoat called 'Seamus? Seamus!' The woman inside snapped her fingers. 'Baldy, the punch! Simon, put him down if he won't do.' The one-legged man dropped the little boy from a height above his own head onto the rushes of the floor. As the child knelt coughing for his breath, the sailor reached down absently to fluff up his brown curls. 'Ye're a lovely boy altogether,' he murmured.

"I saw all of this. Yet she had taken up my hand, and I stood lulled by the fire, the bright heavy skirt of shimmering colors, frozen with longing; not wanting her thick warm fingers to leave me go. Once, after the lad had crawled across the floor and pulled himself up on the open half-gate, he turned to look at me, child-to-child. He hesitated. But then a slender arm reached in from the darkened street and tugged his coat. There was a swing of striped petticoat, and he was yanked out into the street again. At that same moment the woman bent down, holding a warm cup to my lips. Ale and cloves poured from her breath as she cooed, 'Never mind, drink this now, darling.' And that was the last cup I drank on Ireland's soil."

The Irishwoman pauses. She lifts her shawl to adjust it and a pustulant odor wafts from her direction. Peter Coote flexes his fingers, wrinkling his nose involuntarily. He glances up. What an exceedingly pointless tale, he thinks. A waste of time and good foolscap. The only possible value might be that reverie will make her careless, and then secrets will out. "All well and good," he says blandly, "but will you soon get on to the conspiracy?" He reflects a moment. "The traitorous and murderous conspiracy which you knew about and aided?" he amends, writing this down for all posterity. Looking up he notices her eyes are blue. Raised to the light: a pallid, plain, and empty blue they seem to him, shot with red veins. "Biddy?"

But she is staring out the window at the becalmed garden. "The ship," she says, "was the *Falconer*, a slaver out of Bristol. I woke up in a cabin, on the floor, in a sort of nest of rags. I had been sick in them. There were nine females on that journey, all in the one cabin. I was the youngest, the last to be brought aboard just before we sailed. The others slept two to a bunk. The Captain locked us in each others' company against the crew and the men who'd sold themselves, or had been stolen. He wanted we girls fresh, he said, to command a higher price. Besides, he said, nine women would not go far among his crew, randy lads that they were.

"But there was one man of the crew he sent each morning for our slops, each midday with dry biscuit and salt meat, and each evening with our ration of water. This man was a castrate called Spaniole. No matter how we cried his name as we heaved our bile, or water slithered from the bilge over our ankles, or rats squealed at us from the corners, or a woman slid against the wall and gashed her head in the storm, he would not open the door except at the appointed times. Spaniole's nose had been lopped off, and then his private parts, the Captain said. He attended us in silence, but for the air sucking in and out of those great black tear-shaped nostrils.

"We saw the deck of the *Falconer* only twice during our journey. The first time we'd been out from home for several weeks already. One night, after Spaniole brought the water, we noticed that the sea rolled us less like live fish in a barrel. The next morning Spaniole tied us loosely to each other, the last to his own wrist, and led us up the shallow steps to air. The ship had anchored.

"The Captain came on deck to us. He stood at the railing in a fine blue coat with golden buttons, his hair tied back in powdered curls. His face was powdered too. It made his lips seem red and swollen. His eyes seemed rimmed in blood, he was so white. He looked diseased and elegant. He was a young man for a Captain.

"'For those who speak English,' he called in cultivated tones, 'we have put in here to take on fresh supplies. This,' and he swept his arm out to the side, 'is the Virginia colony.'

"'Sir, is this where we will be put ashore?' one girl called.

"'Did you sign on for here?' asked the Captain sternly, turning to stare at her. But none of us had signed on at all. We whispered and translated among ourselves, and looked down, confused.

"'If you did not sign on for Virginia, then Virginia is not for you,' he said. 'But if you were taken by the Spirits of the Night, then you belong to Night, and I shall deliver you to Night itself.'

"The Captain went away up to his deck with the spyglass. 'Come here to me,' Spaniole wheezed through his black holes, 'I am to show you some 'at of the colonies.' He drew us over to the railing by our common lead. The day was fine, the sea hard blue in choppy peaks. Before us the land lay, a strip of beach and gardens—toy roofs, a fort, a quay, pressed against by the dark flank of forest that led into those unfathomable lands. 'Look!' cried Spaniole. 'Do you see the fort? Can you mark our soldiers walking on the walls? There is a trading post within those gates . . .' One of the women began to wail at the sight of human habitation. I peered into the slapping waves, willing the merman or the white seahorses who can tip a boat, to strike at evil and take us off upon their backs. But they did not swim so far from home . . .

"Our gaoler paid no notice to our frantic babble. 'Over there!' he directed, 'at the quay. D'ye see our dinghy? They are taking on fresh meat. Wild fat hens are found a-plenty, and deer by the hundreds, such as some of those lads below deck was sold away for poaching. But here we trade the savages a handful of gewgaws for an entire carcass. Haw! And freely given is the water from that little crystal river leading inland . . . see it there, right by that copse of elms?'

"'Please? Pleasepleasepleaseplease please,' sobbed the last girl, tugging the rope that bound her to his hand. Another girl called futilely to the shore. 'Help! Help me!' A half-mile of stern sea rolled back at her.

"Then the Captain was at our side again, folding his spyglass into itself. From the hold below the stolen men kicked and pounded at the ceiling the deck made. The Captain said, 'I see Virginia colony appeals to you wenches, and you would fain remain here. Well, you will find the Indies even more to your taste. You have been sent out to begin a new life. And which of you,' he asked, looking us each slowly up and down, 'is not ready for a new life? Slatterns all!' He reached forward and tugged my hair, winding his hand in it up to the wrist then spreading the strands on top to peer into my scalp.

"'Nits!' he exclaimed in disgust, flinging my locks away. Then he began to pace. Wailings and pleas turned to quiet shiverings under his indifference. 'You will eat. We are taking food on board and you must fatten. You must look like you are good for clearing trees and planting fields and working like a man. The rough seas are behind us in this season; let your weeping and puking be behind you too, and wax well, for remember—the master who pays least, values least; and that without value is treated roughly the world over.'"

"It was early February when we lay off the Virginia colony. They let us scrub our cabin with icy seawater. Then Spaniole barred the door again and we heard the hold open and the lads led out, as they had been each day the storm was not so fierce that it would blow a man not tied to the mast into the sea."

Peter Coote yawns. The heat makes him sleepy. It ruins his appetite; on the other hand boredom piques his desire to roll something refined and memorable on his tongue. He feels the stirrings of both nausea and hunger, and belches discreetly into a cuff.

"The next time that we came to deck was on the final day but one. Already we stood anchored out of Hole Town Harbor in the Parish of St. James. And I knew not which I wanted more—to stop and step out onto firm land, or for the ship to heave the seas forever.

"Oh, it was a great surprise, to find that Hell is fair. Like Tir na nOg or paradise or Eden it appears. A great part of its torment is that it is so lovely.

"Once more we were tied and brought up from that sewer where we lay, moaning and squabbling like dogs. Up the narrow ladder, stumping our bare toes against the splintery steps. We had lived for months now in a world of brown and black; the only light a beam of amber soaked up by a wallboard or the folds of a filthy sheet, through the door that opened twice daily behind Spaniole. Now he led us up the stairs, lifting his forearm against the hatch as we emerged into the quivering, singing air. And I knew then—though I forgot it later under necessities that seemed more pressing—that the world here on this island was inverted. For if we were delivered up to the Spirits of the Night, they wore the cruel motley of a summer's day.

"Even now, I remember the colors of the island that first morning. The smooth glass stripes of the sea, ink-blue where we lifted and sank on the waves, but paling to the brightest robin's egg where the water frothed and tugged the strand. Proud mountains loomed from behind a fringe of one-stemmed trees. They lifted my heart and tricked me, for they were green and ripe and gay as the mountains of Sligo where I had gone to horse fairs with my father. Why is it that the scent of the air, the tweet of birds circling the mast as if it were a maypole—why is it that every sense seemed to have a color? And they were the happiest of colors!

"This was February the seventeenth, in 1651. A morning like the first, or perhaps the last, in Eden. Our eyes stung with so much light. Spaniole bade us step behind some screens of canvas hung between two of the masts and strip off all our clothes. During this the Captain stood on the bridge, squinting his glass at the small harbor away to our left where two toy ships like our own bobbed at peace.

"Spaniole ushered us into this canvas cranny, curtained off from the deck and the sailors but open on the wide side to the land. He pointed to three large tubs of water, each with a cake of lye soap and a thick brush laid beside it. 'Take those caps off,' he ordered, 'and help each other wash your hair. Off with your smallclothes, now. Off! Put them in the buckets there, and touch them not again till ye are told.' We were all distraught. Unused to complete nakedness since childhood, even with ourselves, there were pleas and whimperings. Arms were not long enough to gather into hiding all that flesh. There were no bawds among us.

"Spaniole moved to stand guard outside our bath, his pistols drawn against the crew and the few self-sold bondsmen who assisted for the landing. And except for the plashing of the sea against the hull, a few low calls and laughter from the men, the playful harrying of a gull, the morning was fresh and calm. An older girl helped me to bathe. The sun had warmed the water in the tub: fresh water, saved from Virginia for this. I took some in my mouth and tasted soap, and the oils and ashy flavors of the skin of girls who'd bathed before me. After the bath, we sat upon the edges of the tubs, on upturned buckets, on an inverted lifeboat. I rested on the salt-scoured deck, knees tight to chest. We lifted our hair modestly, one handful at a time, to dry; for it was our only covering. But every maiden there had hair which let loose past her hips. Yellow it was, and sandy; even the plainest brown held gold and purple lights, and there was sooty black, and an orange like winter flames, and mine, like apple cider in the sun.

"No one harmed us as we waited on that deck for the next word from our keepers. So that we grew lulled, rocking there together as the sun pinked arms and cheeks. Time lied. It seemed to liquefy and flow until there came a feeling as if harm could never come to us. As if we were nine women in a myth; for between ourselves and what we could see of land, all seemed so innocent, and clean. And beauty has a quality all of its own that seems supreme; that seems above mere men with slaving ships and pistols . . .

"But then the Captain parted our canvas drapes and stepped in-side carrying a chair. There was a cringing and a scatter. One girl ran to pull a corner of the canvas over her belly. Another screamed. The one who'd bathed me reached toward a clothes bucket, tossing out three caps in an effort to find a covering cloth. But I did not move. The sun had languored me. I squatted underneath my hair, which in that crouch hung to my ankles, and willed myself invisi-ble, by all the power of Our Lady of the Seas.

"The Captain sat him down. He bade Spaniole to keep without; and to the men who paused in their work, whose heads we saw lifted toward us as the curtain closed, he called in a dry voice, 'Carry on there, gentlemen, no sense to draw the lash or pistol when so near the fleshpots of the shore.'

"The Captain made each of us come near him, one by one. The second lass cursed him in our tongue, and though he knew not her words he took her by the wrist and twisted it up behind her back until she squealed for mercy. The Captain examined each in her nakedness, gripping the arms and the thighs for muscle. He looked into our mouths and up our noses. 'The black-haired wench is with child,' he called out to Spaniole as he regarded her nipples.

"'Wet nurse then, sir, shall she go for,' the cheery reply came on the tangy breeze.

"I was the last. The Captain held his hand forth with a smile and bade me rise. He pulled me close, parted my hair, and passed his hand down the front of me from crown to knee. He squeezed my kneecap hard; and I laughed, startled, for it tickled. Under his powder in that scouring sun I could see the purpley marks of pox. He grinned. His teeth were slick and yellow in that powdered mask.

"'Ah, but you, you are the prettiest of all,' he murmured. 'Bend down.' He checked my head for nits. 'Better. This is lovely hair. You speak English too, do you not?'

"I nodded yes. The Captain took me on his knee. One arm about my waist, lightly, he raised the other to unbuckle his short cape. He swung this around my shoulders. 'Translate,' he ordered. All the while that, through me, he ordered the women to wash their garments in the bathwater and turn them to dry quickly now, he ran his hand idly up and down beneath the cape. The woman who had bathed me stared at him with hot malice all the while she rubbed cloth at the tubs. But I willed her not to do so. As I tell you this, my heart remembers: it pumps in guilt and fear again. For I looked toward shore and all the lovely strangeness there, then I looked at the Captain's face so close to mine. And I willed him to keep me, just me, and not send me off to that broad strand where hundreds like him, like Spaniole and the crewmen and the men below held off with ropes and chains, could get at me. This is why I smiled up into his chalky face and yellow teeth.

"The Captain murmured 'Mmmmm? Mmmmmmmm? My filthy little mouse?' And then he set me down. With a smack against my buttocks he lifted his cape and pushed me toward the others round the tubs.

"Our clothes dried quickly. At the end, to hurry us along, the

Captain sent Spaniole inside the nook to watch us, with his heavy breathing. Spaniole took us back down to the hole. Our sun-stiff petticoats scratched against our sunburnt legs as we went down the stairwell. In the cabin's close darkness, the bile and blood and slops and tears and phlegm of the journey were conjured up again by the high heat of Barbados. Later we heard the men taken out and walked. Along toward evening the sea shifted beneath us; and later all among us stopped our frenzied unsuccessful prayers and speculations to listen to the faint but clear strains of some sailor's concertina, above us on the deck.

"I have heard that on the night before great battles soldiers often do not sleep, but under the eye of death take on a last wondrous animation. That was not so with us. We slept. We tossed and snored and spluttered; whether in exhaustion from the unaccustomed sun, or in hiding from the shame of prying hands and the memory of the crew's eyes, glimpsed through a slit in the canvas drape, which shone with the same empty muscular hunger as a bucketful of living eels. We slept until Spaniole thumped a longboat oar against the door. He opened it and cried, 'Freshen up, demoiselles. Your hour is come.'

"There were four sailors in the small boat below the sisal ladder. Each wore an unsheathed dagger at his waist. Spaniole explained to us with gestures what they and we must do. As the ship bobbed above the black hills of the sea, we were carried down the rope ladder and set into the boat. I think it so strange now that although we all believed in a better life in Heaven to come, there was no inkling of hastening that day by leaping to our deaths. I never thought of such an avenue until I met up with the Africans. No: we had been taught to see ourselves as Heaven's supplicants, not Heaven's instruments. Not Heaven's tools emerging from the fire and the blows.

"In silence we were carried down and set on benches by our guards. We were left untied, for we must wade ashore from the swells and not pull one another down like awkward weights. Hope . . .

hope it was, bred into us, that made us think a better day surely must wait onshore. What the Africans have is more . . . apt, wiser . . . than hope."

Peter Coote gives his head a little shake. He has almost fallen into a doze to the lilt of her unceasing voice. He's stopped writing; but now he hastens pen to pot and then to paper, for he has heard her link herself with Africans for the first time. "Stop," he commands. When he has caught her missing words or what he imagines them to be, brusquely he says, "Continue."

"Water," the woman Cot replies.

A wave of ill humor washes over Peter Coote. The breakfast fruit has soured his mouth and furred his tongue. His hand is cramped, the top knuckle of the middle finger stained with ink. He flips his cuffs well back. "No," he insists. "You will speak until I have had enough, and then be done for today."

The woman is silent. He finds her wide mouth sullen. "Don't try me, biddy," he warns.

"You are right," she says. "'Tis ye who are trying me, is it not? On behalf of your . . . master." She draws herself in under the shawl until she seems to have no shoulders: she has a slight back to hold so many lashes, he thinks. He sits there, pen poised, prepared to learn of Africans and the treachery which took root in her small, primitive Christian soul, sent to be obedient to her betters on the island of Barbados. But she returns to the story of the girls: "We put out in the small boat. We were going to our doom, and we knew it; the black-haired girl called out to Christ to receive her.

"Yet how could doom be upon us? For the sailors were conversing merrily as they rowed. And halfway to shore a silver school of dolphins joined the skiff and danced beside us. There were two longboats of indentured men already up ahead of us toward shore. Those few who had signed on sat unmanacled, rowing beside the crewmen. The others leaned, lashed together loosely at the waist. Some held their heads down, some looked bold and brave ahead.

One man cursed steadily as if he told a litany. One young lad, I remember, was singing about a place named Drummossie. I recall that place-name although not one of the girls' names I billeted with on that long voyage to hell. Only the colors of their hair, sprayed out around their caps by the sweet breeze.

"Yes, I remember best the colors. For there is a glow to hell, and from it came so much light that while my mouth stuck shut with fear, and many of my fellow humans made noises like grieving animals, I was transfixed by the blue bath of the sea and the gilded arcing fins of fish which sliced the air then plunged again.

"I felt nothing, save for cool spray on my forearms.

"I heard the clacketting of palm leaves on the shore over the tears of women in my boat.

"I marveled at a thread of yellow in the rigging of a sloop in the bay ahead of us; an orange banner snapping crisply above a Dutch low-bellied trader; the tan sand below the ever-paling water, which our prow now shot onto.

"'Take hold! Clasp hands!' a sailor called, as he leapt out holding the line, up to his waist in water. When the next swell had sucked back out to sea, we jumped and lifted our soaked skirts. In my small fists I clenched the hands and skirts of women on either side. When the next wave came they lifted me between them and kept running. I remember how one called, '*Fair amach dos na miola mora!* Look out for the shark! Look out for the shark!'

"Then there we were on the beach. But even then, while the men waited tied in a coffle ahead of us under a guard of seamen who pointed muskets and pistols, even then I looked away from our certain plight. Looked toward loveliness. For fanned around my feet— yellow and red and coral pink, pearliest white and the black of Vulcan glass—were tiny stones and curly shells which the clear water waved and winked at me like baubles . . ."

·   ·   ·

"Thus came ye to the island of Barbados on February eighteenth, in the year of our Lord 1651," overvoices Peter Coote. "And a long morning's telling of it too. You give your history great importance, biddy. Return now to your mat. Dip the cloths I left you in the medicine and wrap them over your back; but take care to remove them before they stick to your weals, or you will rue it."

The woman stands, but does not thank him for his expertise. This sours his remaining bit of goodwill. He screws the lid onto the inkpot at an angle. "Lucy! Lucy!" he shouts. When the slave appears, far too soon to have been at her appointed tasks in the garden cooking shed, he orders, "Take the prisoner back to the sick-house, then fetch my lunch. I shall want lemon in the water when I bathe my hands, to get off this blasted ink."

II

When he was twenty-five Peter Coote came out from Oxford to make his fortune in the Indies, after investing the entire younger-son's portion of his father's holdings in an up-and-coming shipping concern with offices in Bristol. The company provided him with a post as ship's surgeon for the passage to Barbados. That had been fifteen years ago, in 1669; a year when excessive rains hard on the heels of drought resulted in a scourge of epidemics among plantation workers. Coote had judged he was arriving at a most propitious moment, for while hundreds of lives were lost, hundreds more were saved through treatments like his own tonics and cuppings, purgings and lettings, and luck, of course, herself. The value of good medical men to plantation economics was thus established. Coote had been appointed Apothecary to Codrington and Cornwall—two of the largest holdings, with hundreds of acres in sugar and tens of thousands of pounds invested in primarily African bondsmen.

But the thrifty managers of these plantations took great care that outside services were utilized with parsimony. Fifteen years had passed, Coote attaching himself to one owner, another manager, most recently an Anglican priest with a wealthy congregation; yet he barely eked along between the goodwill of them all. He still held no acreage of his own.

Then at last year's Christmas ball the Anglican—one Reverend Aynes—had introduced him to a weathered man in rose peau de soie and a lustrous brown wig.

"Governor, may I present the finest young apothecary to come to us from London in many years? Presently he tends the slaves at Codrington, and . . . Colonel Stede, Doctor Coote."

To Aynes, Peter noticed, as to all the wealthy planters he had met, his own existence on the island seemed to begin at the moment he made their personal acquaintance. Peter held out his hand and bowed. His fingers were not taken, and he curled them back toward his chest in a graceful gesture. When he straightened he found the new Governor chewing a sweetmeat and gazing at him with wet black eyes.

". . . the latest in surgical techniques as well," muttered the minister.

"How do you regard your labors with these creatures, sir?" asked Colonel Stede, catching a drop of nougat on his lower lip and sucking it in, froglike.

"Your Excellency, I feel I am protecting our investments . . . guarding our profits . . . ," the younger man began.

"You say 'our,' Doctor Coote. I don't recall your holdings: Is your family here upon the land?"

"My inheritance lies with a consortium of shippers based in Bristol, Lordship, and my investments, in that sense, depend upon the land. But when I say 'our' I mean all Englishmen, whose colony this is." His voice, in this utterance, swelled boldly in proud affiliation.

"That it is *not!*" the Governor snapped. "Many an English rogue shipped here in chains has been freed from servitude to foul our shores. Up in the northern parishes they multiply like hares . . . thieves, swindlers, lewd livers. Problems. Problems, to be sure."

"That ilk, of course, sir," Coote hastily replied. "Though Cornwall and Codrington have, conversely, successfully employed English freedmen as militia against the ill will of the blacks."

The Governor shook his withered jowls and incongruous ringlets from side to side. He dabbed his lips with a lace-edged handkerchief and tucked it up his sleeve.

"Yes—a necessity," he mused. "Chancy. One that must be dispensed with soon. 'Swounds, how am I to watch it all, to hold them all in check out here at the ends of the earth? Yet with the blessing of Divine Providence, it will be accomplished."

The Reverend Aynes nodded with pursed lips. "There must be limits. Strictest limits."

To what, to whom, did he refer? Coote mused. His own plan, back in '69, had been to rise up quickly through the ranks in Barbados. To become a landholder, not merely to increase and guard the wealth of others. But to date his own options had been limited—just enough to keep him in the required sort of lodgings; just enough to stable a nag to ride out on his weekly calls to the sick of the two plantations, and for medicines to carry on rare visits to the gentry. There was scarce enough left to keep up the necessary appearances—a beaver hat, fine linen shirts, and satin waistcoats by which one gentleman could recognize another sweating gentleman.

The merchant company in Bristol was foundering. Suicide and sickness among the trepanned Africans had devastated its anticipated profits. Pirates had attacked an important cargo of ivory off the Gold Coast, and only two years ago three ships laden with barreled rum and muscavado sugar had sunk in a squall off the Carolinas. The income gained in other years was reinvested. Coote had agreed to this rather than take on more investors who would only share the profits of the future, while he had shared the losses of the past.

Then suddenly last month a messenger had appeared in Bridgetown at the rooms of Peter Coote. "I mus' bide for your reply, sir," said the youth. At his desk Coote slid a tapered fingernail beneath the thick red sealing wax. He read,

"Doctor Coote, I am in need of an Apothecary-Surgeon at the Speightstown Gaol. This post will hold my utmost confidence, for some of the prisoners here are high traitors from the northern parishes. A great deal is hoped to be learned from their testimony. They should be kept alive until it has been given. Please consider. Your part-time duties at Codrington and Cornwall might be continued if so desired, but need not be, as this position brings with it a commission and an annual purse of 60 gold guineas: also a house and carriage, two fine mares; fowl, slaves, sows, and other stock to provide for your needs. Should you accept, I must know at once. An important batch of prisoners has recently been delivered. I am most anxious to learn what they will, or what they will not, tell of matters of a planned rebellion."

There had been nothing, really, to consider. To gain a commission without soldiering in the disease-ridden jungles of the Indies was amazing luck. But to become the King-appointed Governor's own man was best of all, given Coote's Anabaptist family roots in England. After the restoration of Charles II to the throne, these had become the wrong roots.

"Your Excellency," Coote scripted hastily while the lad tossed stones idly in the dust outside the door, "I shall be pleased to serve you in this and all things. I shall plan to quit my lodgings and await your word on my removal to Speightstown and the Gaol."

Now on this Tuesday morning, after a night with little sleep due to clicking lizards, whining insects, and the infernal heat, Coote feels peckish. He bids Lucy bring him a glass of hot coffee, well sugared. His impulse is to interrogate the Irishwoman as roughly and quickly as possible. She's the last surviving rebel: why humor the bold jade by penning her full and dismal tale? But an inner voice warns him:

be cautious. The Governor is seeking subtle links between the Irish and the Africans. No more names, really. By the time Peter Coote had ridden into Speightstown that first August morning, the bodies of eighteen rebel leaders already dangled overhead like sides of beef, twisting black and amber in the sun. He pushes the memory of flies feeding, of beaks pecking cartilage and ripping human gristle, from him now. "Lucy," he mumbles around the acid rising in his mouth, "Get the Irishwoman."

"Cot Quashey," Lucy replies, looking down upon him as he struggles with his bile behind a napkin. When she leaves the room, he reviews what he knows about the case. The proven slave leaders had been hanged for conspiracy to treason and revolt. Three Irish abettors had been executed down in Bridgetown. One Irishman had also been held here in Speightstown; but tortured too vigorously, he had expired before Coote's arrival, his lips still sealed except for "Feck yeese. I commend my soul to Christ."

The Governor thinks the Irishwoman, having been in bondage twenty years, having been bred with Africans, and by her female nature weaker and more fearful than the men, might provide information useful to future governance. Coote is to attempt to accumulate some understanding of how and why England's vassals in Barbados have thrice gone against their fellow Christians to align, against God and nature, with black Africans.

The woman had been apprehended two hours outside Six Men's Fort, a bundle for market perched on her head like an African wench. She approached steadily, past soldiers, past four black prisoners being led under the noon sun down to Speightstown for certain execution. The foot soldiers, parched, inquired of her burden. "Only green fruit of the paw tree, sirs," she'd replied. They were thirsty, hungry, bored. "We'll save ye the long walk to market, you smelly hag," one offered. But she would not hand the bundle down and retreated, muttering, when they went to take it from her. They requisitioned it with bayonets. When they set it on the ground and opened the unclean cloth, they found four pistols and a small swamp-cedar box of shot at the bottom, hidden by the bulbous fruits which leaked orange milk and wet black seeds. The Irishwoman was then tied to the file of agitated blacks, and marched along to gaol.

All lies, her first testimony that an unknown Irish huckster had traded her the weaponry for food, and that she was now bound for the capital to sell these pistols to some fine gentleman she knew only as "Ned." For over thirty years the Irish on this island had not been permitted to buy, or trade, or own, or sell a gun: any gentleman would know this, would report a breach, and would confiscate the guns.

At first the Governor insisted on the truth. His tack had changed, however, after eighteen dangled; yet each day the interrogators brought new names, in an ever-widening jigsaw of treason between Africans and the indentured, free Creoles, and those released redshanks who now lived under bushes and foraged for survival. In briefing Coote, the Governor had said, "I've hanged enough now to make clear the futile consequence of rising up against me. Better, perhaps, that the dregs who swarm this island believe a paltry, mad eighteen made mutiny, instead of ten score like themselves. D'you see? But between ourselves, man, we must find the links that give them the same vision . . ."

Coote himself had cut down the Irishwoman after the ritual of public whipping for violations of the Proclamation of 1656. He himself prescribed unguents for her lashes and powders against the fever that was inevitable, given the island humidity and the shock effect of thirty cuts. That day on the platform, sweltering in his plumed hat and brushed dove-colored gloves, Coote, as the Governor's representative, faced the crowd in front of the platform while behind him the prisoner was tied, her scarred back bared for the spectacle like a used canvas awaiting palimpsest. Cut down, she sagged face-first onto a mound of straw. So only yesterday, during the interrogation, had he assessed her full-face across his desk, eyeball to eyeball. A tough and stringy nothing, he's decided; without the strength or wit to mastermind rebellion.

Now he hears them coming, feet patting the stones. As they enter his presence, Lucy is guiding the smaller woman lightly by the elbow.

"Sit down, biddy," Coote orders irritably. "Lucy, you must make haste. Before you bring my lunch, you and the old man must drag the pallets into the sun, scour the flags, and lime the sick-house walls." During the night there have been two more deaths due to the bloody flux.

Lucy nods once, humming lightly.

"I will take a thick slice of that ham which Colonel Stede sent, for my noon meal," he instructs her receding back. Then, hurriedly, he turns to write, for the Irishwoman has begun to speak without his prompting.

"At first I thought this was the Devil's island. Look there"—she is pointing through the open shutters to where the sapling fruit trees shiver lightly in the morning breeze. Involuntarily his eyes follow her finger to the soft blue sky. An oriole draws slowly into shape within a leafy recess, tilting its black eyes from side to side.

"There were signs that seemed so definite," she explains. "Each day dawned with perfection, even in the rainy months. Birds caroled and the air threw perfumed nets of fruit and nutmeg. Every time the sun rose, it lifted my heart high with it—only to dash me further down with the full remembrance of my plight like blood returning to a sleeping limb. Desperate, the pain of that returning life.

"I was sure this was the Devil's land, for through his tricks with light Lucifer is Prince of Darkness. In a like way, although Barbados is a land bathed in warmth and sunshine, here, sir, do dark perversions bloom. I came to know the fierce vertigo of panting up into a blameless sky, only to meet the black swoon that came from too much heat, too much work, too little food. I came to see how, on this island, fertility becomes a monstrous thing. Day after day we whacked at crops and weeds that sprang back overnight. Ah, how beautiful, those scarlet-flowered vines that choked the trees to death; and orange and violet butterflies, lilting on leaves as sheer as silk, that tempted our eyes from work to pleasure, and drew the sudden shearing of the whip. Things brought the opposite of what they promised. And sometimes, when I had been betrayed again by beauty, I saw Satan's pet, the serpent, swimming away through the tree branches . . ."

Coote pulls toward the vision her words paint. He knows she speaks a truth he shrinks from, for he has ridden empty plantation roads at jasmine-scented noon, heart thumping with an inadmissible fear. But hearing her soft, full, wrinkled lips describe it now makes him angry. That this common slut should touch his own experience . . .

"You need not demonstrate your bardic family tendencies," he drawls. "Move toward the purpose we are in this room to accomplish, if you please. You stood in soggy petticoat on Hole Town strand when last we spoke." He dips a new nib in the ink and draws it toward him across the blotting sheet. It catches on a fiber in the paper and two tiny globules fly into the lace at his wrists, unnoticed.

"Arra," she mutters, "there were spirits—weren't we spirited away? And the best folk here, there, and everywhere draw the evil eye—and what about the number seven? Quashey's people also hold it sacred, they walk seven times around the holy stone . . . But I misread the signs, I held up the wrong lantern . . ."

"Biddy!"

"We were on the strand, then. It was a moment like forever. We turned toward the water whence we came. The young browned sailors in their red kerchiefs and rolled knee breeches were drawing the longboats tethered in their fists to shore. The Captain stood making notations in a small leathern book as Spaniole counted off the men tied neck-by-neck together. Before them marched the four-teen wretches who had volunteered for servitude. Wretches: for they would find their rations and their shelter, their work hours and the lash, the same as we who were impressed.

"The females followed all, flanked by Spaniole and the Captain. We were not tied. Our captors understood better than ourselves that fear was our tether: we would not even think of springing away into the trees, or forming colonies in caves in the mountains. Alas, we knew less of how to survive the wilderness than we knew how to survive in servitude to men. And with all that there were the scents of fruit on the air, and the nuts of the tree we learned was the palm clustered and crowded on their stalk, and certainly the sea behind us writhed with fish for the taking, including some that skipped and whizzed a ways above it—in spite of all this bounty, you see, so strange was the land that we turned in terror, with no ar-gument, toward the rise above the strand. For there we saw Chris-tian humans like ourselves, or more verily like our Captain; and they were bent over the edge to espy us, like curious people anywhere.

"Past them we were led, along a path dug deep and dusty by naked toes like ours, some of which lay molded in the stiffened mud. The residents of Hole Town who came for their first peek sped shouting ahead of us, until we all entered the little square that used to be there. You would not know it; now it has been built over with warehouses and market stalls and offices. But then there were, at the sides, two pens for holding cattle, or Africans, or Irish. To-ward the rear was another small rise, which on the day of my arrival served as a natural auction block. In front of this rise, tracks from the north and east and Bridgetown met, and a crowd of servants could gather to tend their masters' carriages and carts.

"We were taken to a large corral, all the unwilling lads and girls. The volunteers were auctioned first. Right eager did they look, to start their seven years ticking off behind them so they might sooner walk free to sign the forms for their own rich payment-parcel land. But of course, sir, you know that by 1651 no land remained to reward the loyal servants of Barbados.

"Of course no one Barbadosed understood that then; so from the aspirations of those volunteers many of us took what we called hope. But we learned it was not hope. Hope is when there is a real chance that what you long for will come true. Otherwise, we learned, what we'd called hope is cruelest self-deception. But those who sought our labors did not disabuse our hopefulness, for it made us docile; whereas oncet that truth had dashed our hopes, that hopelessness would work against our masters. Docility, sir, among we bondspeople, is a thing that we discourage even little children from. One ought to know it if one cannot better one's own lot, though every dog must avoid kicks when it can."

Behind in his scribbling, Coote is looping the final letters of these words when he realizes with a start that here's information of the sort the Governor has demanded. The temper of insurrection! But it's too late to stop her: she has turned into another verbal alley where he follows, hand racing, confident for the first time that bit by bit this foolish woman will let her loose tongue betray herself and all her scurvy kind. He feels contempt for her loquaciousness at the same time that its folly excites him.

"There were about two hundred in the stock pen, plus the sailors with their pistols and swords, guarding us. They sat us down around the railings of the corral and tied the men and boys to the posts. Myself and the black-haired girl spread our skirts together in the dust and watched the auction as it commenced. Throughout the afternoon the gentlemen on horseback, the carriages and overseers with their mules and carts, kept arriving. There were, in those days, only a few women—and no ladies—resident at Hole Town. I saw females fanning on a balcony, but only men strolled under sunshades on the auction green that day. Although the heat was wilting, they wore tall beaver hats and surcoats of satins and brocade, damask waistcoats, and breeches of the finest wool, buckled at the knee. They wore hose of cloth, not leather, like Spaniole and our Captain.

"The Captain led the auction, crossing and marking in his small book while a skinny lad held a violet umbrella over him. The Captain's face seemed almost ghoulish in its shade. At first, as I have said, he sold the volunteers. Although they mostly had professions, and so went for more than common laborers, from them we learned the rules of what awaited us. One sale I recall was of a Scots cooper and his son. The cooper was competed for. The Captain displayed barrels and a wheel he'd made on board our ship, with the result that in the end the Scot was sold for £9, and only for five years. This was unusual: almost everyone was sold for seven years. In increments of seven years, sir, the sprites also kidnap folk whose work or beauty they desire.

"The Scotsman's son, though, was a matter that brought a spasm to my heart, and to the pregnant girl's who held me in her lap. He was a small lad, eight years of age. And although his father argued that the boy had been apprenticed for two years already at the cooper's trade, he was sold as child, not adult. Which meant he went for £5 to the age of twenty-one: thirteen years, instead of seven, of his life belonged now to his master, in payment for the food and brogues the master would provide.

"With one hand in the pocket of my father's surcoat, clasped around my mother's flute, I whispered my fears to the dark-haired girl. You will remember I was then about eleven years of age. To be sold as child would mean I would belong to someone for almost as long as I had lived already. But sold as adult, my servitude would be for seven years. Án Cailín Dubh, I call her in my memory: she advised me to carry myself tall and pretend that I was thirteen, full a maiden, not a child.

"They gave us nothing to drink. Thirst made us sleepy and I drowsed upon her shoulder until the Captain called for her and she eased my face off from her sweating neck. I watched her go, and it was like before, her beauty freezing out the hellishness of things: for as they moved the gate aside for her, I admired the green sun through the bushes dappling the coarse weave of her skirt, and how her hair hung clean and sooty to her waist, like the proud daughter of a cottager on Brid's Eve. They led her to that little hill. She kept her eyes shut while the Captain sang her praises to the gentlemen who plumped and prodded her. I meant to do the same when my time came, but either I forgot, or I was of a different nature—curious. For £8 they went: herself as laborer and wet nurse; and the child to come, for its first twenty-one years.

"Soon after, I was led up to the auction block. 'Bring the poppet,' the Captain called out to Spaniole, and smiled. Some of the gentlemen smiled too. Lining the little track up the rise to the auction block, many bent toward my face. I remember how my heart thudded. A fish's thuds like that once it is caught and knows there is no out—so hard it makes the breast flop. The walk up was again in different time: very slow and floaty, yet not long enough. I had seen brides led to altar in Galway, and always thought that sort of time belonged to them.

"I was a small girl. Except where eyes and teeth bent down to me, I walked through two columns of shiny well-dressed stomachs, reaching hands, jabots and wigs draped around necks and shoulders. At the top the Captain waited, like a most genial host. 'Gentlemen, I start the bidding high for this young morsel.' There was a spatter of laughter from the crowd. The Captain told them I spoke English well and could translate to the other Irish. That because of language and a passive character I was fit to train as lady's maid—had they any ladies. More laughter at this remark. 'If not,' he said, untying my cap and lifting out my matted curls, ''Twon't be too long before she's ready to breed servants—and *you* may choose the father.' His eyebrows flew up in merriment at this statement. 'Hear hear!' cried someone jovially. 'How old, then, are you, poppet?'

asked the Captain. I was ready. 'Thirteen,' I cried in a loud flat voice. He fixed me with an interested stare. 'So small for thirteen,' he whispered. 'Have you yet begun your courses?' I lied to the whole hillside that I had. There was some scoffing, but also interest that one so childish might be woman too. One among these became my first master, Henry Plackler.

"They argued over me. 'So frail,' murmured Plackler. I knew to not look at his face, but kept my eyes fastened on the needlepoint of roses climbing trellises on his waistcoat. His hands as they gestured were ivory and small. 'I seek a girl for dual purposes—to work the fields unless my wife is visiting, and then a lady's maid . . .'

"The Captain tilted up my face toward his in the livid light of the violet sunshade. The air was stifling. His face was chalky, like the dead, like Amadan na Briona, the fool of the firth. 'This little damsel cannot leave my side for a farthing less than eight gold sovereigns,' he cooed. 'I should be paid double for keeping her fresh for the plantations of Barbados, for I was fain to tear a petal from her rose.'

"With every word he spake the laughter round us thickened, a laughter with a stench to it, like rotting teeth. But my new master did not laugh or take up the Captain's bantering. 'I will give you eight,' said he, 'but you must make me a sound bargain for those two gaolbirds tied to the post, or you are no friend to Barbados and her plantations.'

"They led me to a cart that waited and helped me crawl under a seat for shade. My master never approached the cart. It was the overseer, Jenks, who gave me corn cakes and told me to make my water over the side; 'For if you step onto the ground the snakes will attack you to settle their score with ould Saint Patrick,' he warned, waggling his finger. 'Although this island, where they were banished to, is much more to their liking.'

"I lay there hiding, tucked under a shelf against the corner. The sun was swallowed by the mountaintops, and the land turned blue.

'Seven-sixpence!' 'Ballocks your sixpence! Seven and twelve shillings!'
'Seven-fifteen!' sums were called. The Captain's voice grew gritty ex-
horting gentlemen to buy. Feet stumbled in the dust, stepped onto
the wheel rim, weighed it down, and hoisted another servant onto
the bed of the wagon where I waited.

"It was twilight, glowworms flickering here and there, when the
Captain came to settle his accounts. After Jenks had transferred
coins from the plantation purse, the Captain asked for me. 'Oh
mouse . . . my little mouse?' he teased until he found me. His was
the only face around me that I recognized, and I almost loved it,
suddenly. He took my hand in his and squeezed it as he winked at
me and smiled. It was that old, unclear gesture of my father's, so
that instantly I returned the squeeze, still ignorant of the bargain
struck. The Captain turned toward the overseer. 'You should pay
me thrice the sum for her,' he laughed. And heart racing, terror
against terror, I wished the Captain would take me back to the
sunny deck, the ghosts of fresh-bathed maidens all around us, and
sit me on his lap under the cape, and comfort me, and keep me
from these strangers. But when he walked off chuckling to himself,
I stoked my pride for comfort. For although I was deserted, I spoke
the language of the gentry, I was worth £8, and a man with all the
power of a Captain said that I was worth much more.

"God knows I have paid for the innocence of that pride.

"In the end, for Master Plackler's Arlington, the cart was filled
with a volunteered Scots carpenter dressed in black, two Irish lads
fresh from gaol for poaching geese, and two English vagabonds sold
as common laborers. The Irish lads were called Paudi nOg and
Paudi Iasc. Paudi Iasc had been a fisherman in Ulster before his abduction, and he commenced at once, in our own tongue, to advise
the other in the stealthiest of tones about escape. They would steal
the cart. They would clout Jenks into the ditch and steal his pistol
and tinder horn. But then where could they go? They would steal a
boat and find the pole star . . .

"And there was me, lying under the wooden shelf as we jounced through the dark countryside while the bats squealed and dived toward our heads . . ."

Coote holds up his plume for silence. He refers to the sheaf of notes of the testimony she had given before his own arrival at the gaol. "Where is this Arlington again?" he mutters, searching.

"Ah, 'tis all gone now, sir."

"Sold? The name changed?"

"No, abandoned. Sunk back into jungle. Already when we came there it was a failing outfit. When the mistress arrived, for a brief while it seemed that they would make a go of it. But Master Plackler was a gambler: that was how he came by the purse to buy us from the *Falconer*. Well, he lost us soon enough, and more. Arlington lay on the rich black soil of St. George's Parish—flat, without mountains, far enough from the sea that the rivers rarely flooded over, yet there was plenty rain. But at the end I have heard that there was not a mule to plow it, nor a duck to lay the master's breakfast. When he died of smallpox in the '60s, his wife Eugenia abandoned all and sailed back to England. No inheritors. She married again over there, but died childless. And there is nothing now, they say: just a cobbled carriage lane leading to columns that no longer hold a roof."

Peter Coote makes a mental note to inquire of the Governor, at the right moment, whether this acreage is for sale. "Make haste. Make haste, biddy," he says irritably, detained from scheming toward his future.

"A biddy is a laying hen," replies the woman flatly. "My name is Cot Quashey." And suddenly he knows that she is mad. What prisoner who in her lifetime has received almost eighty lashes—whose very life will float, in less than a week now, in the leaky boat of the Governor's whimsy—would speak so boldly to her interrogator? To the man who will . . . interpret . . . her to an indifferent Colonel Stede? Amazed at her imprudence, he clears his throat and smiles. "Is that so, now?"

"I did not see my master Henry Plackler very often the first three years I was his slave at Arlington. He kept residence in Bridgetown, at the town house his wife's father had given her when they came out in '45. The best of everything was there. The matched Arabians and the carriage were always returned to the Bridgetown stables as long as my master owned them, some said because he was afraid his slaves would eat them, as they had once done his ox.

"I have heard they had a larger staff at their town house than the twenty-two of us who worked the land at Arlington. They had bakers and grooms, a seamstress who was also a midwife, and a little black castrato who sang French carols at Christmas. But never did I see those fancy servants, nor the chandelier of Spanish crystals, nor the formal garden maze, for Master Plackler gambled his Bridgetown goods away during my third Easter with him. Indeed, that was what brought my mistress home to Arlington at last.

"In some ways those years at Arlington did me the most harm, although until the end I was not physically beaten. Usually a new-bought servant was put out upon the ground of his new home, in a place where he might build a shelter from the twigs and reeds around him once his daily labor for the master was complete. And usually, in the place the new slave was put out, there were other cabins of people like himself—Irish, Scots, English, Fon or Fan or Ibo—to draw toward and cluster to. But that was not my lot at Arlington. First of all, I was a child; not capable of living shelterless, nor knowing aught of how to build a shelter. But also, Arlington was a smallholding. As I have told you, much had already been lost at dice. When I was purchased I became one of only four white female servants. There were other females, members of a family of Africans led by a queenly woman the master had named Salome. Salome had two grown daughters and several sons by her two husbands, who lived with her in harmony. Africans were not yet common in St. George's Parish, but Master Plackler had won these and a dozen others some years past, during his greatest gaming venture.

They say he'd gambled at cards on that occasion with the captains of two Dutch traders bound for High Brazil. Salome's daughters were in the second gang with me at first, but we were 'promoted,' they to the fields, I to the house, as you shall hear.

"Servant breeding was strictly controlled on the plantations in those years. Master and overseer would discuss the desired outcome of servant matings as thoughtfully as they would plan which cow to calf, which bullocks to geld for oxen, which stock to raise up dry for meat. I was placed at once under the supervision of Dora, the Scottish overseer of the second gang. Dora lived in a small outbuilding that had been the ox shed, but now there were no oxen—no field animals of any kind. Instead the first-gang bondsmen did the hauling and the plowing with their own thighs and backs.

"Dora and two Scots girls shared this shed between them, but Dora would not have my 'Irish arse' amongst them. 'To kill us in our sleeps,' she spat at me around her missing teeth, 'as ye martyred the poor Protestants in '41.'

"So I was locked up come night into a pantry hung with curing hams. I slept upon the earthen floor, with my father's woolen surcoat to both pillow and cover me as best it could. Yes, I was safe and covered from the rain. But also . . . well, I was alone.

"Even though I joined the eight other young people of the second gang in the fields every day but Sunday, I was alone. Jenks and Dora did all that they could to see that bondsfolk went in suspicion of each other at Arlington. I remember that first morning when I walked barefoot behind her, pinching a fold of her skirt whilst hoping if a snake should writhe across the grassy path, herself would step upon it first. The sky was black and soft as we hurried toward the far field that awaited. Then gradually below the slender stars a thin line of yellow began to separate the heavens from the shaggy toss of trees. A calm day was a-dawning. Dora's low tones carried well as she warned me, 'Ye're right to waddle at my tail. Them Africans ahead is cannibals on special occasions. Now that the animals is gone.' She told the tale of the last ox, found roasted where it was felled grazing in the field. 'Just the hide and bones, scattered on the ground. Jenks whipped them good but could not make them talk, until Master Henry says Stop, be wise; we must now get the ox's work out of the Africans.'

"She muttered on, 'And keep apart from them African girls. Shameless hoors they are, rolling their eyes and laughing, near naked in the fields.'

"'As for us Scots—we're onto you Irish and your sly tricks, and we'll have no shite out of ye. And don't you think that you can trust them new lads from your old place, and get together and whisper this and plot that. I tell you, they'd as soon tip you upside down in the field as would the Africans. You must keep clear of all of them—a little thing like you! If you don't die from the starvation, you'll surely not possess the strength to fight off men when their nature is upon them.'

"The sky was filled with rosy light by the time we reached the field. I thought it was a class of corn I saw, silhouetted tall and tasseled against the brimming heavens. 'All right, set to,' Dora called out to the others. 'Here is tobacco,' she explained to me. 'Tie this across your face.' She handed me a broad leaf and a creeper. 'Hereafter pick a wide leaf every night. The sun will scar a girl of your coloring without you wear a mask.' And I suppose I owe her thanks for that, for though the sun dropped me many times in a stroke or fit, the mask has kept me from getting corpse's lips, as you will see on so many white field-workers."

He looks vaguely askance.

"Arra, surely you've seen the men and women out from Europe who've worked the fields without face cover? The sun will burn and blister us in no time, sir, the skin pulling back from the teeth as the face pulls into tight and stringy scars, like any burnt flesh will." Coote recalls, and nods impatiently.

"Dora taught me how to top tobacco. The taller youths went up and down the rows with little knives, chopping off the flowers and tassels that would mean a slow end to the leafing of the plant, while I and the other smaller girls bent behind them, parting the huge dull-green leaves to look for tender suckers which would sap life from beneath. We pinched these off each day, stopping the cycle so that all the sap went to the leaves, which flourished monstrously. There were over thirteen hectares planted in tobacco at that time.

"Never did Dora call us by our names, but only 'You!' and 'You!' and 'You!', swishing her hempen cat so that two or three would jump toward the task, not knowing who she meant. All of Dora's admonitions, and the unsocial way we worked together, frightened by her rope whip and the hefty welts it left, plus the fact that I was quartered every night and Sundays by myself, led me to develop—habits."

"Thieving, wasn't it?" Coote asks mildly.

"The habits of a child abandoned to great loneliness. Where I was born there is a saying: '*Is pol dubh doite e an t-uaigneas, ach ma dhuunann tu suas e, dunfaidh tu amach go leor eile ata go h-alainn chomh maith.*'"

"Pray what does that mean in human speech?" Coote snaps, hiding curiosity.

"We say, 'Loneliness is a burnt black hole, but if you seal it up you close out all that can be beautiful as well.' I was a child, though, and knew not how to use the wisdom I was reared around, oncet I was cut off from its source. But anyway, in truth, although Dora and Jenks said things and fomented squabbles to keep us well divided, they but inflamed a divisiveness already in us.

"What I mean, sir, what I want you to record, is that you do not trust even your own, once your own have sold and bought you. And then there's history; a river of gall that widens with the centuries between those trampled and those whose patience is tried by the constant bucking of the trampled, trying to get up again. Among us there at Arlington, more recent fears were sparked between those of the different Christian faiths. But the greatest differences which lay between those of us who shared that one lot in life, seemed in-stinctive—natural and therefore insurmountable."

After a pause Coote drawls with boredom, "Kindly yield up its nature to me."

"I remember those first mornings in the field," the prisoner muses, "how hard it was to stay bent to my work—although the air was cooler near the ground—because the Africans were dressed, both lads and girls, in only a brief canvas skirt tied between the legs. And their long gleaming muscles, the bareness of their dark chests and backs and thighs—these were both mesmerizing and alarming to someone from the Christian north. Yet did many masters believe it was the black man's disposition to go about naked in his native forests; and so the cloth across their loins was first thought an over-nicety, like covering a sheep's bum with a nappy.

"Of course, as you know, time has revealed the error of this. Because you gentlefolk now each float thousands of fresh, frightened, handcuffed Africans across the sea each year—Africans who have been proved to bleed and chill and die as fast as any farm hand from the northern lands—masters have learned that Africans too want covering, both for health and modesty."

There is something almost instructional in her tone which Peter Coote does not appreciate. He teeters between amused logic—most assuredly she's mad—and a deep resentment, when her speech is less than subservient. Still he holds fast to the Governor's goals: one must be tricky in extracting subtleties. "You wander, b . . . Mistress Daley. It is, perhaps, useful to hear you state the inborn differences you perceived between yourself and savages. For this natural difference, created by God himself, seems to have been per-versely set aside several times by your race and other Christian blackguards in Barbados."

"No," she answers thoughtfully, "the difference you are wanting me to speak about was *not* natural. I had been trained to see it. And so at first I thought their colors and their features unrefined, being not narrow, pale, and bright." Coote notes the Irishwoman frowning to find apt words. Her hands rise from her lap, and draw apart and around, as if trying to form a little globe. "It was like," she says, "that last time I saw the Captain. As he walked away there was this flooding in my breast as if he was my dearest friend. But all it meant was my fondness for the familiar, the fondness we are trained from our mother's apron to feel for a clan we learn to recognize as ours. This is . . . well I suppose it is indeed a lesson the world over. For as I first stared at the huge black eyes and short stiff hair of the Africans, so did they stare at me. And at the Glebe, where I spent twenty years and there were many children, the babes of Africans howled at my smile and smell—which they found unnatural and ugly—and buried their faces in their mothers' necks. So I believe that every tribe of people think themselves the yardstick of Creation, and feel fear and distaste and suspicion of outsiders. But still, I tell you this is learned."

"And you unlearned it?" Coote asks in honeyed tones as he ends one full page and sprinkles sand across it. He sweeps a clean sheet toward himself.

"In right circumstances, things like that melt away like morning haze," Cot Quashey tells him. "We revive them only if we fear some harm, or as a weapon if we have nothing fair to fight with."

The new morning sings as it passes the Apothecary's office window. The cicadas begin their anxious chant. Cot Quashey tells the Governor's surgeon-scribe, Peter Coote, about her first years on the plantation of Henry Plackler, married to Eugenia, eldest child of the Earl of Orkney.

"As I have said, I rarely saw the master during my first three years at Arlington. My days were spent with the second gang—the young gang—in jobs about the place. Dora supervised our labors with the tobacco. We planted it and weeded, we topped the pink sticky suckers, and when it was ripe and harvested by the first gang—the grown, strong men and women—we sat outside the barn, sorting it into batches by the size of the leaf, for hanging in the shed to dry. That was heavy work, the sorting and the tying. It hurt your wrists. The leaves were wet and sandy, and while there were only nine children in second gang, thirteen doughty adults carried the harvest to us in baskets.

"Sometimes Dora brought lanterns to the boards we stood behind, and we worked on in the dark. The leaves must not be left out in the dew once they are cut or mould will spread on them like pox. This meant that someone had to bring the evening ration of corn cake and dried fish as we stood working, and that the first gang must wait in the shed to haul our tied leaves up into the rafters, where they dried. Usually it was the African boys who went for victuals and carried the leaves off to the barn: we young girls were said to have the swifter hands for sorting and for tying, while the lads were said to have the backs for loads.

"When the crop was in, Jenks advised the neighboring planters. Their holdings, so much larger than Arlington, had regular business in town. Someone would take word to our master on the next run to Bridgetown. Master Plackler would come down to the plantation with the buyers, after the harvest had been cured. I see him now— that fine cherrywood coach, the matched blacks frothing up the dust as they galloped down the lane. They tossed their heads and rolled their eyes . . . I could have told him that the bits and harness were too tight.

"One of Salome's husbands had known horses well in his own land. He tended the stallions while the master was in residence. And soon, on Master's heels, would appear the small cart of the buyers, their delicate weights and scales bound in bales of hay for cushioning; and behind them, a chain of wagons to haul the crop down to the ships.

"The buying took up several days after the rains had passed. It was another time we bondsfolk barely stopped to breathe. For we must take the bales down from the lofts and carry them to where the merchants sat under an awning. We lifted the bales into the weighing cradle; then down again; then over to the wagons, where we loaded them under the orders of the draymen.

"Master Plackler had a carved armchair with yellow cushions carried out onto the grass, where he faced the merchants, watching everything most regally. I seldom looked upon him in those years: it was my way of trying, as children will, to be invisible, for it was clear to any observer now that I had lied about my age in '51. But one morning as I helped to drag a bale to the merchants, I did so. He sat that chair as if it were a throne, fist curled over an ivory stick as if it were a scepter. His hair was brown and as long as the wigs men then affected." She glances at Coote's balding brow. "One of the merchants had been smoking a mix of leaves from different bales. They did this to grade the quality, of course, but also to be sure no mould or mustiness had settled in the crop. The merchant puffed, then made a sour face. 'Ah, Barbados,' said he. 'The plant grows well here, but there is something lacking in the soil. Never is the taste as rich as that from the Virginia colony.'

"The master barely looked his way. 'Nor is the purse you pay as rich,' said he. 'Get on with it. You know my terms.' He seemed so mighty, Henry Plackler. I was proud that he was mine. Or I was his: for as a child I had these things somewhat confused."

Coote, as he records this, recalls that the prisoner was said to have had a liaison with Henry Plackler when she was sixteen: one that got her sold off for another seven years. Involuntarily he glances at her. She seems so pale and plain. What about her had the Captain of the *Falconer* desired? Why had Henry Plackler looked beyond the fine flanks of the earthy African women? The latter are to Coote's anticipating tastes. Somehow Lucy's quietude swells the effect of her voluptuousness; he catches himself thinking of the seductiveness of silence.

"That is what slavery will do, at first," she interrupts, looking beyond him to the garden. "You search for something to belong to that is high—that can make you *mean* more than on your own you do mean to the world around you. Which is nothing. And does that not seem a way of looking for a new tribe, once one's own has been ripped away?"

The question catches Coote unawares. For a second he almost considers it. The next evening it will return on scented breeze, through a lace curtain.

Cot Quashey tells him that every year after the crop sale there would be a feed: the master would buy a sheep or a fine heifer from a neighboring herd, and Jenks would have it slaughtered. It was Salome who knew best how to pit-roast the meat: which stones should line the earthen tunnel and not crack when baked in flames. Which leaves to lay over and under the carcass so that it stayed moist, rather than singeing dry and bitter. Cot and the other young folk dug the pit, following Salome's pointing fingers. Then, while the meat was roasting, they gathered twigs and boughs and fallen branches of the palm, and built a high bonfire against the twilit sky.

"At Arlington the master never attended the feast days of his bondspeople. Jenks would appear with a little barrel of spirits which he handed over to Salome's husbands. In spite of her moralizing, Dora could not be trusted with drink; and the rumor was the Irish and low sort of English servers would guzzle till insensate. But I tell you," said Cot Quashey, "Salome's men liked the spirits well enough. They would not part with the little keg, I remember that. If the two Paudis went to beg to take it up and pour a measure, they would shrug their shoulders as if they didn't understand, and sit upon it. There were at that time eleven African men, and only five Christian bondsmen. Salome's men shared the liquor fairly among the first gang; we of the second gang were judged not to have earned, yet, such a pleasant gift.

"At Arlington there was no fist-fighting among the people, which was somewhat unusual, for we were as different from each other as Clydesdales from Arabians from Kerry ponies. Five lan-

guages were present, and a great hibber-jibber and rolling of the
eyes and waving of the hands when people needed to communicate.
The quirt of Jenks stood between raised fists. Still, while there were
no blows, at the feeds on holidays, people pulled as they will into
little factions. Voices dropped and eyes peered at each other across
the flames as night grew late and the keg sank low.

"There was no music there at Arlington," she wandered. "If the
Glebe was a place of sudden, unexpected violence, it was also a
place where people's liveliness rose up from time to time. At Arlington once, one of the Africans had built a drum out of a fallen
tree and the skin of a creature that had been roasted. But Jenks had
hacked the drum up with a small axe. Abomination, he called it,
saying it would call to serpents and other things of Satan.

"On one occasion, Salome and her older daughter sat on the
ground swilling palm juice they'd distilled, from a calabash. That
daughter was only after her conscription to the first gang. They began to sing. It was a song that sounded much like taunting, and the
new husband and the single men not of Salome's clan answered it
melodiously. Then the other daughter rose and shuffled in the
shadows. With her back turned she made her legs stiff and twitched
her rump quickly, like a peacock will in May. Salome growled
something and they laughed among themselves. I sat alone, admiring that language between them—the mood they'd entered, all with
music. Many was the time, in my six years among the folks at Arlington, when quick excitement would wash through my chest, and
I would want to steal to my sleeping shed where my father's surcoat
lay wadded, the brass ha'penny pipe deep in its pocket. I wanted,
too, to be a girl making music and dancing. But I never did. For as
soon as I imagined myself twirling out of that shed, whistling a
reel, I would imagine someone searching my earthen bed under the
mouldy rashers once I was in the fields, and stealing my whistle away.
I never played my mother's flute at Arlington until the night I left
its sight forever.

"The only music we heard at Arlington was caroling at Christmas. Jenks and Dora urged the Scots people to sing, lined up in their rags like beggars while all the others felt embarrassed for them, and turned away their eyes. The English rakes knew a good few tavern tunes and they would sing them on Sundays if Dora and the Scots maids were going for a walk around the place. Like proper ducklings they walked out, the fools. But these Englishmen ran off after a year, stowing on a vessel Cromwell had sent to subjugate the other islands of the Indies . . . please, I must pass my water."

Coote directs her to the garden and shakes out his wrists. In the background, he hears her meager stream. He draws out his pocket watch, queasy from the heat but in need of food to replenish him after the restless, moody night. It's almost one. Surely Lucy should be coming with his dinner.

"Enough news of the entertainments under your first master," Coote says peevishly when she has resumed her stool. "What intercourse beyond the musical had you Irish with the Africans of Arlington, or of the other plantations which surrounded you?"

"As I have said, we did not mix with them at all, unless we hoed the same row or helped in the felling of a tree or carting of a bale. We did not share a language. They had been given house-land on a different spot than the Irish lads, so that there was no commonage where their lives might cross on Sundays, as they tended their little gardens, or roasted the small birds we were allowed to snare.

"On the big plantations it's a more usual thing for slaves to visit others in the evening in the slow season. At the Glebe, the first-gang men and women were sometimes rented or lent to other sugar houses too, once our own crop was in. And trusted women workers there kept a Sunday market at a crossroads between the houses, having passes to do so. But at Arlington . . . by the time I came there, the only animal stock left on the place were fowl and swine: we had no need to bring the animals to stud at other farms, and no stock to sell at mart. We numbered only twenty-two at Master Plackler's holding: twenty, once the English rogues ran off to join the navy. We were too few to work the land. There were thirteen hectares in tobacco, and some in indigo, and the master had us clearing more to try out cotton. Altogether there were fifty-eight hectares and only twenty folk; so the master never lent a soul to another harvest, nor had he silver to rent the slaves of others. It was ourselves who took the place of oxen and drays in ploughing land and carting loads around the place. For all these reasons we never met anyone from another place. And 'mongst ourselves—beyond the usual human clannishness—I have told you thrice now that our overseers kept us apart through inspiring fear and loathing. We were a little colony of suspicious factions there, in an Arlington that the ghost of ruin-to-come already lay over. Bad will hung thick, as if something angry was watching us, and just about to fly into our midst."

Coote stares at her.

"It was like the *siogue* had been riled; yet we could not see them on this new island. Where I come from, although we may not want to, folks *can* see them. What you can see, you have a better chance to appease or foil . . ."

Coote's stomach rumbles. The Irishwoman rubs sweat from above her lip. Is it the heat? Her narrow cheeks have taken on the faintest flush. For the first time he notices the small soft cleft in her chin.

"Nor was anybody sent off the grounds for breeding," she adds. He tips the nib of his quill to the side: a neat man, he wants it to last the morning; and his letters are already becoming wide and slightly blurry. Where is Lucy? "The first year I was at Arlington, one of the Scots girls died. It was consumption. Dora said the lass brought it with her from the highland croft they took her from, for Barbados air is warm and soft. But I have known many, including Africans, who succumbed to the consumption, and they fine and hearty their first years here. At any rate, once that girl had died, there was only Dora, exempt from childbearing by her overseer rank; myself, a young slip not yet in her courses; and the other Scots girl, to breed between four men. In those days they only bred Christian with Christian unless a master or an overseer made a by-blow.

"The surviving Scots girl was named Ardiss. She would have been fifteen or so at the time. After the second harvest of tobacco had been taken and the indigo was in the ground, the master and Jenks decided to increase the Plackler stock by breeding two females—the Scots girl and Salome's daughter. A man among the single Africans was chosen, and he moved into Salome's cabin with the daughter. Those people test the way of things between a man and woman anyway before they build a hut, even in their own nation. The Scots girl, our betters determined, would best be mated with the Scots carpenter, who now served as joiner, cooper, and cobbler as well. Wheels he mended, and a gate; he made forks and locks, such things.

"I see him now, that Scotsman. Every Christmas we were given lengths of simple undyed canvas. The Africans were given less, to wrap around the waist and through the legs, the tag-ends hanging down. But Dora and the Scots lasses and I would stitch new breeches and jerkins, and petticoats and waists, for those who had been brought out from Europe. I myself, I only got a skirt, not yet being formed like a woman. The Scotsman, who had come over in a suit of stiff black wool, did his work like all the other northern men in bare chest and canvas breeches. But he had kept his black surcoat, as raveled and mouldy as it was. At the harvest feed and holidays he would don this jacket. He was a slight fellow, and he grew slighter on our rations, for he was not much at hunting birds, and he would not taste the lizards the Africans cooked as victuals.

"He was smaller and shorter than Ardiss, the Scotswoman they bred him to. But once when he stood at a fire eating roast, the fat dripping down his poet's wrists, his hair and eyes as black as his suit coat, he smiled at me with all his teeth and I found him right handsome. Dora said, 'He keeps that surcoat for the day his time's worked off. He says he'll walk free in it, the eejit.'

"When girls were old enough to breed, they were also considered strong enough to join the heavy workers, the first gang. Jenks took the Scots girl from the ox shed and put her, alone, into another. I was in the yard one night, getting water for helping Dora with the loblolly, when Ardiss came in from the field. Her step was jaunty! The shed she had been given, she said, had a floor of dry planks to lie on. The first gang seemed a real promotion to her; 'my own housheen,' she laughed. She had lovely dimples when she smiled, that one.

"Then one evening Jenks told the Scots carpenter to get his things and billet with the lass. I saw the two men walking down the hill from where the slave cabins stood, through the yard past the big house and Jenks's cottage—which the master stayed in for the few days of auctioning the crop—to the work sheds. In one of them, Ardiss, unwitting, waited.

"Each day before dawn, when the morning star hung over all," Cot Quashey tells Coote, "the Scots girl threw back the door to her shed and stepped out to fetch a bucket from the pump. Over a little fire before her place she boiled water for their breakfast gruel in a broken pot her man had mended. Sometimes she sang. 'That Ardiss is a right hoor,' grumbled Dora. 'She takes to it like rats to corn.' When the first gang passed on their way to the fields, the Scots girl joined them. The carpenter did not, if there was a job awaiting in the yard. But it was whispered that when he too went to the fields, they took their midday rest together in the grass, his head upon her lap while she stroked his hair. At night we heard them laughing.

"So it was with surprise that folk began to mark, in spite of all the signs of love, that the Scots girl's belly was flatter after six months than it had been before. Then the master came for the third sale of crops.

"On the afternoon when the merchants lumbered off down the road, their wagons laden for the London ships, we slaves were sent to clean out the tobacco sheds of mildew, rats' nests, snakes, the like. As we carried out the trash to burn, we saw Jenks and the master seated underneath the trade awning, deep in conversation.

"After some time they called Ardiss to them; and Dora also, to question her. Next the Scots carpenter was summoned. The story was brought back: never in all those months had they lain together but as a sister with her brother. The carpenter said he would not force her. 'Master Plackler, I would marry Ardiss when I am free,' Dora mimicked, as if this were something cunning and posh to say. But Jenks had answered with a guffaw: 'Yer willy will not function better when you've put a ring upon her finger.'

"Dora said the master spoke with impatience. 'You have wasted almost the entire time of parturition for one child,' he cried in disgust. 'We could have had two off this lass by the time she now bears one.'

"We in the shed did the best we could to catch the tale unfolding in the yard. The Scotsman was sent down to their little shed. We watched him trudge, shamefast, up the track to the cabin he had left six months before. The black coat was underneath his arm. Bad sprites hung in the air like mist. You can take a green reed and make a ring of it. If you look through it, you can see what those who bring the ill luck look like. But it will blind you in the eye you see them with, and seldom is it worth that much to know. Yet to foretell what brought Ardiss and the Scot, and Paudi Iasc (he notes that she says *iasc* means "fish" in the Irish tongue) so much bad luck, they might have gladly paid an eye to know." The Irishwoman jerks her head, as if she has been nodding off with her eyes open.

"Suddenly Jenks moved toward the barn. We hustled inside and made busy. I can see them on the rafters, Paudi nOg and Paudi Iasc, standing with their legs balanced akimbo, dirty toes curled around the beams as they bent to haul the bales of fodder we were hoisting to them on the forks. That fodder was for the dry season, after which, by the grace of God, two sows would litter. These would be gorged before and after, and the bonhams soon weaned for sale.

"Paudi nOg and Paudi Iasc were strapping men—twenty-one? twenty-four? at the time. They had been gaoled for poaching fowl—Paudi nOg because the hunger came on him as he walked the land, looking for a *spailpin's* place. Paudi Iasc went a-poaching, though, because he'd married his sweetheart, got her with child, and had been trying to keep her fed. But he was a fisherman. And the mackerel had not swum up the bay that year. He had no land to sow. No stock to breed. Yet all around his cottage ran rabbits, the streams were choked with salmon, the *boherin* shone speckled in the morning with the spoor of roe deer. And gobbling and pecking through his cabin yard waddled the sleek flock of His Lordship's geese . . ."

Before he hears Lucy turning from the cook shed into the corridor, Peter Coote sniffs the scent of ham. At last, he sighs, his right hand crampy. But the Irishwoman rambles on.

"'You! Paud Iasc!' Jenks cried out as he entered the dim barn. Everyone turned, stopping in their own shadows. Jenks picked me out among the others. 'Cotlin. Tell Iasc to get down at once and come with me before the Master and the lass.'

"I did so. Paudi Iasc sprang from the rafters to a bale on the ground, for the glory of being in his prime no doubt. Also it was that Jenks might whip the men until they bled, but his joints would still nevermore be vigorous enough to let him leap down from a loft. I was beckoned along with them, out under the awning. The ground lay littered with golden tobacco leaves, already souring from the damp.

"I do not know what Paudi Iasc expected. Some arduous task, perhaps. When Master bade me tell him get his things out of the cabin he shared with the others, the girl began to whimper, and the color rose on Paudi Iasc. He had a fine head of ginger curls, had Paudi. Redheaded folk color up like October apples.

"Paudi Iasc began to wave his arms. He pushed his face right up to Jenks and shouted in our tongue, 'Arra, leave the girl alone, or stick her yerself, you ould hoorson! I'm a married man already, with a babe by now. I've made my sacraments!'

"With my eyes down I told them Paudi Iasc could not go with the Scots girl for he already had a babe and bride. But Master laughed. He waved his cuff at Paudi. ''Tis proof that he's apt stud.'

"Jenks then grasped Paudi Iasc by the neck, pushing him toward the cabin for his kit, and saying, 'Ye thick bustard! He's a thick bus-tard, sire; a child off him mought be born an eejit . . .' Then there broke out a little scuffle. Paudi Iasc pushed Jenks's arm away with his tilted fist, and the overseer almost toppled in the dust. For that they clapped Paud in the stocks and doled out thirty lashes, to be administered after the Scots girl had caught, but before the busy season. For Paudi Iasc was a man who worked hard just for the pleasure of feeling his muscles stretch; that was why they chose him for the breeding, and why they could not harm him with crop time ahead."

A shaft of sunlight strikes the pewter tray Coote's meal rests upon as the slave comes through the doorway. The napkin tented across the dishes is the same blue as her wrapped headscarf. Coote sands the paper he's been writing on as soon as she appears, piling his supplies quickly at the top corner of the escritoire. He rubs his hands together and sighs with anticipation and exhaustion. "Rest," he instructs the prisoner. "Lucy will come for you when I am ready for more testimony." The two women file slowly from the room as he takes fork in hand. Under the napkin lies the purplish slab of meat; also cassava cake and pickled okra.

After the heavy meal, Coote retires to his private chambers. He re-moves breeches, waistcoat, and his one remaining good Irish linen shirt, donning an older one, frayed impossibly along the neck and cuffs. He uses this as a nightshirt. As soon as he slips below the mosquito net onto his cot he sinks into a deep and drooling sleep. A shutter banging at the window awakens him. The storm's already passing, leaving a cool current of air to lave the middle of the room. Peter feels almost drunk from his greasy meal and viscous sleep. But once he washes in the fine porcelain bowl his mood shifts again: much better, almost hearty. He pulls on his hose, feeling the darning at the heels when he tugs on his snug breeches and slides on his shoes. Then he draws the good shirt over his head. As he raises his arms to tie once more the jabot, he notes, in dismay, his cuffs.

Stitched of fine Irish lace and linen, both are grimy-gray along the edges of the hem. Now Coote notices two smears of ink on the right one, tiny blobs until dragged across the desk as he scripted. "God's bloody teeth," he curses tightly, feeling the undercurrent of rage and frustration which has been swelling for fifteen years now, in the tropics. A freed woman in the village has been recommended as a seamstress. Coote has ordered two shirts made on account, based on his rank as the Governor's commissar. But higher ranks and commissions must be satisfied first: the seamstress has been finishing the bridal ensemble for the wedding of the daughter of Newton House. And now, for the Governor's banquet tomorrow evening, a complete new set of table linens is being hemmed and embroidered with the crest of State by a circle of mop-capped skivvies, under the seamstress's sharp eye. The apprenticed slatterns seem able enough to Coote, but she herself would embellish the emblem of government on every napkin with cloth-of-gold thread; would embroider the plantation daughter's sleeves herself with silver. Only between times has she begun to wind fragile ivory threads between tiny pins pegged to a board, fashioning the lace for Peter Coote's new shirts.

Friday week, she'd said, or if not, surely Saturday. But spreading the sheer cuffs of his soiled shirt between thumb and forefinger, Coote is distressed. He is invited to the Governor's banquet, which will occur tomorrow night. A newcomer to their circle, an unknown among the famous planters and senators, the shippers and slavers and merchants also on the guest list. Stede will be waiting for an update on the Irish investigation. They'll bend together in close counsel. He imagines the Governor taking his arm and bending to listen or chuckle, and . . . and himself in tatters! He lifts the small bell he carries everywhere at the gaol, and rings it too vigorously. "Get the prisoner," he orders abruptly when Lucy appears. He lifts his waistcoat and drapes it over a chair back. Why should he dress himself like a lord for Africans and criminals this muggy afternoon? Instead, he hangs the dove-gray surcoat over a ladder-back, buttoning it to block its form in the soggy air.

He brushes it, considering. It looks fresh enough. On a waft of breeze his spirits lift and tilt toward optimism. Dinner is late in the tropics. By candlelight, or strolling His Excellency's grounds in the shadows of flowering vines, who will notice old cuffs? They'll look passable, no doubt; and by the weekend the new shirts will be done. He carries the small bell with him to the office where the Irishwoman should be waiting by now. It jangles faintly once in the corridor, although he does not shake it.

"The mistress came home to Arlington after my third harvest. Christmas had passed, then Easter. I recall this because I had a new canvas petticoat, and I had painted on it with those red beans in the long pods which the Africans used to decorate their loincloths. Little flowers I'd wrought, like vetch—so simple in design, all along the hem: I was standing in my father's open surcoat in the yard, feeding fowl from a palm shell, when we heard the carriage coming.

"It was a rosy evening. Lovely. Ardiss and I were chasing the pigs. The sows had littered, and wandered the plantation with yokes nailed around their necks to stop them from rooting up the pigeon peas and seedling cotton. Behind them trotted their piglets, squealing for the teat. Dora had come up to us with orders for the Scots girl, too big with child to do the work of first gang in her last weeks, when the fine red carriage with the Orkney crest thundered into the yard. We scuttled onto the grass, Ardiss and myself, but Dora pushed the wisps beneath her cap and stepped forward. Jenks was running toward us from his cottage up the yard by the time the driver stood down, opened the carriage door, and placed a footstool in the dust. When Master Plackler had alighted in his deep plum coat, he held up his arm. A woman's cuff and long white fingertips slid onto his sleeve. It clung there as a swish of gray silk skirts stepped uncertainly onto the stool. Our mistress looked around—at the sighing trees which fringed the fields, the evening swallows darting through the pinkening skies, the poor-kempt flowerbeds by the steps before her, and finally past Dora and myself, to linger in a blank way on Ardiss. 'Cover her shame,' she said to her husband. 'My dear?' he asked. 'That young thing, where is her bodice?' the mistress said pointing at me although her eyes were still on Ardiss. 'Ah, 'tis just the child I bought to serve you as lady's maid,' he smiled absently. The mistress had already turned, clutching her skirts to ascend the steps to her door, when Jenks caught up, crying 'Sir, I was told you would come Sunday week, I had no notice, the house is not aired.'

"But the master only replied tiredly, 'You must do the best you can for the night, but have them fall to it on the morrow, for my lady has come to stay.' They went inside. The groom began to unlash three large trunks strapped across the ceiling of the coach. Jenks had moved to help him when we espied another shoe, another knee, pushing skirts of dark blue calico through the open coach doors. 'Mary?' the mistress called from somewhere in the house; and her voice raised at the end with a note both querulous and sharp, like a mad child playing with a razor.

"'Comin Mawdam,' was the reply, and I drew in my breath. For the woman who stood now in the ruddy lane had the rich sound of home. I stared into her face, and she smiled and winked at me as she gathered up small cases, hatboxes, a fan, and hastened toward the stairs. 'Will one of ye not help me?' she invited. But the bar wench in the Donkey and the Tankard had smiled and winked kindly, so I hung back while Dora simpered forward."

"I take it," Coote interjects, "this 'lady' you speak of was Mary Dove, she who was executed after you revealed her plot to your master."

Suddenly the prisoner cries out hoarsely, burying her face in dirty gnarled knuckles. Meanwhile Coote records his words as if they have been her admission. "May God forgive me, for sometimes I cannot forgive myself," she sobs. This is her first real breakdown of composure. The room grows utterly silent but for her jagged weeping. Coote finds himself disconcerted: even after floggings and now the likelihood of worse, the prisoner's loyalties seem to lie with the fomenters of sedition, dead now for many years. He pours himself water and drinks.

"Eugenia Plackler never set foot again beyond the Spanish tiles of Arlington's patio from the time she alighted from that coach, until her husband died," Cot Quashey continues in a bit. "Arlington was the holding her father the Earl settled on her at the birth of their firstborn son. But that son, Mary told me, had perished just weeks beyond his third year, and none of the mistress's other eight issue had survived more than a week beyond the womb. Eugenia Plackler had retained a surgeon in Bridgetown to help her bring forth an heir. But now that her husband had lost their property in Bridgetown at the gaming, she had only Mary and me to help her build the strength to attempt the ordeal again. From the beginning the mistress hated to look upon Ardiss's comely belly, but my own swaybacked childishness drew her watery smile. She sent for me to train under Mary as lady's and nursery maid.

"And Mistress Plackler's first orders to me were delightful! She herself gave me two lengths of blue calico, and set me to cutting a skirt, a bodice, and a cap much like Mary's. I was to sleep on a pallet, my father's old coat with the pipe in the pocket to pillow my head, and a patched linen sheet to cover me. This pallet was placed outside the boudoir when the master visited her, but at the foot of her bed when she slept alone. For then, almost always, ghoulish dreams of wailing babes would wake her. It was my task then to bring the sleeping cup Mary had brewed, and sit by her side as her pale nails dug red crescents into my hands. How she babbled in terror at the darkness, repeating their names. I remember some of those names to this day; the ghostlings that had followed her from Bridgetown cemetery to this desolate plantation where her husband's dicing excesses had exiled her.

"But in the beginning every day was a joy to me in the Big House. I arose before dawn to help Mary set cook fires in the fieldstone kitchen. As the biscuit baked we spoke our own language, blessing the hearth and asking for redemption, to mark our own day inside the day that owned us. My Mary came from a townland up around Slieve League, and had been parted from her seven children and their father, a great rebel chief."

A sort of tingle floods through Coote as his prisoner lauds the rebel as "great." It is a detail which will pleasure the Governor; which will suit *his* point of view, fulfill *his* expectations. But also this admission holds something for Coote himself, if he can remember to jot the idea down in the book which contains his hypothesis: recalcitrance seems bred into the blood of certain races, while others are much more sensible and resilient. . . . But ponder that later, for now she is musing, ". . . and no African ever set foot in that house, nor fertile Ardiss, nor jealous Dora; and the groom went back to Bridgetown to deliver the horses and himself to the winner-at-cards. So you see, we were there alone with the mistress, and sometimes the master, and it was easy for me to pretend childishly that the house was mine: Mary's and mine. And would we not be safe, inside what was our own?

"How the senses delighted as I knelt upon the floor, my new skirts spread around me to admire as I polished sun motes into the planks. The scent of citrus oil and tallow, the proud cold swell of a porcelain vase as I dusted on hot afternoons, the wink of the haughty brass lion-headed knob that emerged from my cloth as I shone his cheeks and nose . . . all these brought alive again something that had been stunted that Wren's Day when I entered the Donkey and Tankard," she says. And stops, seeming puzzled. Then she mutters, "Beauty. It was beauty."

"I do not take your meaning," Coote frowns. But the words she speaks next somehow create a small diorama for him, and he too envisions a maid, sprouting winsome from lanky childhood as the seasons move past. Unaware, as she crosses the yard on an errand in her blue uniform with hair and skin scrubbed clean every Sabbath to please her mistress's nose, of narrowing eyes which measure her figure, now rounding on rich table scraps. Eyes noting the blush which rises to her cheeks, the sometimes mirthful, sparkling young eyes. These are the colors, the sparks, of too much ease, clean satiny floors below bare toes, uninjured fingers culling ripe fruits and sweet flowers from the overgrown tangle surrounding the house.

"The mistress," Cot tells Coote, "had me adorn her bedchamber every morning with flowers. A vase of them must be placed at the side of the glass where we made her toilette, washing away the nightmare sweats and poppied sleep. I would comb out her hair, sometimes rinsing it with cedar bark boiled in ale for the burnish.Oh, she was worn to the bone by the time I met her: stringy from fallen health and pallid with grief for all those lost babies. Mary, who had been purchased as a slave for life by the mistress's father . . ."

With agitation Coote interrupts. "As I recall, his Grace the Earl of Orkney reprieved the ungrateful Mary Dove from swinging at the side of her man and sons!"

"Ah. Gratitude. She was a Christian, like yourself, yet her life was the Earl's to bestow or dispose of. And because of his rights over her forevermore, she was gifted to mistress on her wedding day and brought out to Barbados. And anywhere the mistress would go, that was Mary Dove's destiny too. And if the mistress would give her away, or lash her, or starve her—that too she woke to evade, every day of her life. But be that as it may, Mary could remember our mistress from the days when she was fresh and lovely and gentle. Except in adversity. Not many are gentle in adversity . . .

"But there was ever adversity by the time Mistress was brought to us at Arlington and I stood behind her shoulder combing the night snarls from her hair. We would look into the glass, she and I, as if into a tableau. From the vase the red lips of hibiscus reflected some color on her gaunt cheek, the purple vine flowers suggested their own color to her deep-set eyes. I could see at such moments that her beauty—now a near-dried-up well—had once been uncommon. But it was in that same glass she too began to see the beauty arising in me."

Coote is astonished! The tart, the hag! "We are entirely aware of your sluttish escapades with Sir Henry Plackler. Are you hoping to justify your betrayal of your mistress by demeaning his poor Lady's looks?" A bubble of bile from the Governor's undigested ham explodes, scalding his throat.

"She herself set the stage for that unnatural relationship," the prisoner replies, aloof and bitter, but without shame.

Coote changes tactics. Smoothly he urges, "Very well, tell us, how did she do that?" His tones are evoked by a memory of the Governor, licking a gob of creamy nougat from his pouty lips. He ignores a small secret pulsation inside his breeches: "unnatural" secrets, things "to be revealed."

"As I grew up and my form changed, the Mistress began to grow short with me. Mary Dove bound my chest and bade me hide the coming of my courses. The first time her Ladyship slapped me was on a fine June evening. The Master stayed away a good bit of the

time in those days, visiting other planters. All the gentry were con-
ferring then about conversion to the new crop, sugar. We were alone
in the house, the gangs still far out in the fields, when a keening
came up from the yard. It was Ardiss with her time upon her. The
Mistress sent myself and Mary down to tend her in that little shed.
How well I remember: the planks beneath us grew wet and slick. So
much pain seemed to surprise the Scots lass, her eyes bulging when
it came like someone whacked from behind with an axe.

"When the baby was delivered—a lusty son—Mary sent me to
the Big House kitchen for rags. The mistress had risen after a nap.
Through the window where she liked to sit she watched me crossing the yard. Sometimes she waited a week of afternoons at that
window, for Master's return. 'What are you about?' she called that
afternoon from the top of the stairs. 'Please madam, soft rags to
wrap the new babby,' said I. But before I could take them I must tell
her of this child—its sex, its vitality, and most pointedly its looks.
Indeed, its looks were distinctive, for it was born with Paud Iasc's
ginger curls matted all over its wee perfect head.

"Later when Mary returned wearily to the house the mistress
called her also to her side. 'Fetch the child to me,' she fretted. 'I must
see for myself.' But Mary spoke in calming tones: 'There is no need.
'Tis an Irish wee'n.'

"'Do you swear it? There is no mark of him in it?'"

"'Nil, mawdawm, the child has the hair of Iasc, the fisherman. I
swear.'

"At this the mistress quieted. She credited Mary's word, for they
had been together for a dozen years."

"And in the end see what that trust brought her: almost the loss
of life and home!" Coote interposes sternly. "Do not deviate. Continue your dark tale."

"The mistress quieted," Cot Quashey repeats, "but was not truly
reassured, for that very evening as I plaited her for bed, her eyes nar-
rowed upon me in the mirror. 'Pray look at you!' she cried. 'You're

getting fat. Did I furnish you with fine new clothes just to have you bursting up and out of them? Did I?' 'No Lady,' I said downcast. But she had raised the heavy silver brush from her dressing table, and swung it backward into my face. 'Your physique does not become you,' said she. 'You shall spend some weeks on field rations, I'll see to that.'

"Thus began the decline of my happier days into the pit of her madness. For she would starve me, clout me, scratch me, then the next day turn and feed me sweetmeats between her own fingers. I grew gawky, so confused I blinked and stuttered. Still, the house ways were much better than the fields, until she lost the last child.

"The master was pleased with Ardiss's fine son. In time Salome's daughter bore a child as well, and he beheld this increase in numbers, this generation of his fortune without the slightest effort on his part, as a promising new plantation industry. That summer Paud Iasc was meted his overdue punishment for insubordination, then returned to quarter with the northern lads while Ardiss nussed her wee'n. But in spite of himself, Paud took pride in the child that had been forced out of him, as it learned to laugh, and reach, and touch. The ginger curls of birth fell out, the small head curved naked and perfect under its father's stroking hand. After the next tobacco harvest, the master stood with Jenks outside the barn and speculated. 'Now is the time to breed more stock. Put the redshanks Irishman in with the girl again, their breed is strong; and bed the two black females with different bucks. As for the child— Cotleen is it?—another harvest, and she'll be ready. Perhaps by then our carpenter will have grown more lusty.'

"So once more Ardiss conceived. My mistress, as her own blood-soaked cloths were scrubbed and hung to dry month after month, saw from her window that no longer did the rags lie drying on the bushes round the Scots girl's shed. After her nightmares she sometimes sang, like a nursery rhyme, 'Sows and Scots will rear their young, / While ladies lose their babies.'" Perhaps his revulsion at these women's matters shows in Coote's face, for the prisoner leans forward and says, "In truth, sir, her bewilderment, misguided as it was, would break a heart of stone. For every evening she made the same toilette, applying scented oils to tired flesh to make it gleam in the kind candlelight. We pulled her still-fine braid of hair over one shoulder and bound it with a bright silk cord, in case he came.

"We lay her in the carved, stepped bed, on those chaste, infertile sheets, and if she woke alone in them her mood was rash and foul. But happy were the evenings when he came to call and stayed till day. Then, I believe, they still had hope that something would restore them to the kind of life they might have enjoyed, had their firstborn lived and Henry Plackler, a mere squire, had through paternity become the true master of our lady's father's place at Arlington.

"Yes, as they breakfasted at the little tea table in the corner of her room after a night together, there was . . . conviviality . . . between them, and if he rode away then to healthier plantations, she often seemed serene. She would nap, then rise to read her little book of common prayer at the window that overlooked the yard. And piteously, long before her courses were due to flow, she would perceive symptoms of a babe within. Mary and myself rode her sweetest hopes, dark disappointments, and reddest rages every month, along with her. In short, surely at times Mary and myself wished as much as Mistress Plackler that she would bear a child.

"And then the miracle occurred. The courses did not come. Mary confirmed the flat dry nipples budding, tender to the touch. After some weeks I ran with a silver urn each time my Lady's gorge erupted unexpectedly. But after every retching she would smile and sigh, reporting each puke as work well done to Master, who would come to sit upon her sheets and hold her hand as night fell. The change was great: we heard them laughing, saw their heads held close together in the taper glow."

· · ·

"Then the day came when Mary and I were in the kitchen, boiling the linens and smallclothes: it was a Monday. In the big houses in the north countries they only do this twice a year, in good drying weather. But as you know, sir, we must launder often in the tropics, for the stench of the body, heated by cloth, develops quickly, even amongst gentry." Coote flashes with sudden shame upon the shirt he wears, and will have to wear next evening. So strong is his desire to sniff for subtle and insulting odors that he misses some testimony, until, ". . . there stood the mistress in her nightshift and bare feet, slumped against the pantry door. She said dreamlike, 'Mary, what is this cold wet thing on my leg?' and stretched forth a hand full of clumps and blood. I got her into bed, while Mary sent Jenks to the next plantation for the master. But by the time he came it was all over. They figured five full months she'd held this one, much longer than the time before.

"The mistress lost both blood and will. The doctor came from Bridgetown. As we had only fowl and swine, the mistress of another Big House sent a bullock, which the Africans knew how to drain daily for blood, yet keep alive. Our lady had to drink a goblet of warm blood twice daily. I held the crystal cup to her weak mouth, and it sparkled like claret in the firelight of her room. She was always cold, and we sweltered till we felt faint in attending her. The master would not come into her room. Less than one week after her mishap he rode off on his mare to Bridgetown, not knowing full well yet if she'd turn septic as do many highborns in the tropic countryside. But Mistress healed to rise again.

"She rose again at sundown on an evening fair as any other. I was sweeping out the courtyard from the afternoon storm's blow when Mary, more whey-faced than the mistress leaning on her, came through the open door and in a low voice told me, 'Get Ardiss.'

"Gaily I skipped through the sunshine of the yard to where the Scots girl, just back from the fields, sat in the door of her shed, dandling the fine fat child she'd borne the previous summer. 'Ardiss,

Mary needs you,' I sang, and returned to finish swishing leaves into the ditches. Ardiss, baby on her hip, followed along. Meanwhile Mary had sent a pickaninny running for Jenks. He arrived hot and panting, breeches unlaced, blouse in one hand. He had been shaving.

"'What is it, Mistress Plackler?' he inquired.

"'Take that child from its dam,' she ordered sternly, 'and fetch the mule cart.' There was confusion. One by one we surmised, then rejected, her meaning. Jenks brought the cart around, tucking his shirttails down his breeches. The mule closed its eyes and chewed cud as it waited.

"'Please Mistress . . . why, Mistress? . . . No, no, no, Mistress,' Ardiss cried as Jenks pulled the startled baby from her arms. Up the hillside in their huts the gangs were squatting at their evening rations when they heard the fierce commotion, saw the tugging, heard the child begin to cry. Just as Paudi Iasc reached the bottom of the incline we all saw Jenks thrust the screaming child into the straw on the cart bottom and at the same time, watched Ardiss raise her hand to strike the mistress.

"It was Paudi Iasc who caught that hand in midswing, cursing; he who saved Ardiss from having the new life she carried flogged away. It was Paudi Iasc who leapt toward the cart, almost unseating Jenks with one rough push. For this he earned two nights and one day in the stocks, in the full sun of the yard.

"The mistress gave her orders to Jenks. She told him to command the best price that he could for the baby somewhere along the way. Remember the child's length of service was to be a full twenty-one years, as a bargain point, she said. Jenks was, in all events, to carry on to Bridgetown, after selling the child, and find his master. He was to bring him home where she had need of him: or else she would sell more of us, her stock. Those were the words she used.

"How, wherever we each are scattered now, will we forget that sundown—the heavens pearly blue and gentle pink—which made all future sunsets haunted by a disappearing baby's shrieks and its mother's answering wail?"

"It took a week for Jenks to find the disbelieving master, coax him to come home, and for them to return. In that time Salome's daughter and her child were also sent to block with the suboverseer of a neighbor, whom the mistress called in to maintain order while her own men were away. Mary said the mistress imagined Salome's babe exceeding light for Africans. It was like hell, a view of hell down in the yard, the black girl's man rolling his eyes and sweating as they loaded up his kin, Ardiss shrieking in tongues to condemn the farmhand who drove the cart away. But the mistress was not satiated. That very evening, she had me whipped.

"'Come here you sully slut,' she said to me, as she watched the yard with one eye from her window. The morning before had been like someone else's life, her ladyship offering me a jellied bonbon, and as I combed her, holding a silk riband to my cheek and murmuring, 'Look how well this suits your eyes.'

"I will not lie. I wanted that blue riband, it was true it suited my blue eyes and ginger hair better than it did her own." Coote frowns up fiercely from his scribbling.

"But I did not take it. And the next afternoon, after she had cloven the young African family apart, she called me to her whilst Mary stood by looking at the wall. 'Look,' screeched Mistress, 'Mary you are my witness, this girl is a thief! Thus she does repay my kindness!'

"My poor poor Mary. Grimly she stood there as the lady lifted the blue silk riband from beneath the gray surcoat-pillow on my pallet.

"How swiftly, how completely, the course of my life changed in that one moment. In the next, despite my croakings, the neighbor's suboverseer had me by the wrists, dragging me through the yard to the horse stable. My hands were tied to a spike high in the wall, and I received ten of his sound-muscled stripes. Before full measure had been given, I fainted.

"I came to in the straw, my blue bodice folded neat beside me, the grain sticking in my flesh like needles. I was sobbing in the dark when I heard a noise. The door swung inward. The master had arrived with his roan mare. When he perceived me, Master asked me what had happened. Only a child as young as I would have opened her gob and spilled out everything. I told him what the mistress had accused me of, and that she herself had planted the lovely riband in my bed. Wiping down his horse by the silver light that crept through the narrow window in the stall, he laughed out loud at this. But in the end, when the horse was quietly chuffing feed, he came toward me through the bales. He lay his ringed hand on my forehead. 'You are too warm,' he murmured.

"'No Master, I am very cold,' I shuddered. And he commanded me to make myself a nest in the hay, he would send Mary to bring a blanket and tend my wounds. 'You are a worthy lass,' he told me. 'I will not see you spoiled, you can rest certain of that.'

"Poor Mary came to wash and heal me in moments stolen from the mistress. Ah, how she begged my pardon for the part that she was forced to play, in witnessing a theft that never happened! Though in the shed he'd laughed when I told him of his lady's plot against me, when his wife accused me to him he was most serious, Mary said, of mein. 'My dear,' he told her, 'you must not be vexed by such inconsequentials. The maid must be returned to fieldwork; trouble no more about her, but rest so that your health returns.'"

Coote has a notion. He indulges it. "Did you report Mary Dove's plot because she had borne false witness against you?"

"Did I take vengeance? No! None of us owned the right to tell the truth, we all understood that," says Cot Quashey. "The truth was the creation of our masters. Everybody knew. But we also had a duty to, in small silent ways, do what we could to behave *other* than the masters' truth."

"You babble," Coote reminds sternly.

"For not keeping right behavior—this is why I've had to bear the guilt of Paudi Iasc these many years. For once my back had healed and I returned to second gang, I found the other bondspeople accepted me in a way they had not done before. It was the welts upon my back. A kind of respect had come from surviving the ceremony of the whip, like some reversed communion of unjust pain between us. But also, those higher in rank who might have used Eugenia Plackler's ire as excuse to wield the whip, desisted. For the master had begun to favor me.

"Oh, not one word was said directly, but Dora and Jenks could sense that he did not want to see another mark upon me. Yet even from this dually strengthened position, when Paudi Iasc called out to me for a sip of water on his second day in the stocks, I lowered my head and skirted his suffering without reply. Even the Roman soldiers gave Christ a sponge of vinegar. But I would not chance to help my countryman the least, and even glared in anger at his face. For I was afraid.

"I was afraid," the Irishwoman cants, "to lose all I had gained. For once again I felt the manic demiurge called hope. The master had begun to visit me most nights. From the open stable to a disused stall I moved, and Master Henry bade me use whatever was at hand to make myself comfortable. I dragged bale after bale of old honey-scented hay to build my roost. I made a bed of sorts, raised knee-height from the floor to discourage rats; and pushing bales up onto this first platform I made the seat where Master came to sit and talk. From my deserted pallet Mary brought me my father's coat, my mother's whistle hidden still in its deep pocket; and also brought a coverlet which had been set aside for polishing. At my master's orders she brought a sconce for tallow wicks. We hung it from the very spike I had been tied to for my chastisement. Which slowly, so desperate was I, I began to bless; for it was the flogging that had brought me to my master's eye.

"Who do we love, as much as the deliverer?" she muses. Coote glances up acutely. The Irishwoman's staring into some deep void in front of her. "And what pain lingers longer than being despised?

"From my mistress and her recurring madness, he brought me laughter. The first door to shut since I had been trepanned: there was a half-door on my disused stall—this was the door I proudly opened when I heard his boots approaching in the dark. I was a child, a girl child. The first bauble he brought me was the riband, the very blue riband I had not stolen: he fetched it to me. 'There Cot,' he said, 'that justifies something.' He tied it in my hair, then pulled the ribboned coil toward him and sunk his nose in it. Only one week before had he first unbound my cap to touch my curls. 'I remember you,' he said then, dreamily, spreading one hand through my ringlets and snarls. 'That afternoon in Bridgetown when they brought you from the ship, and I bought you, gray rags and all, even then I took note of this hair.'

"In the stable I learned about my looks. My master owned me, truth, labor, and looks. Thus he commanded me to bathe in the stream every Saturday afternoon, and in the stable to keep my cap off, my hair unbound, the riband looped to tie it up. Keep the first buttons of my bodice undone because he found the white flesh at my neck startling: 'That such a one should have such skin,' he murmured, as I sat upon his knee."

Coote's lips tighten and turn down at her words. His trousers rub uncomfortably against his thighs.

"Yes, sir, I sat upon his knee, as he bade me do. I took off the faded too-tight bodice, and laced on the ivory cambric corselet that he brought to me, and by the end I bit my lips and slapped my cheeks for color, just to see him pause outside the pool of tallow light as I held the stall door open, and whisper, 'Beautiful! Beautiful!' But what you think, sir, did not happen."

Coote sniggers, instantly angry for demeaning himself by show-ing such expression before a hag of lower race. He is, according to the evidence, only four or five years younger than herself.

"Nay, it did not. For Master Henry did not crave the natural from me, though with his croonings and his touchings I came to want to offer it. Wanting to feel the hand of comfort more, to keep it longer with me in that sea of fear which was my life in bond. But no, Master Henry liked to talk. To talk and diddle.

"The night he brought his lady's corselet to me he spoke of those fond days when his Eugenia—he called her Jenny then, said he—had been his bride of love. She had defied her father, the Earl of Orkney, with her youngest brother's help, to slip away and marry him. And had gotten away with it, the only girl 'mid four strong sons all bickering for land. In shame to see her married down, the Earl had sent them out to govern his Barbados holdings. The youngest brother got her hall near Nottingham.

"I sat so still upon his lap, my heart thumping with desire to be like pretty Jenny. To inhabit her place in the story so that he would run away with me though we were landless, penniless, because he could not resist my beauty. What power anyone would have, if they were truly irresistible. Rich or poor, we women dream of this road, and of how we'll win it!

"But as I sat there, barely breathing as he absently stroked my soft new bosom above the corselet's fine silky stuff, he grew quite angry under me. Talked about his lady's father; how he, my master, had been hobbled like a slave, by a pittance of retainer in Barbados. 'They say it is my gambling,' he sneered to the darkness of the barn. 'But what galls them is that I'm a man! Not a niggardly mer-chant, but a man! Willing to risk all for a change of luck they'll never know, with their prudent caution. And now . . . ,' he uttered low, 'they mean to break me because my wife cannot bear a living child, an heir of our shared blood. But I will not be broken! I will not find myself evicted from this estate on the day her coffin lowers to the ground. Her great bullocks of brothers will not oust me!

"'I have a plan! I only need a little credit from this one or that among my neighbors . . . then I *will* risk all, you'll see.' Can you imagine my youth, the innocence? Of how I timidly touched his dark long curls, for I was certain he meant me. I was the risk, I thought, or bound up with it in the everything he wanted for himself.'"

Peter Coote lays his quill down in its holder. He is charged with sudden fury. "Who do you think to deceive with your rantings?" he demands. "The Governor? Or only me? Good men may slip in the grease of a slattern's skirts for reasons of no import. But what freeman, let alone a gentleman, would reveal his plans and secrets to a tart, a cow, a lowly slave? What do you take me for, you frowsy hag?"

Now it is the prisoner's turn to appear incredulous. After a moment she clears her throat, and in a voice so mild it's almost kindly, says, "Why sir, the preferred confidante of the master *is* the slave. Who else can be trusted not to turn dark secrets to a tumbling of power? Who else will listen patiently, uncritically, endlessly, admiringly—expressing no objections or opinions? Who else provides the truly captive audience, which never asks for discourse, or even reason, but must agree? Why, masters are not masters because they wish to share, or to collaborate . . ."

Before the storm comes to wash the glumness from the afternoon, the Irishwoman tells her gaoler of that night when Mary Dove crept to the shed before the master. "I thought that he'd come early, and somehow I had missed the sound of his boots on the pebbles of the yard. Quickly I slid a finger to unhook the two top buttons of my blouse. With the other hand I slapped each cheek as I bit down on my lower lip. The wick was in the sconce already, lit by a coal from my cooking fire behind the shed. The door creaked slowly inward, the horse uneasy, nickering, then still again.

"I had not heard her for she was barefoot, as all bondspeople were. Now she held a finger to her lips to caution silence, and moved forward. I remember the oddest things, even now, about that visit. She, herself forced to condone the weaknesses and concede the lies of those who held her life in hand, had never once, during the months after my flogging, asked if he'd had his way with me. I suppose there would have been no point. Surely it was assumed. A bondsmaid has no right to withhold aught from her owners. And Mary would have had no way to help me, any more than she could help Ardiss, or Salome's girl, or myself when I was flogged for growing comely.

"But now she came toward me in the candle glow, and put her hand on my forearm, and said blandly, 'Look at you, gotten up as for your betrothed.' Her hand was icy cold.

"I mistook her at the first, mock-curtsying because I thought she was admiring me, as did himself. I smiled. 'Beautiful. The master calls me Beautiful.'

"She shook my arm once, sharply. 'From this night forward you need not suffer him again,' she said low but stern. 'We will go far from here, no one will know, you will forget, you will have a new life.' She told me of her plan. At first they'd thought that when he left me tonight, I should tip the wick into the hay and run, and meet them in the jungle. But now they had decided not to fire anything. The neighboring plantations would see the flames and smell the smoke. No; they, the plotters—the two Pauds, Salome and her man, several Africans including the small pickaninny who brought my tin of loblolly each evening, and Mary herself—they would hack the enemy in its bed. My only task was to untie his horse, the last steed on the plantation, and lead it quietly into the bush. Someone else would bring the donkey, tethered for pasturage at the forest's edge. That way, no alarm could be swiftly raised, should anyone escape the butcher knife.

"I argued with her," the Irishwoman insists. Coote peers fiercely at his prisoner, then nods in agreement as the scene runs before his mind's eye. "I pleaded for my master's life, for I loved him, the savior on whom I had staked every desperate hope. I told her how impossible it would be—a dozen ill-fed, exhausted serving folk; with what? Stones to throw? A garden hoe, a cotton baling knife? The master and Jenks were said to sleep with brass-fitted pistols and cedar bags of shot beside their beds. Never! Never would we scarecrows see the sun rise if we dast raise hands against our masters.

"And Mary. How she looked at me with pity. A pity which moved her hand over my cheek, cupping my chin in the secret gesture which, ever since my mother, I have hungered for. 'You do not understand yet, Darling. How going free can make us suddenly a match for any gun,' she said, so gently. 'But it's all right. You do not need to understand. Just untie the horse and lead it to the wood, when himself has finished with you for the night. We'll find you there.'

"She never doubted me, my Mary. She was not taken so young that her moral bones were yet unformed. But I had been. And when my master, who'd been cupping my small chin in his hand for many weeks, came to my stall, I found his favor more valuable than hers, or any of my kind."

"By 'your kind' do you mean those of the Irish nation?" he clarifies busily, without looking up. There is the slightest pause.

"Well. Of the Irish nation: or the female nation: or of the nation of all chattel," replies the prisoner. "At any rate, that night when he arrived master brought me a cutlet from his plate, and held a cup of wine, and found no fault with me, but was youthful and merry. He held me round the waist and talked about his plan. It was to stake Arlington—the crops, the slaves, the animals down to the last hen's egg—for wager against a large plantation in Brazil, once its owner—too fond of cane whiskey—returned to Bridgetown. And all the while I was thinking.

"By now, over six years of my bond had passed, according to the Captain's deal. I did not want to risk my release in a year: that lay, sir, at the very bottom of my hot, cold, reasoning. I told him everything."

The interrogation pauses. Peter Coote looks his prisoner up and down with a pursed smile before he asks, "So, biddy, would you say that you were Mary Dove's wren?" The mad bitch spits onto the floor. He masters himself before he asks coolly, "What happened then? Was he displeased with you as well as with your comrades? For soon, I know, you were sold off to the Glebe."

Cot Quashey shakes her head. "Not that it matters, what happened between livestock dealers long ago, but never was I sold to that plantation. This is what happened. In the morning, they led the plotters off hobbled, Mary amongst them. Jenks had run the horse into a lather the night before to raise militia at the next plantation, while the Master had loaded all his firearms and sat in the vestibule to wait. He doused the lights for bed and let the rebels give him time to enter a peaceful sleep. Salome's man was the first to creep in through the door, then Paud nOg. They each received a bullet for their welcoming. I was not there, but I imagine it still, the mistress screaming from above, the master laughing as he often did at moments that seemed not to call for it. The first two rebels different shades of blue in the moonlight, then the tarry blood seeping from them, the loud clatter on the porch as Jenks with the hasty raggle-tag militia leapt out of the bushes with guns and swords at hand. All night I huddled in the hay within the barn, not certain who would take the lead, and fearing either side. I prayed desperately to my fading saints to defend me, then defended myself hotly to those tired saints. But they kept still. Nothing stirred but a rat, munching old chaff. I wafted from the strain of prayer's dry words told on the rosary of my fingertips, to the likelier image of a master I might cosset and persuade: one who could, with his gratitude, wash away my ever-whelming dread that I had murdered my only friend when I gave him her secret.

"Toward morning they were leaving; two ranks of plantation volunteers, the brave of Arlington between them. The master stood there to review them. I opened the barn door to peer at the condemned, already doomed to the remorse that gnaws my gizzard still, almost thirty years after the day. The morning was as mild as milk. Dora spilled the corn about the yard to feed the fowl: I saw pregnant Ardiss tied shank to shank with the other daughter of Salome in the file.

"The birds sang silvery tunes as a soldier on a mule swung the flat of his rifle into Mary's kidneys. Then the group began to march forth through the dust."

"Woman, why did you go wrong?" Coote inquires with intensity, hoping to shorten this interminable testimony. "In your early years it seems you knew your duty . . ."

"Ah no. That I did not. But I have spent these last years trying to right the errors of those days." It's an alarming and ambiguous statement: also one that he can see the prisoner will give no swift explanation to. He sighs and dips his quill and waits.

"The master was not rife with me, nor was he glad. The plantation work was abandoned for some days for want of hands. Then other masters thereabouts lent some men to Arlington for the cost of their board, so pleased were they with Plackler's foil. That was how they called it. Meanwhile my own days spread about me, aimless and afraid. Only the children were left at Arlington. And Dora, you might guess. No one came to me, except the pickaninny with the rations, who somehow had escaped notice during the revolt. He kept his eyes lowered as I took my share. I could not tell if he avoided me, knowing my treachery; or if he had known nothing of the role Mary wanted me to play. By the time Master came to visit me again, six days and nights of lonely and remorseful agony had passed. Six eons, in which I tied a limp riband in my hair and sucked my lips to make them rosier to a discerning eye, but no one came, not even the horse to its stall. Then he was there, though brusquer, not pulling me toward his knee, not stroking my cheek and breast, but set on other things, though jolly enough in speech. 'My Cot, how unlike your fellows you have turned out. They who gambled all, it must be said . . . ,' he smiled.

" 'Where are they gone, Master Henry?' I asked him timidly. And he told me who had died of shot, of Mary and Salome and two more bound for the gallows tree. Salome's son-in-law and Iasc had escaped for the time, though they'd be caught and made example of. But the rest, he said, had gone to block at Bridgetown to try some other master's hospitality. 'And we will go to Bridgetown too, my little Cot, in only two days' time. For word's come back that my as-sociate, the Dutch planter, has come up from Brazil. So Cot; ready yourself to see the fine houses of Bridgetown. Down to the river in the morning with you, to bathe these lovely tresses. When Dora has finished tending my poor wife, I'll send her with a fresh skirt and waistcoat for you to wear. My girl,' he said, rising to leave, 'you will enter Bridgetown all in finery.' And I was fool enough to giggle, and curtsy deep. He bade me bundle up my other things—my gifts from him, my father's coat—we would not trouble to hurry back from the festivities, said he. I was certain that I was being raised to him in favor even more. Yes: I knew what was a concubine.

"But for some hours my spleen lurched after Dora brought the new clean clothes. She passed them to my hands without a word, but I felt the scorn pour from her like a foul wind. When she had left as silent as she came, I shook the items out. They were my Mary's annual allotment, sewn at Easter but saved for colder weather. I had helped her stitch the bodice up. We'd laughed and mocked fine fashions on the island then; her scent now hovered in the air around me, like the fey. But I had to put them on, though it was like putting on a ghost. I sat there in the sweltering shed, on the straw throne I had constructed for a Master's courtship, until he himself came to fetch me. I was to bind my hair under my too-small cap to keep the dust of the road out of my shining locks, said he, considering me with his head aslant, a distant smile on his graceful lips. Master was uncommon handsome; but at that moment he seemed cousin to the Captain I have told you of.

"I took up my bundle; the old gray surcoat wrapped around a blue riband, a dimity corselet, my own faded skirt and bodice, and followed meekly to the harnessed cart. The mule was braying at his own demons. Up onto the driver's seat jumped my master, and I scuttled till I sat as close as possible behind him in the box. Across the way, tied to the handle of the rear flap of the cart, a sullen African child they called Hugo slumped with eyes downcast.

"Dora came to the cart with a small list of errands for our mistress, and Jenks spoke quietly about arrangements for the hired crew. How jovial was the sun! Not hot yet, but strong enough to catch the dew prisms on new flowers and leaves, and make the whole clean world flash. To make the buildings around the yard and up the hill seem calm and pleasing, well set out. Then something caught my eye at the window above the circled drive where we sat waiting in our cart. It was the Mistress, drawing back the curtain; she who, in my childish mind, had brought these days of horror on us all. And so, as my master bent forward, shook the reins, and shouted the beast into motion, I reached into the bundled surcoat and pulled out my mother's pipe. I put it to my mouth, and remembered a baby song all children learn in Ireland. I whistled it out, and my master turned askance, then laughed quite raucously. I whistled bright and smart. I wanted the mistress to see I had been saved from her, and was going off now with my lovely master to know better days, because I had been loyal, and completely true. Truly his thing.

"But as I tootled down the road I did not heed that we clipped along the same route taken first by Ardiss's child, by Salome's kin, then by the rebels I had betrayed. I realized it later. For when we came to Bridgetown, my master tied me, like the African, to a tree. We were in a Spanish courtyard, I remember that my tether let me reach a bush of trumpet flowers when I had to make my water. There was all the time and more to think then.

"They played at cards all night. Finally we sat, tied together, the wordless African lad and me, and kept a numb vigil. Then a master staggering with spirits came out to get us ready for the road ahead: not Master Plackler, nor any Dutchman, but a small angry cock of a man, the overseer of the Glebe. My master had gambled all—his final mule, the cart and harness, the African youth called Hugo, myself, and those still back at Arlington—the carpenter and Salome's lads as well. I never saw his face again. Thus I was sold anew, for seven more years in bondage."

III

"The Glebe was my next plantation. It lies in the parish of St. John which rolls down to the eastern sea. The Glebe was seven times the acreage of Arlington and run by companies of slaves who numbered in the hundreds. There were four gangs, and the first gang was split in two, there being many distant fields to attend. Each gang was urged on by Africans—there were no white drivers then at most of the plantations. Men drove the adults in the two sections of the first gang; women drove the younger people in the second, third, and fourth. The fourth was called the pot gang.

"The pot gang were the tenderest of children. They could not cook yet for themselves, so a granny too old for heavy work was charged with boiling up a pot of mush for their midday meal. When the gong was sounded those children used to race from every direction where they'd been pulling fodder or feeding fowl, to the pot of loblolly. What child is not hungry? I remember them so well! Mostly they were young Africans, though a few were European, and some a mix of both. They called out in so many tongues with their birdlike voices, and our pride in them gave us cheer and laughter as well as worry.

" 'Every mouth that does not suckle must earn its feed,' said Jack Vaughton, the overseer of the sugar fields. He and the other overseers had been brought out from England, except for Robert Rigley, who oversaw the sugar mills and the distillery. He was a Scotsman, and renowned at brewing spirits. There was one Ephraim Lye, I remember, who oversaw the yard—the smithy, cooper's shed, the cobblery and pottery and all; and William Butler, who oversaw the tending of the stock. I knew these last only by sight. Because I was gambled for the value of a second-gang fieldhand, Vaughton was the one I must abide.

"It was he who drove me to the Glebe from Bridgetown after Master Plackler gambled me away. He who turned me out onto the ground with the name 'Big Dinah' as his only instruction before he turned the cart back down the lane for Arlington. He lost no time in fetching his master's other goods—two of Salome's younger sons, the carpenter, the sag-backed mule to work the grinding mill—and setting them to work. That man was like an accountant on horseback with a bullwhip."

Peter Coote notes that she is huddling her shawl around her tightly, yet the morning is exceeding warm. He lays his pen in its painted porcelain holder and looks closely at her face. Her forehead and neck are flushed and sweaty. For the first time he notices small rusty wisps of hair sticking to her brow from beneath the wilted cap.

"Have you much fever?" he asks.

"A touch," she mumbles. "The back. Lucy says 'tis not healing at all."

Peter Coote makes a "tcch" sound to demonstrate doctorly concern. "I must see to it myself, then, before you leave me for the day," he replies. The warm swelling comes into his chest; he always feels it when he bends to help someone, no matter how lowly. It is a sensation that embarrasses him, womanish rather than sound and manly. He never heard the teaching physicians tell of it, this almost overwhelming wave; and he keeps its secret softness to himself. Now he leans toward the woman for intensity. "Biddy, as you feel low, and I have many other duties, it would help both of us if you could . . . tailor . . . your testimony on this day to your encounters, your relations, with the Africans."

But she replies, "My entire life at the Glebe, from that first evening unto twenty years, was an encounter, a relationship, with Africans."

Coote sighs. "So be it then. You like your gab," and picks up his implement.

"Vaughton put me on the ground. In this way all slaves and servants were settled in, except those purchased for the house, and ones too small to fend for themselves as I'd been first in Arlington. Thus, as I said, the cook shed and the stable where I slept at my first plantation were luxuries, for they were ready-built.

"In general, though, when slaves arrived for seven years or for a lifetime, they were set upon a spot of earth; and on that spot it was their task, after a day in field or sugar mill, to build themselves a shelter of what materials they might find at hand. I was put out of the cart just below a rise. A track led up over that rise. The time was evening, but the gangs had not come in yet from the fields.

"I went into the bushes by the track and made my water, and took off the tight corselet my Master Henry gave me. Then I stood peering through the leaves and curling vines. And still it seems right odd to me that among all that strangeness I felt not desolate; only numb and dumbstruck. I looked about the Glebe. It seemed a village, not a farm. There on a low plateau to my left stood the three-storied manor, with a circular lane of crushed red stone leading to its pink marble half-moon steps. Two black girls with suds and brushes were on their knees, washing the mud of the afternoon showers from the porch. At Arlington, blacks never worked at the house.

"The house was freshly plastered, I recall, one white wall lit coral by the waning sun. Roses were planted along a walkway near it, and lemon trees and limes, cut into boxy hedges.

"The work yard was central to my view. At day's end, from that vantage point, I could hear the clank of hammer on hot iron coming from the smithy. There stood an open square of wooden and stone sheds. In front of the one which I learned was the pottery, a lone African in a patterned orange cap sat at a wheel slapping clay he spun. There was a well in this yard, a small pond, and two larger ponds, fenced in although their gates swung open at the time. Down further in a small declivity there stood sheds my nose told me housed animals. Later I learned which ones were for cattle, which for horses, which for sheep. There were also small houses for the fowl and another one for pigs. Pigs thrive well on sugar trash. Their flesh turns sweet and cooks up crispy.

"But that evening as I spied the holdings from the brush, the animals were out to field. I heard ewes bleating to their lambs now and again. These were the first sheep I had heard of in Barbados. They made me sick with longing for Ireland even after six years away, and seemed treacherous, like trusted beings from a peaceful realm who lead the dreamer, unsuspecting, off of nightmare's cliffs.

"Further below, toward where I stood, was the heart of the plantation—the sugar works. I saw the offices, the gray stone mill beside the muddy river; the great boiling house, the curing barns, the still. Many small paths crosshatched from that enterprise to the cottages where the few white house servants and the overseers lived, just below the blind where I was crouching. A dozen servants—waged after indenture, this being 1657 when kidnapping Irish, Scots, and poor English was already giving over to kidnapping Africans—slept in long rows of pallets inside their houses. Not so the overseers.

"Their houses were two-storied, whitewashed, with bright chimbley pots. The overseers had use of slaves and servants, so their yards were planted with vegetables and native flowers, the grass cut back with sugar knives to keep out snakes and rats and those brown spiders who nest in sheds and shadows, and whose sting can kill a six months' pig.

"All about me and above me on that dusty hill, the shacks of Africans and the few indentured field whites were built; and just below them I could build my own, Jack Vaughton said. I was looking down at my hands in a puzzlement that blocked all thought or action when I heard the folk returning from the far-off fields. How to build? What to build with? I was wondering. But no answer passed through my mind. Only wind, and the image of my body lying under it while the rain soaked into me. In this vision I had nowhere dry to go, and the strangers in their strange abodes would not open their doors to me.

"Then I heard them singing: one clear male shout and an answering chant behind him. Marching from a field beyond the big house came half of the first gang, hoes, digging sticks, and shovels perched upon their shoulders. This crew was about three-quarters men, the rest women. In those earlier days of planting sugar, few women were imported. The masters did not know then that the men were lazy."

A little laugh. She disguises it straightaway as a cough. Coote is astonished. A feeble woman, fevered with festered lashes, discrediting the diligence of men. Incredible. But then, she is demented. There is documentation attesting this.

"Big Dinah told me, and Quashey too, God rest him, that where they came from, women made the fields. Did the planting and the weeding, the harvest and the cure, and the preparation of new seed. But the slavers did not know this. They'd brought in women—whether Irish or Ibo—mainly for the breeding and the housework. That was it, so."

Quill scratches over paper. The third morning flies by. Coote sprawls across his desk, braced upon his elbows. For a while the rhythm of her telling and the rhythm of his writing join like breath. The Irishwoman, Cot—then seventeen years of age and relatively coddled at Arlington, so that she knew not how to build a house, nor had anyone to help her—talks of sleeping under a banyan tree the first six nights. Of hiding her belongings—the surcoat of her father with her mother's whistle, an extra apron and cap, the corselet, a fraying dark blue ribbon—under the bushes while she worked. She tells of asking for Big Dinah, the overseer of the second gang, which she had been assigned to. Accosting a younger girl from the third gang, "the hog's meat gang," who trudged up the path past where she hid in the bushes that first evening. Straggling behind the others toward the village of small shacks rising over top of the hill, this child gave a little shriek when Cot hissed and grabbed her elbow. She seemed to know no English, though when she heard "Big Dinah" she pointed, trying to break free.

Cot held to the girl's arm for safety's sake among the unknown people. In the yards of the mud hovels on the hilltop the laborers were gathering for supper. The light had drained, and now the orange glow from small, crackling cook fires illuminated faces. The people where the young girl led were dark people. Squatting beside the walls of mud-daubed houses, bending over a fire to stir a pot, kneeling at an open log to smash dried corn with rocks. Passing one yard Cot saw a man rinse his hands in the basin where a baby was being bathed. The man splashed the child and they laughed. His woman looked at Cot in silence, lifting the infant from the water. "I half-raised my arm in greeting, but saw myself through her eyes for a moment. So pale I seemed glowing in the dark, a huge glowworm."

Big Dinah stood before a shack with a small garden plot at the side, pressing her knuckles into her wide back. She answered in English. "Vaughton say you for my fields? You sure?" she muttered, frowning. Cot asked for a place to sleep the night but was refused. "The night looks clear," Big Dinah said. "You rest under the banyan, we find you when we go out early." With foreign words the woman sent a pickaninny into the cabin. He came back to the doorway holding a small dried fish to Cot. "Some pawpaw by the ditch down there," the big woman said, pointing.

Cot Quashey tells the Governor's man that she had joined the second gang, a group of more than fifty youths. "I was with them until Big Dinah died almost three years later." The second gang weeded sugarcane—"It was similar to topping tobacco," she says— and planted food crops—corn, yams, potatoes, pigeon peas. They tended livestock of the various kinds, and during harvest season moved up and down the rows collecting cane trash to fuel the furnace at the boiling house. Outside of harvest, they took the sugar trash to rethatch the cottages of the slaves, and to sweeten the meat of the hogs.

On those first evenings before dark the Irish girl stole around the edges of the yards, shivering as she noted the structure of the houses. Through the treetops she could glimpse the wide sea flowing home. Sometimes someone threw a stone at her or yelled, and she slunk away. By Sunday she had gathered enough sticks to poke into the ground for a three-walled shed. "I remember how my back ached that Sunday night; but as the evening star began to wink, I crisscrossed piles of long fresh branches across a portion of my narrow walls, and made a bough roof to lie under. I had no science then; the walls and thatch became the nest for beetles, flying roaches, scorpions. The Africans know to pat mud and dung over all to keep away insects.

"No one helped me, though they watched me from the corners of their eyes. I was the only Christian in the second gang at that time. The Africans thought I had done something severely wrong, for white female servants were often used for housework by this time. They looked more natural in an apron, the masters thought, and knew a tea cozy was not a hat, and the like. So . . . that was my first housheen. I was bit upon the neck by a centipede just before it was blown over by a storm a fortnight later. But the next time I built faster, and someone from the cooper's shed lent me a hammer. He showed me how to pound the sticks into holes prepared in the ground. You fill the holes with pebbles then, and pack them shut with soil. I never knew his name. The shacks I built myself were never large enough to stand in. Just tall enough to store my rations and my pot and tinder sticks, my father's shredded jacket, and to crawl inside for sleep after the field.

"At the end of that year, Cromwell had several hundred Irishwomen spirited to Barbados. The Glebe bought two for breeding with the Irishmen on the first gang, and they both could weave, cut cloth, and sew. I was so happy when first I saw them unloaded from the cart after the auction; when I heard the silvery sly jokes and barnyard complaints in our tongue which they made about Jack Vaughton right before his unwitting face. Those girls were lively! I cannot say what changed in me so that one day I was planning how we three could build a little cottage altogether, but the next I drew away from where they stood. I averted my eyes as I passed by them. 'The dirty Irish mares,' Vaughton called them, and suddenly I felt them so. One lives at the Glebe still. She married Robert Rigley after his first wife died, dirty Irish mare or no, and was given paid work in the house."

"At the end of the hurricane season in 1657 a rider in a dove-gray suit and hat came out the lane one afternoon. Jack Vaughton, Ephraim Lye, Robert Rigley, and the others, they were gathered on the half-moon stair up to the mansion as we came in from the fields that evening. We had been draining land. There had been a lot of rain, and we were getting ready to plant new sugar shoots. The drivers stood along the path. They were tired too. They told their people there'd be no supper until the gentleman had spoken, both to those who knew the English and to those who could but stare blankly when it was spoken. The rider had brought the Proclamation of 1657, sir."

"I have read it; it serves as the foundation for the laws we keep today," replies the doctor.

"I stood there in the crowd," she murmurs. "A crowd of various black folk, but here and there the new Irishwomen, two men from Connaught who labored in the first gang, the Scots carpenter I'd known at Arlington. I watched them as the government messenger proclaimed from a scroll that people of the Irish nation, being slothful and dissolute, lewd, evil, and pilfering, should have placed upon them corrections for their idle, wandering ways. It was read that if any of us were found out on the road without a written ticket signed by master or by mistress, the nearest overseer was to whip us as much he deemed fit, then convey us to a constable. Constable to constable we would go, whipped, until returned unto our masters. And if any Irish should be stopped, suspected of a counterfeited ticket, that person must be sent directly to a Justice of the Peace, considered in theft of his master's chattel, and liable to hanging.

"On and on the paper read: if any of us should run away we should be flogged and our service lengthened between two years and double. And even after freed, if we were found with no fixed abode the Justice was to take us off the road and whip us sound, and send us for a year to a plantation at whatever wage he chose.

"When the messenger read off the last condition against the Irish race, I felt the proclamation to be in part inspired by the plot Mary had begged me, that night in the barn at Arlington, to partake of. A backlash, if ye like. No arms were to be sold to any freed Irish from then on, and any arms they legally had purchased were to be seized by citizens and neighbors, and turned over to militia field officers in each precinct of Barbados."

Coote focuses carefully on the words she has remembered from the Proclamation. He wonders if there is a way to lead her tale, so that the route from early armed uprisings of the Irish can be traced directly to conspiracy—"Negroes and Irish versus Planters, Free Inhabitants (non-Irish), and Other Servants on the Isle." He writes himself a note of this across the blotting page.

But she changes tack and he feels himself, for some reason, unwilling yet to yank her sharply by the reins. "Up to that time when the Proclamation was read out I had had a bad time with Big Dinah. I could not accept that a savage had been set over me, and with a whip to boot. Were we not taught at Arlington that although we wore the same rags, starved on the same ration, and were all born to serve ye British, that still we Christians were created higher than the African? Was not a 'dirty papist' better than a pagan? Were we not Christian cousins to your King?"

"Sound reasoning on that, at least," Coote murmurs, finishing the page.

But no: Cot Quashey shakes her head. "'Twas thoughts like that made me their puppet for so long."

"Whose puppet?" No reply. Fever, Peter thinks, she's rambling. Wordlessly he stops and pours a goblet of water for the prisoner. Such secret indulgence of his tenderness for the sick in general gives him a fine feeling about himself. The water is not fresh. A mosquito floats upon it which he lifts and flicks away with the feathered portion of his quill. After she has sipped, wincing as she swallows, she continues in a lower voice.

"I pushed Big Dinah to the limits. I spat in her direction and mocked her voice, and once I cried out, 'Here, then, bitch. Strike me!' But she would not, although she made me do my work in any case. Later she told me, 'Something was upon you. I could see it crawling on your neck and shoulders. I knew better than to hit you while you was carrying that.' And she was right. For hatred was upon me."

"Hatred against your master!" Coote exclaims, prepared now to get to the bottom of a conspiracy fueled by animal hatred.

"My master, Edward Lord Cleypole, came to Barbados only twice in the twenty years I cut his cane," the prisoner replies almost impatiently. "For as you know, he was a great favorite at court.

"No; Big Dinah said, after she heard the Proclamation, that she watched me and saw my hatred flying loose as a whirligig. She helped me put a shape around it, for I stood enchanted in the center of it, unable to recall, except as empty words, the movements I had made away from my own heart.

"The first movement you might say occurred when the *Falconer* stood offshore of Hole Town, or when we landed on the strand. And all I would see was the beauty of the place, the soft beauty of the black-haired girl as she was led from the cattle pen, the lovely cloth in the breeches and the waistcoats of the gentlemen. The next remove I made when I deserted my countryman in his stocks, as others once deserted Christ.

"Further I strayed, straining to woo and coddle those unsound, ungenerous beings who held my young life in their hands. The Captain. Mistress and Henry Plackler. I stumbled from false hope to betrayal to numbness. And suddenly, with Big Dinah, a woman who would not be a mother to me, I arrived, a creature surrounded by a forest full of hate.

"Hatred, like loneliness," she muses, "is composed of many things. Yes, I hated the man who proclaimed from the cold stone steps that his nation would rein my bestial spirit unto death, if I, as Irish, did not bend. And I hated the Scots and the English gaolbirds in the crowd because they were not so proclaimed." But the worst thing, she tells her interrogator, was how deeply and obediently she hated herself, for the laziness and dissoluteness, lewdness and thievery, said to have been bred in her: those qualities, all said, which added together made her of lower quality, lower race, fit only to serve her betters.

Coote is puzzled. "But dissoluteness, lewdness . . . those are sins. All Christians have been commanded to hate sin," he interjects. "You do well to hate those in yourself, biddy. Why does your voice ring with such passion over this common burden, while you have shown no remorse at abetting murder and sedition?"

"No! No!" she cries. And then a bit more calmly: "It was not sin I hated, but myself as sin's favored vessel, my race singled out as the dirtiest of the lot. And I came to such a hatred because each night, lying in my small stick-hovel, I searched and searched for how I was at the bone, and found these things truly festering in me. There *was* lewdness, for I liked Master Plackler to look on me in my corselet, while I played the maiden who had never seen the bull upon the cow. And dissoluteness was at my very core. I could find more examples of it than suckers on the sugar plant: look how I had turned away from Mary Dove and Paudi Iasc . . ."

"You are possessed with Paudi Iasc," Coote nearly shouts.

". . . yet curtsied to Eugenia Plackler, told her she looked lovely, listened to her woes about the children, when in my heart I felt terror and loathing and was always looking for a door in her madness that I might escape through.

"And my thievery had begun by then, though Big Dinah once told me that the Africans had a proverb: 'It makes God laugh when one thief steals from another.'"

Peter Coote underlines this emphatically as he writes it down.

"But to steal from one's master is also inviting death. And my own God told me not to steal no matter how great the need, instead to pray for redemption from my hungers—and my greeds.

"For greed I also hated in myself. It choked the better things, and it grew fat on loneliness. I hated the other slaves for the measure of food that was shared between us; they seemed to leave me less. Hated my skin, which bled and blistered in the sun, wherever my ragged clothing did not cover me. Hated the sun itself; and slow time, and every living, growing thing that I must bend over till a buzz rang in my ear and sun-worms swam before my eyes.

"Hated my father for not coming to rescue me from the tavern or the ship, like Hercules, leading a godlike fleet on behalf of innocence." The prisoner's breath catches in her slumped chest as she concludes, "And I hated my mother, for lifting off the cart which covered me in safety as she traded above me at the market; for taking away kind touch, which no one ever laid upon me anymore; and most of all for dying without telling me she could."

There is silence, but for the rapid labor of the pen. The prisoner watches the Governor's man complete his record. When he looks up at last, she says, "You might finish your page by noting, sir, that the one thing I never thought to hate was my master or my mistress. For those who harmed me most were also the only ones who could redeem me from worse harm. Them, I did not dare to hate."

Peter Coote has sent his slave Lucy into Speightstown to negotiate for two hens and a cock. Three laying hens had been devoured by a snake at daybreak, a snake which he has shot and laid out in the garden as a warning, so puffed with venom that the flies will not settle on it. He has been told that the living of any species will avoid a place where one of its own kind lies dead. The slave who will prepare his lunch today is a granny with the complexion, Coote thinks creatively, of an aubergine—purple black, thick, smooth. When she appears at the door to his office, she asks, "Mastah like pig or fish for lunch? A huckstah in the garden wit fresh fish."

"Which one are you again?" Coote asks. "I prefer fish."

"Little Mary," the old woman replies; and as she turns back to the hallway he thinks he sees her chin move into a sort of sliding nod toward his prisoner. But the Irishwoman focuses solemnly ahead; sweating, hands shaking in her lap, though when she speaks her voice is quite composed.

"Big Dinah had a garden plot there by her house," she begins. "I went up to her cabin only twice without invitation. The Hausas did not like anyone but themselves to come around. The first time I went up, I went to steal from her garden." In the garden Dinah grew ground provisions—vegetables and nuts. One night the Irishwoman lay sleepless from hunger and from anger: "I could not separate them, for the two often twisted together into one bigger thing." As she snuck out she heard the forest beasts howling on the hunt. The moon lay old and low.

The houses on the rise stood in shadow layered over shadow. There were no dogs to bark a stranger's coming: at the Glebe, the only dogs were owned by overseers, except a kennel of gouty hounds kept for Lord Cleypole, should he choose to visit the plantation.

Big Dinah lived on the flat hilltop amidst a cluster of houses inhabited by her countrymen. "Hausas," the Irishwoman says, which means nothing to Peter Coote: but it might to the Governor.

Here the shivering prisoner almost chuckles. "I still remember squatting there, in the garden by the hut where I had found Big Dinah my first night. There were okras on the bush, not good for eating raw. I had bit into one. But there was also Guinea corn, the kind that when it's new tastes like a sweet. You can eat the cob and all. So I ripped a couple from the stalk and began to tear the husk when I heard her voice.

"That voice was like a man's, an older man's from her own nation rather than Plackler's, Vaughton's . . . yours. Jiba had a voice like that: they called her Sargeant Jiba. They had voices that froze foolishness, all right."

"Jiba?" Peter asks, brows furrowing together.

But Cot goes on. "That big stony voice said from behind me, 'What you do to my corn I'm a do, girl, to your head.' And she did. She lifted me, with the great ham of her arm, until I dangled above the soil. She lifted me by my hair, and some fell out when she left go of me.

"No penalties existed then—as now—for stealing, slave from slave. 'God laugh when the teef he steal from the teef,' Big Dinah told me, 'but mastah laugh when slave he steal from another slave.'" Always, Cot Quashey said, she had remembered that.

"I did not know why she was waiting up, although the Hausas had a custom of visiting far into the night. Quietly. Nobody ever heard them down in the houses of the overseers and the wage-earning servants, or at the big house. For the big house was staffed as well, sir; always kept polished in case of his Lordship's favor, or the visits of his associates. But on the hill above those handsome houses, the people sometimes visited late into the night . . ."

"Biddy? Were they plotting then? Perhaps assisting those who did?" Coote insinuates softly, thinking to catch her off her guard, so sunk she seems in reverie.

"I wit not, although I never spoke a word of Hausa. I think they talked about their homeland; and certainly they kept watch and protection against the others all the time."

"Which others?" Coote demands.

"Why Hausa against Ibo, and Ife against Fante against Fon against Yoruba. Those they fought with back in Africa; those who stole them to sell to you, sir, but then got stolen themselves. That enmity between them was what caused them to build their houses in little groupings with alleys close-connecting people from the homeland. They did not trust the other tribes."

Again her conversation veers. "I have heard it said that never will a Christian understand the thinking of an African. Well that may be so, although thinking is not the only thing to understand. I know I never understood Big Dinah. Who, though she could not have had me lashed or hanged for stealing from her garden, could easily have given me the dirtiest of work, or whipped me in the fields, or shorted on my ration, or even poisoned it. But aside from shaking me; aside from saying in a voice of growling wonder, 'Oh, I see it on you; it's there, climbing up your chest,' and swatting my arse as she sent me back down to my hut, she did not punish me. Instead she took me with her to the market."

Coote dips and wipes and scribbles rapidly. Sunday was free time for all, except good Scots and English who must spend their day at prayer. But as for Irish bondspeople, "There is no Mass here on the island, as you know; and we can hang if we're caught gathered, praying. I became quite lost from worship as a young girl in Barbados. As I have said, my own sweet household saints rolled up their eyes and wrung their hands at the cruelties here. They became, somehow, like we lovely maids after our bath upon the *Falconer.* Not able to credit the future that was to befall, they floated in that mystic place where beauty and goodness defeat time and evil."

On Sunday the bondspeople washed their rags and cooked; they foraged at the forest's rim for nuts and small fruit, and although the wild game belonged to the master's larder, they were permitted to snare lizards, spear frogs, and drop birds with stones.

And on Sundays the buzzing voices grew louder in Cot's head as the day lengthened. Alone she waited to cook her two scant meals, then for the light to wane. Alone she sat, in the dirt before her hut, arguing with herself over dissolution and thievery, cursing the in-bred lewdness in herself that must have lured the master of Arlington, the captain of the *Falconer,* even the barmaid at the Donkey and the Tankard. Haranguing herself, she wove free grasses into mats to block the wind and cover the ground. Everyone who passed on errands to the yard stared at her.

Only after she had woven many Sunday mats, hanging a large one for a door across her open wall, Big Dinah said, "Come, I'm a show you what my garden for."

They walked toward the sea, their tickets in their pockets. Big Dinah had a Sunday pass, trusted driver that she was, and she obtained a temporary one for Cot from Vaughton. "You bring some mats wit you," said Dinah; and as they wended the forest path, tried to show the younger woman how to roll and balance these upon her head so that her hands were free. "I was right angry when she laughed at me," remembers Cot. "But later I too learned how to balance awkward loads above me as if they were not my burden."

Coote can't resist: "Yes. We have heard of pawpaw bundles full of shot and tinder," he smirks gently. "Pray continue."

Cot Quashey describes the market, held at that time in the clearing by the church of St. John's. "We set up underneath a cottonsilk tree. Hausa women are market people, like my own mother was." Coote's fingers race to keep up with the colors that she tells him. In laps of glue-colored canvas and gray Osnabruck, he records yellow lemons, green wild figs, coconut shells spilling amber pigeon peas. Cot spreads a herringboned mat which Big Dinah grunts down upon, placing bundles of Guinea corn and piles of downy okra pods around her. Nearer, nearer to his script Coote bends, stroking out letters for "dried shrimp from the coast," "oil on the fingers from split oranges." He captures blue shadows at the edges of white eyeballs, and sparse purple hairs glinting on the shinbones of black women, before he comes to himself. He says, "What has this to do with treachery between you and the Africans? Women from differing plantations at a market?"

As if entranced, the Irishwoman intones, "She taught me not to block out ugliness by giving imagined beauty false dominion: but that on the other hand, in the midst of hatred and ugliness there is color, there is life, and there is . . . personal usefulness . . . as well. I traded one of my grass mats for a coconut and a pocketful of figs. Another Sunday as we were walking back to Glebe through the forest, Big Dinah told me about trees. 'The market sits always by one of these,' she pointed. It was the kind of tree you call a kapok. She taught me something of this tree, and about the spirits of the market."

Coote cannot control his reserved and stoic pose: for a moment his lips curve in a sneer. "Spirits of the market, is it now?"

The madwoman winks and sneers back! "Once I thought like you myself. 'Poor Dinah,' I told myself. 'Black as sin, and haunted as a child in Samhain, to boot.' But later I lay upon my mat fingering my father's coat and recalling stories of Our Lord, Lazarus and others, always in the marketplace. The healings there. And how in corruption the marketplace got mingled with the Temple; for the Pharisees, who traded in words, were to be found in the no-man's-land between the two. And then I thought of my abduction: how those who stole the thousands like me were called Spirits. How they 'spirited' us away to the servant market in Barbados. Not for the last time did I marvel then, that a simple woman you would say is savage, like Big Dinah, might be awake to more than me. Wherever there's a market there are hordes of spirits seething."

"After Big Dinah died I was the only one among the Christian folk who did not believe she died of dropsy, as the apothecary wrote into his ledger. Yes, it is true she faded very rapidly in head and limbs yet swole up in her belly and her feet. But the thing I saw the second time I visited her unbidden, and what she said it meant, left me uneasy all my life as to what killed her.

"Big Dinah was a stern woman. You may think she was fond of me because she took me to their market, and did not beat me but even taught me something. But she was not my friend. It was just that she was . . . familiar . . . with the thing we would call hatred which she saw creeping on me."

"She was a witch? Is that what you are saying? What exactly was her familiar, then?" Coote demands.

The Irishwoman clears her throat and pauses, frowning lightly, for the right words. Coote watches. The heat these mornings holds them all within its paw. A yawn escapes him. His belly rumbles. Down his powdered face run rivulets of sweat.

"No. Big Dinah was not a witch. But she could recognize a spell like hatred, and she . . . respected it."

Coote writes: "The Negra respects the vice of hatred in the Irish."

Cot Quashey continues. "She was so stern she never had to warn me of certain things. There was something . . . imposing . . . in her body, the way she held herself at times, that kept younger or weaker people back from her, whether myself or the Africans. She never had to tell me to stay away from the Hausa place at night. A few times, after the market or the field, I would want to walk beyond my hovel after her. But she had a way of stiffening and getting taller; as if her body were a door—part open, then shut in your face without a word. I was angry and ashamed that even a dark savage like herself would not have me in the house. I was doomed to cook my cornmeal in the yard of my stick-house alone, with only myself for conversation. Under the moon I'd sometimes rub the rusting little flute with the shreds of the old surcoat, but I never played it lest one of the others envied me, and stole it away. To say this in another way; to befriend anyone was to risk losing my pitiful all. Yet when I thought to intimate myself with Dinah, she found my risk not worth the having.

"I could not go to market without Big Dinah, for there were no Christian women in that circle under the Sunday cottonsilk. The tribeswomen from all around thought me Dinah's assistant of some sort. They would laugh and taunt me in their own tongues sometimes, but mostly they ignored me. I would not dare to enter their circle on my own, even if I had a pass. They had so much more power than me, you see.

"Then two Sundays went by without Dinah coming to my hut to collect me for the market. In the fields she looked on me with fierce red eyes when I asked why. 'Bend your back into that field, girl, and lift them rocks,' she snarled. I looked up from my heavy task, watching her huge, strong arse rock slowly underneath her skirt as she moved away across the field. 'Ye dirty hoor ye,' I hissed beneath my breath.

"Soon after that, one night, I stole up to her hut. I had come just to devil her, for she had picked my trust up and then dropped me, herself a lowly African, while I, though cousin to the race that Masters sprang from, had no recourse against the pagan slut. Thus did I reason."

Peter Coote, though he continues writing, feels a sudden bitter sympathy for the insult that it must have been to be placed under a heathen's supervision. One would think such rancor would spawn strict division; how then had these rival groups—Irish and Negro—island-wide, bridged their resentments to plot treason together? It's this great puzzle which the Governor wants solved.

"It was very late on the third Sunday of no market. I climbed up to her yard. No one saw me go, though some sat out for the breeze. The weather was sultry, just before the time for summer storms. I kept to the shadowed brush which edged the yard. I came up to her partly open door, its covering mat rolled almost up.

"Everyone knew Big Dinah had a group of little pickaninnies she was raising, but they were not in the room. I thought the whole place empty until I saw the darkness writhing slowly in one corner. I heard the richest grunting and the lightest, softest breath. Standing there, I sent my eyes into the night-filled shack until I picked out a narrow back—certainly not Big Dinah's—squeezing in and out like bellows. Then I heard footsteps.

"There was a rattling at the side of the house, as of a gourd with seeds dried in it, and something flurried through the darkness. An object hit a stone beside the hut with a cold clink.

"Big Dinah had a fancy man. It was he in there at her, until they heard these subtle sounds and froze their limbs. She rose out from beneath him like a breaching whale. Fat and strong and naked, she was on me at the door, and shook me like a rag: but she was looking past me at the night. The thin-backed man hurried past her, tying on his drawers. It was he who stepped on the thrown thing and made a dismal cry. Then I could tell that he was young—perhaps only the same age as myself."

"What was this object?" queries Coote.

"The night was dark. I could not make it out as anything I knew; except that tied to the top of it was the raw and glistening organ of a smallish animal. If not for that object she would have clouted me senseless, and worse. But now she ordered me to pick it up. It was wet and cold against my skin. She yanked me in against her hard fatness and whispered, 'Who throw this in my house? Did you see? Who throw this in my door?'"

But the prisoner had seen no one. Then Big Dinah reached inside the room and drew out half a coconut shell. She bade Cot put the thing inside the husk for her. The next evening after fieldwork, Big Dinah took Cot to the woods. "We knelt down under a tree with silvery skin and high boughs, like a massive beech or ash. The birds sang so sweetly—river orioles. I never heard a more dulcet song. They sing like cousins to the linnet."

They buried the object in the earth, Big Dinah speaking Hausa speech rapid and low. As dark descended and they hurried back again out to the path, she told the Irishwoman that the buried thing was poison. The thrower was an Ibo woman of childbearing age, who had been given to the same young Hausa man Cot saw rocking on Dinah. "I thought then, what did he want with Dinah, fat and mean and ugly as she was?" But there was a custom, Dinah said. A man learned to be brave from war and forest and animals. He learned to be a friend to other men, in secret houses with men his own age where no one else could go. And only from an older woman—a widow—could a young warrior learn to be a man with women, before he took a wife. The men of her people took many wives; the women but one man until they were widowed.

The Hausa warrior had sought out Big Dinah. For many evenings had his tutelage gone on, and then the Ibo woman heard of it. It was time for him to breed with her, make her a cabin: Jack Vaughton had said so. This young Hausa man was liked by many women, Dinah explained. Yet their lessons, instead of coming to an end, became more frequent. The young Hausa groom-to-be spent almost every night with Big Dinah, then all day Sunday, until the orphans she was raising must be sent to visit neighbors for weeks at a time.

The Ibo woman, who spoke some words of Hausa, began to

stand beside the path as the crews returned from fieldwork, accusing Big Dinah: "She holds my man by sorcery, until he thinks she's young and shapely, like myself. She means to wring him dry," the impatient bride denounced to everyone who'd listen. Many listened. Many laughed. "She has shamed herself, that's why she hate me so," Big Dinah brooded to the Irish girl.

Coote writes this with an equal mix of curiosity and revulsion. It was not that the young man meant to reject the Ibo woman (although her words were sour), but that each Big Dinah lesson led to others. The prisoner explains, "As when you ask a question, but the answer holds within it one more question to be asked. On and on like that." The Hausa youth kept putting off the day when he would go to his appointed woman. Then one evening the Ibo bride stood across the path and shrieked witchcraft at Big Dinah.

"Your overseers, they knew none of this?" Coote verifies.

"No sir. When Jack Vaughton made the pairing of the Hausa and the Ibo, he did so just for issue; but it were better, in the harvest season until June, if every worker could lift and bend far into the night. Thickening women slowed things down. So Vaughton would not come to push the union until late summer. The overseers and the higher servants did not mount the hill unless there was good reason."

"What sort of reason?"

"A feast, the funeral of a person important to the Africans. If they were looking for a runaway—the like."

Before Little Mary carries in Coote's lunch, he has described in feathery script the fading of Big Dinah. How in the fields she had slumped and grayed, till at the end "she always looked afraid. The apothecary came to nurse her, for she was considered very valuable. She knew the tasks of second gang for every season, and in all sorts of disasters. She spoke four languages of the Africans, as well as passable English. She knew every ruse for the sick-house and so never let us slide away from work. In short, though she was past childbearing age—as far as I knew, never had she borne one—Big Dinah was strong and vigorous. To season another for her work was going to be costly.

"But the apothecary came too late. The syrups and elixirs he spooned into her mouth dribbled to the mat as she turned away. He wrote down 'Dropsy' as her cause of death, for the master back in England to take note of. But the young folk in the second crew whispered 'Obeah' while she still stood over us, gray as a dusty ghost.

"She died on a Friday in the rainy season. She had risen from her pallet and came among us in the field, mumbling orders in some arcane tongue. There was a big wind that day. Jack Vaughton took an African, a Fante named Mercy, from the first gang, and was already touring the yard with her explaining what he wanted, when Big Dinah swayed and dropped. The second gang had gotten behind its work in the confusion of Dinah's final days. I was afraid to work beneath that woman, Mercy. She was very nervous and had little English. Vaughton had given her a barbed cat-o'-nine-tails to carry in her belt, and even as he pointed here and there from the yard into the fields, she tapped the handle of that whip against her thigh.

"Jack Vaughton told us to remove Big Dinah's body and prepare it for the funeral. The rain was thick and green. The first gang was, at this hour, still out in the field, digging shallow ditches so that the seedlings would not drown. So we of her own second gang had to lift Big Dinah and carry her up the hill. She was on a canvas sheet, and with the weight of her the cloth began to rend. For a moment the stretcher began to fold shut in the middle, sinking toward the ground. I stepped away, a coward to touch the limbs of death, then felt a splash of shame as the young Africans lunged together to push her back up from the mud.

"We laid her on a plank inside her cabin, and I sat over her and fanned the flies away until the Hausa women came. That was at nightfall, when they could no longer see their fieldwork. Jack

Vaughton came up the hill on his yellow horse and circled it round. The yards and paths were slushy. People were building little fires inside their open doors, in rings of stones. It was a dismal evening. Some of the senior men came out to where the horse was milling. 'Half-day for the funeral tomorrow,' Vaughton said. 'All of the overseers will be in attendance.' This was a high honor for Dinah. The Africans were jealous that even their enemies should attend the funerals of those principal among them.

"Big Dinah had been principal among her people because of her position as a driver, for the English that she spoke and could interpret, and for the things she could see creeping behind the open eye we know as day. Jack Vaughton told a first-gang driver, Pawpaw Jack, to come down to a shed and bear back to the women in attendance a length of red calico and some rum.

"I did not want to touch her. But I squatted in the shadows until the Hausa women threw me out. Then I went into the garden, and right in front of them I ripped two ripe ears of Big Dinah's corn from the stem. I placed one on the ground beside her plank, then went below to my own house where I gnawed the second, cob and all."

At that juncture, Little Mary shambles in with Coote's meal: a fine fish on a platter with cassava cake and yam. He sighs, throwing his shoulders back irritably. "Does it take this long to roast a fish?" he scolds the old slave.

She retracts her neck between her shoulders in their rags. He wonders how his new shirt is progressing. "Naw suh," Little Mary ventures so timidly that he is sure his eyes deceive him when he glances up momentarily. The granny-slave is leading the prisoner back to her sick-house pallet. He almost thinks he sees a wrinkled hand scoot from below a filthy apron and pass, by the tail, another, smaller, fried-eyed fish. But then it's gone, a trick of the Caribbean light. The two women look to be the same elderly age from behind, shuffling along the narrow hall. By the next morning, Thursday, Coote's humor toward the prisoner will alter somewhat, based on events yet to happen on the night of the Governor's tensely awaited feast. But at the moment he merely feels spiteful, and longs to justify it.

They are strolling round the garden. Blue twilight sharpens into night. "Your grounds are beautiful, Excellency," Coote murmurs, humbled by the harmony of elements assembled in this place hacked out of jungle. Clouds of jasmine scent puff past on warm air currents, a rich warble of frogs rises from the artificial pool which ripples with the reflection of the evening's stars. Stede nods, glancing toward the glowing windows of his house.

"Let us head back to my guests, shall we?" he says, on the tail of a belch. "This has been both an enlightening and refreshing talk. You understand why I did not want to discuss such matters at the dinner table, do you not?"

"Certainly, sir, matters of State don't aid digestion," Coote responds, with formal cheerfulness.

The Governor snorts. "If you mean politicking has no place at table, you do not understand the reason for this gathering, sir. No, I mean that among the loftiest at my table there are those who'd like to see my hand before I play it. Who'd like to take my island from me! Yet I must play the ignorant, forever courting their goodwill! Fah!"

They are promenading toward the mansion as the words "my island" jolt Coote into boldness and a sense of time-running-short. He blurts, "Sire, is it true the Orkney lands at Arlington have gone to ruin? If so, with your favor, I should like to make a bid for part of them."

The Governor thrusts his face mere inches from Coote's in an attempt to read the younger man's motivation. "Don't plague me with your interruptions," he admonishes sharply. "I was saying! There are those at my buffet tonight who would gladly pull the carpet from beneath my feet. Take your old employer Codrington. Or Andrew Lambert. And Hinkley out from Bristol, too. But I will bide my time. They will not know how firm is my command; how little I need British gunboats. Strength lies in those merchant vessels clustered in the bay to buy our 'Bajan' crops. The days of monarchy are a corpse cold as Charles Stuart, though for form's sake we must bend our knees an inch or two."

Grasping Coote's elbow, Stede rants, "More than a few inside there with my hired whores, pretending they are gentlemen with ladies, would give a purse of gold to know that I'm in weekly consultancy with Willowby of Montserrat. And we've now begun relations with the man we're sure will be the next governor of Jamaica," he harrumphs.

In the awkward silence after this unwarranted and volatile confidence, Coote seeks the essential words to cloak his shocked sense of propriety. "But Governor Stede, believe me, every gentleman of sense stands in gratitude and admiration of your benevolent administration. We loyally . . . ," he scrabbles. The Governor cuts across harshly.

"Men admire profit, not administration. And it is not my 'benevolent administration,'"—in a mincing voice—"good sir. It is my *rule*; and it shall last my lifetime!" he spits. Then lowering his voice, "Do not forget: pull the wench's tongue and see if you can make it wag. Help me find the link between these black and Irish devils and their island-wide conspiracies, so that"—he points inside his house—"*their* fickle gratitude can swing to me once more. I cannot see that what she's given so far is of much use. Well, if by Saturday she coughs nothing up, we will get rid of her. Quietly; lest it be marked not only hot-blooded madmen rebel against ourselves, but even weak-witted females, ready to be martyrs. The papist slut!" He glances toward the porch they are approaching. A shadow flat against the wall. "Oh say there, Codrington, I am out showing your ex-apothecary my lily ponds. Would you fetch me brandied port against the night's humors? I have some private news of water rights especially for you." The silhouette on the verandah raises its glass in salute and melts toward the French doors of the lit banquet hall.

The Governor quickens his stride, moving ahead of Peter Coote. Just before he climbs the stairs at the path's end he turns to his retainer. "And Mr. Coote? I myself hold Arlington," he rasps. "For quite some years, as others were evicted. Or failed. Or despaired and crawled back home to England. Of every smallest opportunity, I have availed myself. And I can see that although you can heal many malaises, you yourself are victim to the same land sickness I have known." (In *sotto voce*) "I will remember your fidelities, only the first of which, I'm sure, lies with this matter of the Irishwoman."

Coote bows deeply. Upon unbending, he sees that his mentor has abandoned him to the rich-smelling night. He inhales it deeply before he climbs the steps.

The meal is at once a cornucopia of colors, flavors, noise, and a disjunctive display of dainty objects imported to a land beyond their use. Coote, seated between a senator and a lady of the night in satin gown, at first lets his nervous senses float on the bright bounty of the table. The light of three-foot tapers and lanterns in wall sconces shines golden on the crested linens which took precedence above his own new shirts. Behind each carved oak chair a servant stands: sculpted black face under powdered wig, clad in the livery of the Governor. Each holds a six-foot fan: flamingo feathers mounted in bamboo, with which he slowly waves mosquitoes, flies, flying cockroaches, and other pests, aside. The lice, the fleas, are not so easily moved.

The food servers and bearers and footmen at the door are adult men. But the Governor takes great pleasure in the slave who fans his sweating majesty—a lad of thirteen years, in miniature uniform and too-small powdered wig. A castrato, Colonel Stede titters, reaching back to tuck a morsel of roast lamb between silent lips. Soft, and wonderful of voice at Advent time, his master brags.

Coote drinks more than is his wont; but nowhere near as much as everyone at table. So that hours into the feast, when he glances up to see the Governor's face in hot conversation with an Edinburgh trader through a frame of peccary ribs picked clean on a greasy platter, an uneasy and unbidden image comes to him. The quiet fanning servants seem dignified; the wealthy of the island, porcine and debauched. His mother and father, his uncles and his aunts: never would they break bread with such moral riffraff. But . . . he is here now. And of course these raw, rough colonizers in court silks must make their way . . .

The table grows littered with the glut of brilliant food ripped into chunks, then abandoned as something new is set forth. A discreet slave steps forward to sprinkle salt from a silver cellar whenever someone slops wine on the tablecloth of State.

"Look at him, fanning, fanning, as if in a trance," the Governor's companion dimples at the slave boy who continues to stand perfectly still, waving rhythmically now for hours in the heat. And the Governor does look, humoring his Cheapside jade.

"His whole life is a trance," Stede quips. They collapse into a heap of brocaded laughter. The young servant fans on and on without expression. Coote can see the muscles of his forearms quivering with exhaustion. The senator beside Coote says, "Do you not think this claret of the best?" while his lady of the evening yawns, dropping a hand into Coote's lap and tickling him halfheartedly. "His Excellency says you're up and coming," she murmurs in a Midlands accent. "Cot, is it? Peter Cot?"

And something creeps across his grave. "Coote," he insists, and leaves soon after.

The Governor accompanies him to the steps and they wait as his horse is brought around. Stede sags with his arm around the woman he has chosen for the night. He appears to be very drunk. Yet his eyes narrow shrewdly, assessing Coote. Something about Coote.

"Pity you must leave before the music and the games. I have had two of my Negras trained on violins, and one will play a harpsichord." His speech is slurred but his speculative gaze seems sharp. "Can you imagine? On a harpsichord!" the street wench shrieks admiringly. Coote looks away from her. Her accent tells her provenance—herself till recently in bond; but time expired, she's been released, thousands of miles from the crumbling hearth where her family of beggars returns each night to cling together. Released to harlotry in order to survive, with arid hopes of attracting a protector to ward away the whip and gaol cell which here await the vagrant. Something is stifling Coote although the air is fresh. He looks away from her flushed, disheveled breasts. They heave with laughter as the Governor presses his head to their soft pillow. From that soft, sweating shelf, His Excellency peeps out of his eye's side like a wily bird. "Dr. Coote is not enjoying my party as well as you are, my dear," he says coyly, "or he would not leave so soon. Ah, but Coote. There's a long dark road ahead of you. Is there not? Let us meet again on Friday."

Then the horse is drawn around and Coote bows, praising the meal, the hall, the grounds, extravagantly again. But the Governor interrupts, "Come my dear. Let's have a sip of rum from Lord Codrington's finest batch," and the couple lurch inside.

Coote mounts the fine gelding which the Governor furnished only weeks before, letting its calm alertness rein in his own unwarranted sense of panic. The moon is bright, half-full upon the dark clay of the road. Its blue light dwarfs the little golden beam of lantern which the servant hands up. A heavy knot coils inside Coote's belly. He tries to unravel it as he clucks the steed into

motion. It is a knot of revulsion toward his social betters on this island: their behavior has not been refined or gentlemanly. Particularly
the Governor. There is a grossness, an uncouthness; his father would
not have kept a stablemen that loutish about the place.

But this knot of revulsion is cinched with a tight sinew of fear.
Suddenly Peter Coote, come out from Oxford fifteen long years ago
to become a merchant prince, though landless still, sees himself
strolling with notable gentlemen through a series of lavish tropic
settings: Codrington; Cornwall; the Anglican named Ayres; so
many others. In waking vision, he matches their diverse paces, their
tones of speech. Hoping to fall in with them, the unimpeachable
band who rule this primitive place with letters of credit, muskets,
grim brutality. The vision proceeds to this very evening, in the
darkening gardens of Colonel Stede. Coote sees himself, slim still,
bent to listen, over the splash of water from a marble cupid's
mouth. The Governor at first conversing sensibly enough. But suddenly he's glaring, spittle flying through the air as he rants about af-
fairs of State, coalitions with the ruling class of other wild colonies
against Coote's homeland. Where civilization had been born. Their
dear England.

How smoothly the Governor had turned from his tirade to greet
a courtier upon the porch! As if they had indeed been discussing
lily ponds.

The placid mount approaches a bend ahead now in the midnight
lane. Cool moonlight bathes only the highest sighing limbs of
trees. Below, the path into the future lies buried deep in shadow.
Coote hears a gecko click, insects whirring, a brush like air through
wind chimes, suddenly. Why does the horse seems to be moving
slower, almost rocking its head from side to side, with a dancing
gait? Sweat sprouts from Coote's neck. He remembers the prisoner's
testifying words. Her faded robin's eyes as she fixed his in bewilderment, insisting, "Why sir, the preferred confidante of the master is
the slave. Who else can be trusted not to turn dark secrets to a top-

pling of power? Who else will provide the truly captive audience, which can do nothing but agree? Masters are not masters because they seek their equals among servants."

Or some such rubbish. He shakes his head, to clear it. But the reasons she's given as proof keep hissing through Coote's ears, which begin to hum and deafen as if he's going to faint. He induces vomitus. Afterward, he feels weak but stabilized, although the weak flame of the lantern snuffs out in the process. The horse, oddly unperturbed by human tensions, ambles forward into the tunnel of a night that could hold anything.

IV

"Jack Vaughton rode his butter-colored horse into the fields that Saturday," the prisoner relates. "The land lay under white mist after the cool rain. People working saw a dark hat, blond mane, wide wheat-colored chest muscles galloping through the fog toward them. He had gone to inspect the third gang first, and seven African children jogged behind him, the new driver Mercy urging them along. She shouted Fante words none among us understood.

"These children had been taken from the meat-pickers gang. Their work was light work: picking livestock 'meat'—grasses, reeds, vines, beetles, and grubs—and tending smaller stock and fowl. Jack Vaughton had examined the entire crew, and determined that the seven trotting through the mist were strong enough now for the work of second gang.

"We of the second gang were damming up a ditch with stones, the shortest standing waist-deep in muddy waters that had overflowed a side branch of the river. It was crucial that the ditch not flood the field roods below, a field planted with fragile cane, already in danger of red rot due to the cold that came in with the storm." Cot and the taller workers of the second gang saw this apparition galloping toward them over the banks of the drain. The mist had muffled the animal's hoofbeats until Vaughton was practically upon them.

He did not dismount, but waited until Mercy's body, running behind him, caught up to her disembodied shouts. She lined the seven children straightly on the bank. Cot heard them panting. The horse snorted. "Get out of there a minute," Vaughton told the second crew in his flat voice. In their mud-soaked clothing they struggled up the ditch bank, clutching at roots and the branches of small bushes. Some helped each other wordlessly. There were thirty-two of them, Cot Quashey tells Peter Coote: it is the fourth day of interrogation.

"He never touched us. He pointed with the quirt. Those who were tall, or even squat but robust, he sent to Mercy. She had been trained well—or perhaps remembered how she herself had been chosen—for she felt our necks and arms, looked in our mouths, had us bend and stoop, and then she shook her head or nodded. If she nodded she said one word: 'This.' And we were drawn aside.

"They took two lads before me, and then it was my turn, But I knew not what for: just that I had come to his attention, a place I did not want to be. Because you see, just as Arlington had protected me in ways from the full measure expected from a slave, whether for seven years or for life, so had Big Dinah's second gang been a better corner of the house of misery.

"Oh, I knew what the first gang did, from eavesdropped tales and my own eyes; and also that the lot of mature bondsfolk was to join them. But I was slight, and like a child in that my emotions—petulant and sulky—were weak. I knew myself not strong enough for adult dealings, to wit I had no impact on the adult folk around me. They seldom spoke to me except to curse my clumsiness or push me out of the way. Do you remember, sir, that I told you once about the last day on the *Falconer*, when we kidnapped maids were bathing and looked, naked, on this island glowing in the sun? How time lied and seemed to say, 'Forever: ye'll be like this, enchanted here forever, nothing can harm you'? In second gang, time seemed similarly frozen. My three years of work with Dinah were not dangerous, and with her helping me start to shake free of hate's spell, I believed Providence had hidden me from the most evil eyes. Real harm had passed me by.

"But when that woman Mercy grabbed me by the arm, the world flew up in shards all around me again, the way it had when I was whipped, or when I was gambled off. Do you know extremes of fear like these yourself yet, sir?" she leans forward to ask Coote.

How dare she affront him so! As if her base and ravaged sentiments and his were linked in any way! But then a sudden image of himself last night upon the horse, immediately before he made himself empty the banquet from his belly: a thought, a mood, a terror he'd had then but could no longer grasp. Gone. It was gone, thank God. Related to the Irishwoman, though. That much his flesh recalls. Something shifts. He feels both cowed and resentful. To compensate, he lifts his quite-patrician chin and peers down at her sternly.

"When two more had been culled, Jack Vaughton stated, 'Ye will join first gang, come Monday,' and rode away. We went back down the ditch, then, all of us. The mist burned off into a strained, bleached sky. Mercy shrieked and pointed orders at the small new workers, who stumbled under heavy rocks. It was late afternoon when the dam held sound and we straggled back across the field to our slave huts on the hill. And though I walked among the rest, somehow it seemed that I was also watching from above, behind; as if I were a spectator on a hill viewing a procession during Holy Week whose meaning is unknown.

"Suffering. Fear and suffering. Hunger, ailments, desperation. Those were what I saw. A nightmare procession which could never disappear beyond the mind's horizon; for it moved with us: we carried it."

"There was tension at the time of Dinah's death among the African drivers and the Northern overseers: if more heavy rains came soon, the new seedlings could wash off, or at the very least decay. The fields themselves might soak with water and the damage come much later from drowned roots. Yet Big Dinah was important to the Hausa. And even if the Hausa were enemy to other tribes upon the hill, a slight to an important funeral would have been a slight to all the Africans. Work had to stop. A proper wake had to proceed."

"I imagine such a slight may have . . . united? . . . them?" Coote probes.

"Yes. So we were given time to wash with river water. The adult Africans tied on fresher clothes if they had a change. I myself followed the motions of the others. I put on the rags of my Arlington house-waistcoat, for it had color, and tied Mistress Plackler's riband in my matted hair. Then I went on up the hill.

"The Hausa women had sat up with her all night, and now they ringed the open pit which had been dug. I was pushed aside somewhat by the crowd who groaned and keened, until I stood beside the Irishmen from Connaught. One tipped his chin at me in greeting. He said in Irish, 'It should've been the boss.'

"Big Dinah was carried out on a canvas sheet. She wore her double petticoat and canvas waist, which tied across the front. But she had over that a new vest of pretty red calico, with thick black swirls almost like writing over it. Around her head, in place of the canvas cap which all we women wore, a hank of those red goods was wound and tucked. They bore her to the edge of the hole, which was dug beside her garden; in fact, in the middle of a route or walkway the Hausa used to move between their houses. There were people carrying palm branches, waving them. Others lit two bonfires at both sides of the grave, for the evening was now deepening to night.

"The men of her people stooped and strained, setting her bulk into the grave without a mishap. She was a queen, that night. They had wrapped her still-fat neck with several strings of beads striped like the rainbow. These come from the Job's Tears plant. She also wore bracelets of palm oil tree nuts, interspersed with carved dog's teeth. The teeth shone like ivory in the firelight, I remember. The men adjusted her while the wailing of the others grew to ululations that waxed and waned, like fire fanned by breeze.

"They made the *olagon* like we make in Eirann. Until the corpse is laid out, women keep their silence, tending it. But then, caring for the dead as if it were a helpless child, the loss, the terrible sorrow that the dead have left us all, builds up in a keening cry straight from the hearts of the women. In the midst of all that crackling and blackness, shrieking and warbling, Big Dinah was set upright in her grave, facing toward the east. Her hands were drawn up by her cheek as if she were sleeping. To one side, in a loud dull voice, Robert Rigley read verses from the Scriptures in an accent no one but a Highland Scot could comprehend. In front of my eyes, bodies darted to the grave and back. I saw arms place a loaf of cassava bread, a noggin of rum, a gourdful of tobacco in the pit. Then Jack Vaughton himself stepped forward to lay a new white clay pipe at the graveside. I knew this custom. At home the common people prize the *duidín*, that little clay pipe with long curved stem and flat-bottomed bowl. Later Quashey—himself a Coromantee—had Mama Chiva explain to me how Big Dinah was placed to face the old port of Benin, where the dead find their canoes waiting to carry them across the sea to the spirit world beyond the sky. He told me they'd put sensible treasures into the grave with her, that she might enter the kingdom of her ancestors well-prepared for traveling.

"But at the graveside then I did not understand their ways. I looked with contempt at their savage differences. Yet at the same time, the whole crowd keening cried out to something with no name that had been growing in myself day after day on this island of Barbados, or maybe even since I had been orphaned by my mother's death. Oh, I felt most riled up and confused.

"After they had closed the hole, the overseers handed over a jug of rum. The Hausas spilled most across Big Dinah's grave and drank the rest off, no thought of sharing with we who stood there watching. Then we all draggled back to our own abodes, except the Hausas, who had rituals to keep through that long night. This had been the first interment of an important bondsman I had seen, since landing on Barbados.

"Whilst I was at Arlington, Salome's older husband had expired. He was important to his own, but not enough to warrant killing a scrawny pig and furnishing rum for. And Eugenia Plackler could not bear the sound of tambours. When she heard them, she dreamed, eyes open, of spirits coming for her. But the Saturday evening of Big Dinah's interment at the Glebe we wandered to our skimpy rations knowing that on Sunday, folk would rise to prepare a great funeral feast.

"I could not sleep that night with them screeching up there. The shadows on my hovel walls seemed unfamiliar. On my mat, covered by another mat, I lay holding my bundle of rags and whistle to me as if it were a child. Alone in the close darkness I speculated on the first gang.

"At the Glebe, as I have told you, the first gang was split with over fifty men and women in each crew—each a rough and wiry lot in order to survive, for none could look out much for another in the cane fields with the overseers pushing all to reach the quotas. I lay there as the stars scooped round the world outside my cabin, and a waking nightmare of evil sights and tales came back to me. Women puking and fainting in the ditches, struck down by the sun while the harvest hummed on brightly about them. Once when I was herding kine, a driver hurried to the yard with a young man, bent over, holding a big leaf to his eye. 'I spear up in a cane top, I spear up in a cane top,' the hurt lad screamed, blood spurting from beneath the leaf. The sharp cut cane had stabbed him through the eyeball. Arra, they laid him in his hut and sent to Bridgetown for the apothecary. We had no sick-house like yours then: the sick were only given leave to return to their cabins, where their kind might care for them at night. But I have told you that the ordinary slept on clay itself; or at best on bare planks above the ground. And you yourself, sir, know why you do not. Crawling with vermin were the cabin floors. And something wet about the air here—the swelter of the afternoons—the body sweats continually, wounds fester open like evil blossoms.

"He lost that eye. On a Sunday morning while the birds drew song across the cane fields Vaughton brought a jar of whiskey, then rode back down the hill. In a worker's shanty his menfolk soused him with the liquor, but his roar still shook the valley when they dug into his flesh and burned the socket clean.

"And everyone knew of others who had simply disappeared, put to ground without a ceremony. These would be folk like me, folk without kin or clan who had been taken by pestilence, snakebite in the ditches, or by slow starvation. The managers tried to keep such cases from us lest we run amok.

"Had I not also seen the man called Yeaboy howling in the yard until his voice went hoarse, holding his ear? Which had been cut half off by another African working as his partner—one in the cane row, the other in the trash row. A partner who, beneath the broiling sun, cane rash crosshatching from his forearms to his armpits, blistered fingers, back pulled from bending low, had grown impatient when clumsy Yeaboy tripped him and he fell upon his sugar knife. In an instant his arm arced against the sweet blue of the sky, and Yeaboy's ear fell to the trash ditch.

"So I was afraid, sir, to go into the sugar field with first gang.

"But also, as I lay there, it was as if the sod of my dank black grave weighed upon my chest. For I ceased breathing when I thought about the breeding. Then all things together whirled, until the shrieking and shrilling that knifed the air from Dinah's wake both expressed and heightened my worst fears.

"In the breeding we went to whomever they chose for us, and that was that. No thought of sacrament or family, as we were raised.

No choice or right to stay with the same stud from child to child, though we had heard of mergers: servants who, bred, were allowed to stay on with each other, and after servitude took to the road together as a team."

Coote sees a team of oxen, pulling, on all fours.

"But the breeding was an extra duty after a full day in the fields. Once the woman stopped her courses the man who fertilized her would be taken from her cabin once again. It was the woman who bent over a thickening waist to the same field tasks, who ate the same small rations while something inside sucked them from her. It was the woman who must force the stony skull of a child from between her thighs without drowning in her own blood. Who, upon her pallet on the damp clay floor must evade putrefaction and get back to the fields within a week. Still, a week for parturition was a new privilege in my day, brought in to coax the Africans to breed, for they were wont to lighten their bellies with spells and herbs, or bury birth-wet infants in the woods.

"Over in England our master, Lord Cleypole, and the merry clerks who advised him on such things, had read their ledgers and deduced an unprofitable infertility of stock. So they'd decided on a program of increase. The accountants of England advised that we be given eight days' rest before returning to the fields, and special foods—chocolate if we felt weak, a taste of rum in the last month— and one length of cloth to coax us toward the future. As for myself, I got two silver coins, but my case was somewhat different, as you shall hear.

"So the night Big Dinah went into the earth, in my own way I waited with her spirit too, picturing bloody heads like cannon hot exploding my flesh from inside, while in the night outside the Hausa women trilled and cried. Christ, how I wanted to escape my fate, which stretched its arms to take me."

Coote almost smiles. From this point on we'll trace her mutiny, he thinks. He puts his quill down, flexes his back discreetly, and baits her, hoping to break his boredom. "But your saints, biddy, is it not true your idols can wreak miracles to defend you—virgin martyrs and the lot? Your nation has killed Protestants on their advice. Why not call to them for aid?"

She bristles. "I have told you. Even the most stalwart saints were shocked dumb at the horrors of these lands." Her odor and her shabbiness try him more each hour. She is so . . . failed. He takes his quill again and drones, "Shocked. I see. Let us proceed."

"In the afternoon two drivers, Pawpaw Jack and Bacchus, riding donkeys, dragged a slaughtered ox and five boars o'er the hill to the slave quarters. There was much elbowing and trilling among the African women as to who would roast the meat. I saw that I, an outsider, would be given nothing choice whether I labored or not. So although I remembered Salome's roasting pits at Arlington, I did not help to cook Big Dinah's funeral meal. Instead, I crouched upon a fallen log to watch the goings-on.

"At first I sat there talking to myself in the way I had grown used to. Under my breath I was arguing, as I'd not dared to with the Hausa women who had chased me from the corpse of Big Dinah. Now I told them, great hussies in my mind, what great friends she and I'd become. I whispered the story of the object she and I had buried in the wood. And when I saw that Ibo woman slinking round the meat, arms folded tight across her naked chest, I pointed at her, raised my voice, and cursed her as an tAbhirseoir, the Devil. As usual, sir, no one paid my madness any heed.

"But as the evening darkened the men passing round the tin cups full of rum from the big full barrel Jack Vaughton'd sent handed one down, unheedingly, to me. And I had my first taste."

Why does he want to needle her? For daring to assume that he and she share a kinship through common feelings, such as fear? Coote inquires, "You were then . . . around twenty? You who come from that nation famed for drunkenness expect me to believe this was your first acquaintance with spirits? Next you will tell me you brought forth your bastards through virgin birth." The depth of contempt in his tone jolts him inwardly: where has such bitterness come from? He was not reared to speak so to any female, underling or not. "But go on. Do."

Young Cot had drunk and drunk, empty of belly, empty of heart and hope, fear trickling through her every cell. "In later years when I was drunk I lost the memory of episodes, and nights, and weeks. Yet I remember well that night, my first grand burial feast, with hundreds in attendance all milling by the tall red fires. I clasped each cup and drank it fast, hoping for courage to do something very wrong. Something to make the Hausas scorn me publicly, that I might fly into the faces of those I thought more bestial than myself. But instead, what seemed like magic happened.

"On my tongue, rum was a foul stinking thing, like the mouth tastes after a long fever. It made me flinch and shiver. But once it sank below my gorge, my blood began to dazzle. Never had my limbs relaxed so. I was reclining, long and heavy on the stony ground, yet my limbs seemed light as hair.

"Every cup that passed within my reach I clutched at, and between them thought about Big Dinah. From the angle of the grog she seemed ever more kind and friendly. When in fact she was not friendly but concerned for the survival of her own, and only meant to tame that thing she saw on me, for it endangered all of us."

"Biddy, do you say she saw you were possessed?"

The prisoner's impatience with him is almost rude as she responds, "For Christ's sake no! I only say the rum and I were ardent since our tongues first met. There I lolled as the mourners gathered in their clans around the food pits. It was somewhat like a Galway market day . . . legs and feet going by. Some dark and bare and dusty, or in floppy canvas trousers, or inching along under hiked petticoats. A driver strode past in his unlaced boots. I saw the knobbledy knees and bloated belly of a lost child, crying in a strange tongue for a parent in that moving forest of Africans. Now and then some redshanks passed.

"They dug up the meat. I saw as in a dream Big Dinah's people cut the carcasses and place the best parts on her grave. I watched them splash gourdsful of rum onto the mound. Then they took charge of carving, handing chunks of seared flesh round to all the people. But I, though always ravenous, cared nothing now for dripping roasts. I roused myself, and weaving through the crowd I searched for drink. The head people, however, as the rum barrel drew low, bore the rest away to their huts for the rites still to come. I found no more.

"Instead I found their faces, as before I had seen only legs. A sea of heads and faces swiveling to every angle, bodiless below the shoulders; or rather, become one undulating body set below the bobbing wave of shoulders and heads that talked and chewed and looked about. The Hausa group began the rhythmic chant. A woman sang a line. The other Hausa, all together, sang the same. They went on, taking turns, until those who spoke in different tongues began to imitate or hum.

"Quite soon the tambour men who'd squatted on the earth between the crowd and the tomb took up their thumping, and the whole group drew back to form a ring at the very edge of light. We stood not in a clearing, but formed a tight oblong, backs pressed against the bushes on either side of the path down to the sugar works as we surrounded Big Dinah's grave, now strewn with gourds and meat, and a death-blind ox's head. We bridged the empty space that divided the Hausa from the next tribe's compound.

"The drummers, Hausa men, rapped and tapped on logs set upright or laid flat like miniature canoes. We, the ring of bondsmen, stood back from them. At the long narrow center of the group sank the grave, framed by flame. Now, to the rapid slap and slub of wood on skin, people began clapping. A child in a woman's arms jogged back and forth. And suddenly a young man leapt onto the sandy soil of the mound. His dancing had been summoned by the drums. Even I could see he and the drum were conversing, but that the drum was master."

Coote's stomach rumbles. The lunch seemed greasy. He is bored, irritable, fascinated, in different layers of himself. He sees the garden of the night before. He and his Governor, the common appearance of two colonial gentlemen conversing; but beneath the image of mutual respect, the Governor, dissolute, rapacious, is master. Shocked, he drives the vision off.

"Many people danced before me, one by one. Strong agile youths; old women who limped around the yard by daylight feeding the fowl, yet lifted from the waist and swayed like princesses once they partnered with the drums. The hands kept clapping, voices chased each other eagerly in song. Two hundred sets of feet stamped the ground. Something rose in me."

". . . Something came upon you?" Coote asks, dipping for fresh ink.

"No. It was my own, of me, but it would have had no way out had it not been invoked by Africa, that way of dancing, which set it free into the world. The music let me speak with people whose words I could not understand. One moment I stood peering between nodding heads. The next I elbowed forward, my legs were flipping me across the swath of earth toward the drummers.

"The Africans I've seen dance from the shoulders and the waist—a looping, leaping sort of thing; all looseness and free movement. The dance of Galway was straight up and down. The last time I'd had call to dance it had been on Wren's Day when I was kidnapped, though I still recalled its merry and sweet steps. But now, to Hausa drumming; to four hundred hands beating against each other. I felt a deeper language in that dance. The marriage, sir, of wordless protest with high spirits and with grace.

"Over and over I kicked. Rigid neck to hips, but lashing out with feet. With my feet I refused! Refused the first gang's dangers, and the breeding; refused our mouldy rations, the hours bent to pluck the sun's gifts for another's bounty. I kicked over the table of gamblers who had traded my life for a throw of dice in Bridgetown, and I stamped on the inconclusive lusts of Henry Plackler. My legs lifted higher, thumping down firmly as the mistress told Jenks, 'Whip her.' My heels stomped 'no' as the ginger-headed baby was dragged screaming from Ardiss's breast. Whirling, I spun off the Captain's knee on the *Falconer*. Knocked his cloak onto the deck, and leapt into the sky."

She stops. Peter Coote looks up. "And then?"

"Then ... then ... that was all. As something had drawn me out to dance, it left me crumpled in the sand when it had finished. I went down to my stick-shed in an hour, for the ceremony became wilder, my head was aching, and my stomach sick. Once the dance was out of me, despair began to settle once again like dust."

"Once the rum was out of you, you mean," Peter Coote corrects rather primly.

The next part of the testimony is confusing but quite brief. Cot Daley, he notes at the end of it, has only patchy memories of several years. Could there have been an alcoholic swelling of the brain with prolonged consequences? An undetected fever? he questions in the margins.

The day after Big Dinah's funeral dance, the Irishwoman had gone straight into the first gang, where she stayed for several years. Because already the overseers suspected networks of rebelliousness building among the men of Ireland, she was kept from the crew where the Connaught lads worked. That had been in August 1659. In March of 1660 the prisoner had stolen food from an unlocked storehouse. A large cheese, a crock of butter, smoked salmon, a fine-milled loaf, and a large, sharp silver knife. For twenty years the law had stood that thievery of goods worth twelve shillings or more must be tried as a capital offense. Not only were the goods in question worth more: Jack Vaughton had gone pale at the proceedings, for the foods, imported all the way from England for an Easter dinner at Lord Cleypole's largesse, were irreplaceable at that time in the colony.

Cot Daley was found guilty, her accurate penalty death by hanging. Jack Vaughton argued long and hard with the tribunal, concerning this servant's worth as a worker, to be increased by issue as many years of breeding stretched ahead of her. In the end they concurred: if by her execution Lord Cleypole would suffer double theft, that was not just. The Irishwoman received seven years' added indenture, plus twenty public strokes in Bridgetown once the harvest was complete. "There was a roaring in my ears as I stood at the whipping post the second time," the prisoner tells Coote. "I did not faint so easily as when Jenks fell to, but seemed to float away and watch myself, writhing, begging, as a crowd of gentlemen and ladies, tended by their servants, watched with me."

"What did you take the knife for?" Peter Coote asks.

"To spread the butter, sir," she grins.

Later that year, when her wounds had healed, Jack Vaughton ordered Cot Daley to prepare to breed. By that time planters and their managers had begun to reconsider the wisdom of breeding purely Irish stock. Since her years at Arlington, two island-wide uprisings had been masterminded by the Irish, and uncovered just in time. For this and other reasons, Jack Vaughton hesitated to appoint her stud. Recently the first experiment of offspring bred between Irish and Africans had reached early maturity. Lighter-skinned and softer-haired than pure blacks, the girls among them showed especial promise to be handsome, thus more suitable for special duties than ordinary girls.

Therefore, after consideration, Jack Vaughton bade her submit herself to Pawpaw Jack, the driver of her field crew. "But I could not, *could* not, bring myself to do this," Cot claims tersely. And silently Peter Coote approves.

"He was a small and thickset man who watched me all the time. Whilst scolding me to cut cane faster, or having words with other Africans, his eyes had a skinned stare when they fell on me, as if they might pop and explode.

"I have told you that I was alone there at the Glebe. I had no friends as once I'd had in Mary Dove. I was the only Irish in my field crew, so I had formed the habit of talking to myself. Sometimes as I worked away, babbling in Irish to myself, Pawpaw Jack would hunker down beside me. 'What you say, Red? What you say?' he whispered. I slashed away beside him with no answer.

"That was all he wanted from me, at least at first: to know what I was talking to, although I would not speak with him. He was a man who liked those best who liked him least, while Master Plackler, for example, was the opposite sort of man: the slightest deviation from his whims, spoken or not, he found tiresome."

Coote sees no point in commenting on the idiocy of comparing African and Englishman, slave and titled planter, as if they were the same thing: Man. He writes on, with pinched nostrils.

She tells how she had held off Pawpaw Jack until almost Christmastime. Up on the hill, in the Ite compound, he had an indeterminate number of Ite women: they satisfied his needs.

"I tell you, he repulsed me. My brain stewed in confusion, seeking this way and another to avoid his clasp. I thought to lure one of my countrymen by creeping to his pallet in the middle of the night, and achieve the breeding that way round. But the lads from Connaught had less than two years to finish out, and turned me back to my own hut. The only other way I came upon was to get sold off again; but then everything would sink to the beginning once more. Myself the outsider, upon the ground again, perhaps worse rations, perhaps a vengeful mistress, a randy master too, a stud even more devilish than Pawpaw Jack himself. The breeding, at my age, must take place anyway. So I gave in."

The prisoner cannot remember how she first succumbed or why, but it was in a shed, not her own hut, nor in Jack Pawpaw's, for there were other women—Ites—living there. The mating only happened twice until Eastertide of 1661.

Easter was anticipated more than Christmas by the bondspeople, Africans and Christians alike, for Christmas fell in wintertime. Winter work was slower, preparing for the crop season to come. Field tasks were routine ones—the tending of the livestock; manuring of the fields, repairing sheds and outbuildings, clearing drains and ditches to expose the nests of rats and snakes to birds of prey. The work was usually predictable then, the field day only from sun to sun. But Easter fell in the middle of crop time. During that time— January to May—gangs worked strenuously in the fields and mills for eighteen hours a day. Accidents happened in this season, when overloaded, sleepless, hungry workers severed not a cane stalk but a thumb. When millers mashed their own arms between grinding stones; and in the boiling-houses, inhaled steam dropped grown men and women to the ground like folded paper, instantly. So Easter was a four-day holiday in the midst of an inferno.

From Good Friday afternoon through Easter Monday, the slaves and servants of the Glebe were released from their labors except to tend the stock. On Easter Monday night of 1661 at a pig roast and dance Cot Daley had swilled several jars of rum, when Jack Vaughton and William Butler, overseers, rode into the quarters to advise their people to settle down, for another workday would soon be upon them. The weather had been even finer and warmer than usual, and a field of cane stood overready for its harvest. The revelers seemed reluctant to cease cavorting, but slowly, under Mr. Vaughton's eye, they began to leave the yard and straggle toward their shacks. Mr. Vaughton himself then turned his beast and prepared to return down the hill, when the Irishwoman called out, "Feck ye, we have till midnight!" and picked up a stick to lash the horse's withers. Due to her inebriation and the starless dark the horse was facing into, the blow did not connect. But Jack Vaughton had her clapped in stocks right then. In the morning she was given an extended indenture of two years, according to the new Act for the Ordaining of Rights between Masters and Servants, and promised another public lashing when the harvest was all in.

The Irishwoman recounts vomiting the rum out in the stocks, then realizing as the night wheeled to gray dawn, what her life had come to.

"Truly, this is what rum will lead to, especially in the female humors," Peter Coote affirms.

"You'll rarely see a happy person besotted," Cot Quashey replies bitterly. "I cannot describe how the sinking of the night into a dismal dawn pulled me further down in spirit. With the pale coming of the sun people skirted round me with their small yard duties as I had skirted Paudi Iasc a lifetime before, and I understood that I was broken. I would refuse no one, no more."

The prisoner decided that her best course was to pay careful attention to the managers, obeying them to the letter or beyond, if possible. Otherwise, she began to understand, she would not leave her servitude alive. "It was 1661," she counted out for Coote. "I had been spirited away in '50, sold in '51. Ten years, already, had dragged by like the chains of Hades. And now the thing Big Dinah had seen crawling over me had bought me hell till 1673.

"I was twenty-one: I would be the age of Christ when he was done to death when I was released, if I pleased everyone who stood above me from now till then. They let me out to work the fields after two more days. I went straight to the river, where I bathed and washed my hair in the suds of the aloe plant. I also washed my canvas clothes, and slept in the old corselet, lying on the final rags of the old surcoat. The next morning—how can I tell you? I felt queasy with relief. When he came along the row where I was scooping cut cane for the mill, I mumbled to myself as usual. He bent over, closer, closer, staring at my face as if he saw the fey. 'What you sayin', Redshank? What you say?' he asked. 'I'm saying Pawpaw Jack, you come to see me on my mat tonight,' I told him without lifting up. He made one sound. It was like the first bugle note of a rooster's call at dawn.

"I worked late that night in the mills, feeding the boilers. When I crept into my shack, he was waiting. He had brought salt fish wrapped in a banana leaf, and an orange. Afterward I told him rum would make it easier for me. 'Greasy,' he said. 'Rum will make you greasy, I like to slide.' He was with me every night. I meant to bind him to me so he would protect me. Give me easier work out in the field, train me for a second-gang driver, and stand between me and the whip.

"He drove the cart to Bridgetown when it came time for me to take my lashes for speaking up to Vaughton. There were errands for the plantation. Jack Vaughton knew I had accepted Pawpaw Jack, and it mollified him. I took only fifteen lashes, and an apothecary tended to me afterward. We stayed in Bridgetown for two days, while Lye and Vaughton took Pawpaw Jack and Bacchus to inspect a shipment of new slaves from Guinea. These were the Coromantee. On behalf of Edward Cleypole and on his letter, they purchased seventeen. Quashey was among them, and Jiba, and the rest. But Mama Chiva, being from Brazil, did not come at that time. She was brought months later. And Afebwa arrived later still.

"I was driven back with the supplies, and the wagon emptied out before they returned for the new slaves, so I did not see the Coromantee then."

Coote has memorized the notes the Governor has given him, taken during the first interrogations of this prisoner. "Go back to Pawpaw Jack," he commands. "Your relations with the Coromantee we'll return to, you can be sure. But first, did you not have his child?"

She stares straight ahead. "Yes. Pawpaw Jack came to me almost every night. His women hissed at me as I passed in the fields, but I felt a warped pride. He brought me tidbits and rum, and I did the things he told me. They hurt no worse than bending to plant shoots all day, or lifting boulders from the fields. Because he kept his women off me and returned almost every night, I mistook him. I thought he loved me, for I knew nothing yet of love, so I meant to use him. But he came because it stirred him so, that one who hated him would yet do his will.

"I had a child of Pawpaw Jack at the end of '61." The custom was that every child, African, Scots, English, or Irish, would grow up with its mother. But Pawpaw Jack came from a group of people with whom children belonged to their father. A woman could leave or be put aside, but her children would then be taken from her and given to her husband's female relatives to raise. "He told me all along that he would take the child," she says, "but I had never had a babe. In my state, dull, confused, and overwhelmed, he might have said that he would take away my food ration for the day that I gave birth. What did I care?"

The birthing was a long one. They moved her to an empty shed and sent a midwife down to her, for Cot Daley knew nothing of these things in human beings. The lambs fell quickly. Even a cow could birth a long-legged calf from dark to dawn. First she prayed to her mute saints; then gave over and howled. Eventually it was the howling that opened her, so the child could press through.

"But when I took her in my arms there in the shed, the sun rose here, inside my chest"—she points—"and I would not let her go. I knew then that to suffer breeding was not important if it gave me this. Holding my own perfect wee'n . . . and to be a woman . . . under all it was a wondrous, a mystic thing.

"She curled her flower-petal tongue between her lips, and squirmed, and fell asleep. Later they gave her an African name. But although there was no priest, no baptism on the island, I named her for my mother. I called her Moya.

"The midwife sent word of the birth out to the field. That night they came to take her from me, before my milk began to flow. They wanted no milk fever on me, but to keep me to the schedule that they had."

She had shrieked at Pawpaw Jack and the nursing wife he brought along to take the child. "My baby began to wail, and I slapped the woman holding her, bit Pawpaw Jack's nose hard at the tip, and kicked until my blood drenched the clay beneath our feet, where the flies buzzed. Jack Vaughton was sent for. He came inside the shed and shut the door. I recall his dusty boots, the quirt held ever in his hand; like your pen, sir, in yours."

Vaughton paced and spoke about the future. Eleven years lay ahead of her at the Glebe: eleven years of fieldwork, though in spite of a recalcitrant background, elevation to the role of driver or stock-ranger was remotely possible. "After that eleven years you will be more old than young," said he. "But still . . . if you have not been wasted in the fields, and without half-Negra babes clinging to your skirts reminding him . . . a freedman of your type might yet marry you. Before you leave this world you might know peace, and some of the contentment found inside a humble home. But what Irish-man will take on black offspring, let alone the . . . she who bore them?"

Jack Vaughton gave Cot Daley eight days' rest, a length of printed cloth, the promise she would not have to lie with Pawpaw Jack again, and two silver coins. Like Judas, Peter Coote finds himself thinking.

"Like Judas," the Irishwoman echoes him. "Yet she throve with the Ite. She was with them still when I left the Glebe in '80. One of Lord Cleypole's sons was having her raised for himself, and she was proud of it. She got to work in the storehouse. I heard they sent her to Virginia in '82 when he was lieutenant in the King's militia there, but he got killed straight after that. I haven't learned what happened to her after that. My firstborn child. My Moya."

Now gusts of wind begin to blow dust from the garden through the open window as the afternoon showers gather. Some of Peter's pages ruffle up and fly across the floor. "Lucy?" he shouts. She should be back by now. But a bowed old man with a grizzled white beard comes instead into the room. "Christ, Daniel, where is Lucy?" Now Peter Coote is angry. The papers are all scrambled, and in his haste to grab them he has caught the lace of his left sleeve on a tiny finishing nail on the desk's edge. The fragile threads that shape a flower have pulled into a clump of puckered strings, ready to catch on the next thing. "Damn you!" he shouts, whether at the prisoner, the old slave, Lucy, or his sleeve. But within minutes he is soothed and sorted out. The old man closes the shutters and fetches two lanterns to write by, until the rain should pass.

V

Musty and sullen dawns the day. Coote bids Lucy open the shutters for the chance sticky breeze: the prisoner's back smells ever more fetid in spite of herbal washes. The odor makes him vaguely but consistently nauseous. The Irish-woman enters the room this morning leaning on the old slave man whose name he has mislaid. Glancing up at the arched plaster door-way, he sees her framed in tarnished pewter light, but for wisps of coppery hair which resist the dullness. The black wool shawl drawn tightly over her thin shoulders lends her the shape of an unformed girl. The features of her face cannot be seen: only a silvery sheen of light in the wrinkles of her cap and thin tendrils around a raw-boned face hidden as if within a shallow cave. With a gesture of his plume he indicates her seat. Readying the inkpot, parchment, pearl-set box of sand, he notices several heavy flies leave the wall to browse her shoulders, drawn by the cloying odor of decay.

"Begin," he chokes.

She's gazing blankly toward the wall. "Can you picture me there, sir? My life . . . Can you see me day after day, month to year, bent in the fields, cooking my mean ration of cornmeal and weeds at a fire outside my shack? I had built another after the birthing, and Vaughton lent me two black lads and one afternoon, to thatch it. Still it only stood the width of your arms' span, and the roof grazed my hair. From it I clambered when the field gongs sounded, rolling over on my thin elbows on the gravel, the knobs upon my spine like carbuncles thinly covered with hide. My putty-colored petticoat and waist, stitched without care, shredded more each day from sweat and the pull and heave of sugar work. The cloth was so loosely woven that the flesh of my back broiled in a tiny grid like inflamed mesh when I was forced to bend the whole day pulling shoots. The Christmas gift of one new suit of clothes we kept for funerals and feasts, until our older garments rotted into uselessness. But African women have an eye for beauty, and from them I learned to make bracelets from the hard seeds of the Job's Tears bush. I bound these round my ankles and my wrists, and hung them at feasts in my clumped and tangled hair. Oh . . . I can see myself as clearly as if I were a bird flying free above that hank of hair and hide hung with rainbow-colored beads bent tugging at the earth, back itching over the scars of the lash. Rarely did I bathe now. No Pawpaw Jack should look at me again. They'd put me in the other section of first gang once the Irishmen fulfilled their terms and were let go from bondage. I did not have to brush by Moya's father as I moved up and down the rows year after year, back and forth from the ditches to the sugar yard.

"Arguing with myself and the peopled past, beneath my breath; singing the odd snatch of a hymn whose words had been emptied of belief, I tried to be what they thought 'good.' To the drivers, the rangers, all the overseers, especially Jack Vaughton, I bowed my head and stood aside, mumbling 'How's yer health, sire?' Trying to gauge the moment to sidle forward with information, or piously agree with them against the lesser folk. But when they weren't about, splurts of viciousness came out of me against the others of my lot—folk powerless to sort me out." Cot Quashey's voice wavers; she turns from the doorframe to the desk and says humbly, "After each spew of abuse I felt, soon or late, a sense of disgust for myself, and great remorse. Yet these twinges of right and wrong from my upbringing, or from the remnants of my human heart, seemed only to impel worse lashings out against the hapless. I might taunt one being flogged, I might sneer at a child staggering under too great a load. And this was how I tried to keep my masters' wrath off me.

"But though I tried, my days went by as if I was walking barefoot over sharp stones, whilst carrying a large tray laden with the finest crystal goblets. Fear and too much caution . . . they'll make you stumble, sir. 'Tis just a matter of time.

"Then came the feast of thanksgiving after the locust plague of 1663.

"Those swarms flew in on brown sheets which darkened the noon skies. They bowed every tree branch at the edge of the forest like vile fruits crawling 'pon the vine. The grapes of hell, with their swiveling heads and twitching horns and the whining, droning song made when they rubbed their sticky legs together.

"There had been a drought and then a flood before the locusts seemed to burble up out of the ground. They took wing and looked down on our helplessness from the high branches. Still, due to hard work and Providence, half the cane crop of the Glebe was standing at the end. The overseers put the first gangs into the middle of the sprouting fields and showed us where to dig. We shoveled feverishly, creating a wide ring trench, then filled it partway with field trash. Two 'seers were circling us on muddy nervous mares, shouting directions. Already the odd locust, having sawed the leaves and tender bark off every branch around the jungle's rim, was beginning to drop onto the earth to chew the tender stalks of cane, when Rigley and Vaughton galloped up from the yards holding pine-pitch torches high aloft.

"The women and unseasoned males jumped hastily outside the ring, while the men within were given calabashes of water to splash onto the rags tied quickly o'er their faces. Still I can hear the women, screeching for fear the men would be grilled alive. But the overseers knew their work: to their commands, the fire crew forked flaming tinder back across the ditches, or dug the trenches wider and deeper in spots. They coughed and choked; but only one expired from it all.

"But a million insects, drawn to the field, were unable to surmount the smoke and flame. While men fought along the ditches, others took turns plucking the live locusts which had landed from the seedlings. And as I said, a holiday was declared once it was certain the surviving locusts had departed from the Glebe. For half our cane would come to harvest, whilst the crops of many others were devoured to the roots, where the creatures injected new eggs, then went to sleep until their next mysterious hatching.

"It was at the locust feast that I first noticed Quashey the Coromantee, who became my husband."

Coote makes a wry mouth: husband indeed! A buzzing roars by his left ear. He jerks. The recording of a million locust eyes and waving antennae eeries the skin on his arms beneath the gray-hued linen shirt with its unraveling lace. Flies: three of them, move onto his escritoire from the stenchful shoulders of the hag. "Lucy!" he orders. "Get in here now." He rises, slamming the shutters closed, tilting the slatted jalousies open from the bottom at such an angle that there will be some light but few flies entering. Lucy swishes into the room, long neck held high, broom in hand. He motions her to stand behind him, invert the broom, and switch away flies while the interrogation progresses. "Get on with it," he barks at his prisoner. Really! Her stink is sickening!

"I noticed Quashey due to his garments. They marked him as a bondsman of import, for with pantaloons of putty Osnabruck he wore a kind of boot, and though shirtless like all the other men he wore a cloak of wool the sort the navvies used to wear in Cromwell's time. This was broidered with rainbow-colored seeds, as well as animal teeth.

"He was less than usual height, but lofty in his bearing, with skin like polished wood. An unusual raised tattooing cuffed his mighty arms. I did not mark his face at the time, but as he passed me I heard the faintest buzzing, from deep down in his chest. Quashey was given to humming, he hummed his thoughts. I also noted that a woman trailed him to the roasting pit—a most unusual woman, the one we called Mama Chiva. This woman seemed almost old enough to be the mother of the man, yet from the way he regarded her when she brought him food, she was something else to him.

"She too was garbed unusually, in a bodice which beneath its stains had once been red. Another cloth of red partly veiled her hair. But the marvelous thing about her was her smile. For as they sat upon a log beside the fire she gave a laugh at something said, and flashed her teeth, and what a fine mouthful of ivories she had, herself a granny woman! Yes, it is true! Her teeth were made of a fine ivory, carved with what they call scrimshaw. They glimmered like purest pearls in the firelight. In the daytime, though, you could see the fine etchings of tiny sloops and islands in the sea, mermaids and whales, carved in each one. Mama Chiva had been brought up from Brazil and traded by the Dutch, one of whom had kept her as a concubine for years before she thickened after many childbirths. Each of her children had been sold away by their own ardent, jovial father. Himself it was who'd given her the scrimshaw teeth, when she lost her own across the years. He'd take her on his knee, she said, and touching a tooth, tell a tale about its image. He was a sailing man was he, and had been all around the world.

"They said she had ensorcelled the Dutchman for many years, and he had given her many gifts, and money too. The last was true, for when I was wed to Quashey there came a time when only coin would help his cause, and Mama Chiva, who had been his first wife here on this side of the sea, took out what she had hidden and gave it to him. Gave him everything, with a heart and a half. But these things lay far ahead as we sat around the flames chewing charred flesh and preparing for a dance.

"You have heard how it was with me in those days. At the locust feast while the Africans began to thump their tambourines, I hunkered down with a calabash of rum beside the barrel. And at the height of that feast, when the howling had reached its utmost frenzy, I had to make my water. I had been longing, I recall; rum-dreaming: yearning for the days when I'd known Dinah and for a time went among others, other women, at the Sunday market. So half in wish and half in fantasy, I crept into the wood and crouching there to relieve myself, thought I could make out the path we'd trod to St. John's Church. Then, rising in the misty, dangerous night forest, I began to stagger toward it. But I got lost, then cold, then curled myself between the roots of a tree against the late-night dew. The last thing I heard before I fell asleep was a strange sound. A sound as if shells or thin animal bones were blowing in the breeze, chinking together like fairy chimes. And there I lay when the rangers Vaughton sent found me in the morn. Not my swimming head, nor my fetid breath, nor my confusion convinced anyone that I had not made to run away. There was a hearing of some sort that afternoon, but I soon shut my lips, for I felt in my belly the futility of trying to reason with the Spirits of the Night. I was given no lashes this time, but a fully renewed servitude of seven years. Now I would not come up for release until 1680, all going well. And my youth would be behind me. I would be a granny woman of forty years of age, if I should live so long."

The hot tears of pity that rush into Coote's eyes as Lucy waves away the agitated flies are for himself. He himself turned forty several full months ago, and finds himself still landless, brideless, with no permanent prospects in these lonely tropics. He clears his throat into the silence, sniffing. When composed again, he prompts, "Now you have come to Quashey, the traitor who was hanged for his lead in the heinous uprising of 1675. What part played you in all of this?" He records his own well-chosen words with a flourish.

· · ·

"My Quashey, peace be with him," begins the prisoner; and instead of tears of lamentation she smiles the first true smile Coote has seen on her. It's snaggle-toothed and cracked, yet it dimples, lighting the pale eyes like a measure of sparkling water in a clean glass cup. "Ah, 'twas a long time yet until we came together. As you remember, Vaughton had decreed that I need not go again for breeding after Moya, and he seemed, for several years, to have given me up for that. I hoped I might become like Dora at Arlington: a spinster overseer. But others were chosen.

"Before the Connaught lads were freed they bred with Africans from the Horn, and the Irish house girls were mated with Scotsmen and Brits, except she who held out for a pledge from the overseer Rigley. Me, it was as though I were returned to childhood again, except for fieldwork. I had no fleshly obligations; but because I had no child, my daughter living up on Ite hill as if I did not exist, I had no say and no respect among the slavewomen.

"Quashey. Yes, I learned about him over time. At first he had been placed upon the first crew opposite my own, so I rarely saw him outside feasts. But by the time of the first locust plague, Quashey had been promoted. He had become first mariner of the plantation's sloop. At this time Lord Cleypole had purchased holdings down the St. John's River, for the sugar market had grown fierce attractive. Quashey it was who steered the boat from the Glebe's dock across Conset's Bay to the new fields, with seedlings, cuttings, tools, and later stock and people. In pleasant weather he brought the overseers and the odd gentry back and forth. In harvest season he doubled as a potter, making the curing pots they use to drain molasses from the fine white costly sugar. These skills had he brought with him from his home in Africa, where all the men, even from chiefly tribes like his own, took pride in knowing self-sufficiency.

"In the year following my sentencing as a runaway something shifted in me, as things tip, then tilt again in all of us. It seemed too much to hope for—the possibility of my return home to Eire at the age of forty; a cottage of my own, a man, a parish of kind homely neighbors near my sister or my brother . . . if I found them living. I could no longer yearn ahead, yet no longer grieved backward as much, either. Instead, on Sundays and fine evenings now, I began to pull some herbs I recognized from home. Plantain, mullein, dandelion, yarrow; wild garlic and wild mustard. Willow bark, when peeled red and smoked, made a raw throat smooth again. Tea from that winter-smelling thin-needled tree which grows on northern hillsides stopped a cough and lit the fire of life again in an exhausted chest. It became known that I collected herbs: they could be seen drying in the shade of the thatch outside my shanty door. Then came the measles epidemic in '64 and '65, and I was called to help. That was how I first had words with Mama Chiva. She had been taken on as overseer of the pot gang although she was too young for that; but the work kept her close to the yards, where she was known as an herbal granny, a leech woman. And as you know, there were not yet apothecaries on plantations in those days.

"Mama Chiva had more and different medicines than mine. Who knows which worked, and when, and why? We lost more than half of the infected; but many who were dosed pulled through. Through a mix of broken English learned from her Dutchman, and the language of the eyes, Mama Chiva and I compared the attributes of roots we pulled and powdered. That was what we held in common, back then.

"There was a little child, a Mbundu girl who first went blind, then succumbed. I don't know why that one child broke through the hard scab on my heart, but I tried so hard to pull her back to life. The night she passed I brought the old rusty flute of my mother to her pallet, and played, trying to charm her spirit. There was no mother to claim her, perhaps that was the link between us. When she died I didn't know, and kept on playing while a small crowd of whispering slaves gathered round us. Quashey and Mama Chiva were in that group, I looked up and heard his solemn humming; but it was not they who stepped forward to take the flute away from me and lead me from the site so that the child could be prepared for her travel back to Guinea. They called Heaven that. Guinea. Or Zhenna. Or a mix of both, depending upon their own clan's belief."

The testimony rambles on. Coote itches: sweat trickles down his back now that no garden breeze can dry it. The straw broom swishes back and forth, up and down, in Lucy's hands. The air it stirs tickles his ear. Nausea, lasciviousness, impatience, roil in him. He will have them burn camphor in this room, and will take his noon meal at the table in his chamber.

In 1666, the Irish woman says, they witnessed from afar the Bridgetown fire. The sun went red, the sky deep gray for the best part of three days. Among the bondspeople spread a horrid thrill: this was the Judgment Day which every race had heard about. But no; it proved to be only a small judgment on the merchant storehouses and town mansions in the capital. Next came the hurricane, sucking the pillars from plantation porches. Crops were demolished, rations scantier than ever. The island was replanted by drooping skeletons to the flicking of the whip. But afterward had come new and energetic investments in Barbados: Coote realizes that his own embarkation in 1669 rode the latter curve of this wave of rebuilding and high optimism.

At the Glebe, masons were hired to strengthen slave shanties with fieldstone and wood; a sick-house was built, and a part-time apothecary-surgeon hired between three plantations. From Brazil and the French Islands bounced white-sailed sloops with sturdy new strains of cane. The work fell hard on all, bondsmen and overseers alike. Recognizing the need for wholesale improvement, Lord Cleypole's advisors in England established a stepped-up program of increase. Breeding-per-head must be increased among all stock, including human, advised the gentry's agents. And so one day Jack

Vaughton called Cot Daley to him and told her to bathe: he had decided to breed her to the Coromantee named Quashey.

"I reacted with as much scorn as fear and exhaustion would let me express," she remembers now. "But Vaughton dismissed me, repeating, 'Bathe. Don your Christmas petticoats. You have the odor of a week-dead trout, and the Coromantees are a proud lot. Fastidious, unlike the redshanks.' Oh how I cursed his mother underneath my breath. But I went down to the river that Sunday and scoured myself with a crisp, spongy weed which grows beside such places. There was aloe on the banks, and I sudsed my hair. But it was too snarled to pull smooth with my fingers: it had twined like African hair around itself into long plaits. I spread it out beneath me 'pon the grass and lay there for a while, enjoying that drowsy lull a person feels when she's freshly cleaned, and warm. Back at my hut I crouched to boil my corn and chew my dry salt fish. Then, wiping my fingers on my old field skirt, I obeyed Vaughton. I slipped into my newer, unbleached Osnabruck skirt and tied my bodice shut. Then I lay upon my mat awaiting the new stud, as I had waited once for Pawpaw Jack.

"I awoke in that same position, my new clothes rumpled up above my waist. The work gongs were a-throbbing. Quashey had not come."

"Had they forgotten me? Back into my stinking rags I went, more anxious than ever to shrink from the attention of Jack Vaughton. And he said no more. But when a week had passed I was squatting before my hut on our day of rest roasting a turtle I'd crushed with a stone, and I saw Mama Chiva coming down the hill on bandy legs. I squinted as she stopped. She held out a folded length of orange-dyed cloth to me. 'Sister,' said she, 'I have come from your husband to tell you we will bring you to your new home one week from today.' That was the gist of it. I was, you may imagine, astonished. I took the bright cloth from her as she bent, and pushed the turtle meat behind me lest she expect a morsel for the roasting. She must have seen the empty shell nearby . . .

"That night I lay restless. The new bit of cloth, barely enough for a bodice-vest yet the only colored stuff I'd owned since Arlington, lay folded carefully around my flute in the remnants of my father's coat—now only a collar, facings, and one dangling pocket flap. These cushioned my head as I wished uselessly that I could keep to my own hut. Let the man come down to *my* mat, he'd be off me soon as I could catch again. Half the night I lay there tossing, beside myself that they could torture me so; an entire week left to imagine the new home and new mating with mounting dread."

Stiffly, Coote assents, ". . . it is a fearsome fate for any Christian woman to bear, I should imagine . . ."

He means to spare her the need to recite details, but on and on she ruminates. How they came for her that next Sunday morning— Mama Chiva, the first among Quashey's women, and Sargeant Jiba, the madwoman who thought herself a soldier, marching down the hill and barking orders at the air. The Irish girl had watched the two roll up her mats, pick up her iron pot and grinding stones. "I held my bundle of treasures tightly, though, heart pounding dull and fearful as I followed their lead up the hill onto that plateau where the African tribes clustered in their homes.

"Those two I came too late to call my sisters, led me to his compound. There they crawled into a small wattle-and-daub cabin thatched with branches of the coconut tree, and motioned me to follow. Only in the middle of my new cabin could we stand. The cool dim corners, though, were put to use. Along one curving wall Mama Chiva shook my mats open, and the two of them made murmur at my fine designs. Beside the doorway to the left there was a ring of firestones already in place, and there they placed my pot and cooking things. There were clean calabashes from the wild pumpkin shell already waiting, some filled with herbs and dried beans. Over the door someone had scrawled a loopy orange character of sorts: other than that, my small cabin was a dim brown cave with sunlight slanting through the door.

"Jiba and Mama Chiva motioned me to leave my treasure bundle and come outside, but I cowered and showed my teeth, hugging it tight to my chest. After a tussle, Jiba grabbed my ankle as I sat upon the pallet by the wall and surprised me so with her iron clench that I was halfway through the door into the yard again, flute, rags, and orange cloth scattered on the clay behind me, before I knew that I was moving. In the yard, without a word, she hauled me to my feet by the scruff of my Christmas collar. She pushed me behind Chiva. But her push was no rougher than it needed to be, to impel motion.

"I saw that there were four small huts. Quashey had built one for each of his wives according to the instructions of his Book. The one beside mine stood empty. Before these mounded cabins stood a larger one with an awning of straw braced upon poles. I remember, I remember. How sweetly birds were trilling, and that bloom they call hibiscus curled above the entry to this room. We ducked inside. There you could stand and walk about, and there we sat briefly upon a hard-built bench of clay spread with the short navvy cloak I had seen upon Quashey. There were baskets piled along the wall, mats spread to prepare food, a metal basin against the bench, and two stewpots made of iron which I'd only seen issued to overseers. But Quashey, you remember, was at this time already a man of rank among the bondsfolk. As such, he received the confidence of his superiors, and gifts with which they meant to buy *his* confidence. Whence came my bridal cloth of orange—from his own small hoard of riches.

"Once Mama Chiva and Jiba had shown me where to find house water, and which paths into the jungle were useful for my necessities, they took me over to my hut and with a hand-wave bade me enter in and wait. I did so.

"He came to me at sundown, again with those two wives and a young boy, who I later learned was his distant kinsman from the old country. They sat on the floor apart from me, and mumbled something in their tongue, passing the water gourd to me. I was sore frightened with these goings-on. I would have much preferred the quick crawl of a body onto mine, in my own hut down below. I could have looked out to the swimming stars while I was enduring the rut. This hut looked out only on the empty one beside it, and I could not see the sky. When the hocus-pocus had been most solemnly said, Quashey brought from the pouch slung across his breast a jungle hen of the sort they call the Guinea fowl. It has blue wattles and sharp bright yellow claws. Facing the orange mark above the door he bent and sang out more mysterious words, then snapped its neck in one swift motion. He and his kinsman stepped outside into the darkening world. The women came back once to me with coals from a fire to start my own hearth, and pantomimed my plucking. I was left alone again.

"With my stone blade I disemboweled the fowl, which seemed a bedding gift. I crept out for a branch to make a spit, and roasted that young hen, gleeful that from the silence of the yard it seemed I would have her all for my own gob. But as I took her from the greasy branch, the door hole filled with shadow. It was Quashey, squatting there, looking mildly at me. He gazed and gazed, quite calmly. It was his calmness that made me rip one side of the bird's burned breast from its backbone, and hold it out to him."

The consummation, says the prisoner, took place that night; but the quickening not for several months. It was the custom among Quashey's clan that every wife must receive equal attention, so he came to her only every three nights, unless she was in courses. Then he came not at all till she was bathed and her pallet turned. Sometimes he took his meal with her if he came late up from the landing and it was her turn. But other times he supped with Mama Chiva and Sargeant Jiba, who spoke to him with words that rolled like rich tobacco smoke, before he visited his Irish wife. "When I learned a little of the common language, I understood a secret. Jiba, you see, was not Quashey's wife but his sister. The ruse that she was wife was the only means by which he could bring her to his house and try to keep her safe: this was the proud duty of a brother to his sister in the lands from which they came. And so it was that Mama Chiva laid my monthly rags to dry in the strong sun on my cottage thatch with great anxiety. I had been chosen by Quashey over two maidens because through Moya it had been proven I could conceive. You might say my child would be the distraction to please Jack Vaughton in the program of increase, Mama Chiva being past her age for bearing. I ensured Jiba's secret a little longer."

Coote's nose wrinkles as he murmurs, "A most repugnant business . . . 'Twas a human barnyard . . .'"

The light eyes of the prisoner close for a moment. "Ah, so I thought myself at first. But my Quashey lay on me as light as water, moving like a cool clean stream over my limbs. For a long time I made out to myself it was his offerings of food I missed when he did not visit. On Mama Chiva's visits, he went in to her and I could hear their voices sometimes long into the night. On the nights which belonged to Jiba, he and his black wives ate together, then I saw each woman creep to her own little hut, while he slept alone upon that earthen shelf. Yet sometimes it was as if there were other people, unseen, in there with him; for in the deepest dark I'd hear him moan, imploring, calling out in muddy tongues. When he did so I lay awake in fear and curiosity, but with a blossoming concern that let me know the untoward was coming swiftly: I was filling with a longing for a man I did not know, whose words I could not understand, who treated me with nothing more or less than remote mildness."

Coote's lips purse downward disapprovingly: at the same time he becomes aware of a clean heat from Lucy's gingham-aproned thighs behind him. Her broom sweeps through the air, the delicate air currents lift his itchy powdered hair.

"Then I fell with child. They were delighted! Mama Chiva whispered to them that my flows had stopped, she who counted my intervals upon a stick; and they smiled and garbled to each other. My husband presented me with another orange cloth and went to tell Jack Vaughton. But Quashey left off coming in to me at night, preferring his clay bench although he treated me with courtesy. Mama Chiva was sent to me with fresh fish and wild grapes and such, to help the baby grow. Only I was not allowed to eat salt, for Chiva interpreted that among my husband's people, salt was thought to make a growing child tend to fevers once it was born.

"I missed his company, I did. But there was the fieldwork which could not be evaded. I returned to our small compound more exhausted every night. As my breasts swelled and belly bloated, Mama Chiva came to squat with me beside the fire. It was from her I finally heard that I was not merely a broodmare but a wife. She told me other things I did not have the . . . sense . . . to comprehend in all their depth, though I was twenty-four or twenty-five years old by this time.

"It seemed my Quashey was a Muslim. His very name, twisted unrecognizable by the British tongue, meant "strong one," after their ninety-nine-named God. A prophet whose visions had ridden across centuries of sand had spoken to Quashey's father's tribe. To Quashey, this name both called forth his destiny, and bestowed upon him the extra powers of force needed to carry it out. Mama Chiva said it was that clarity of destiny contained within his name, which let our husband nod so patiently to those who ordered him about. Which let him smile with quiet helpfulness as he lifted their burdens, and led him to discover means of perfecting his work. The overseers of the Glebe and the second upriver plantation took his behavior to mean obedience to them, rather than to his own destiny, and God's unfolding plan."

Coote's head is throbbing now with Lucy's heat, the prisoner's stink, and his own unvented excitement. "State what you call 'God's plan' for this rebel," he commands curtly. Cot Quashey lifts up her wet-sparrow head with a wan smile, and leans toward him. Such a soft smile. Such gleaming eyes in her filthy fevered skull.

"His God allowed him to be named Quaco, which the masters, with their uneducated ears, changed to Quashey; because his destiny was to fight Jihad, the Holy War, against the bonds which keep us from The Unity."

An abrupt silence hits the room like the aftermath of an explosion. The broom lowers to the floor, motionless. This is a stillness of alarm, disruption, danger. Coote hears his own wheezing breath from the cavern of his brain. He sets the quill down with a flat slap which splatters ink like a trail across some sheets of writing, and speckles his lace jabot. The chair scrapes as he tilts to his feet. "By God! Now we shall have it from you! After my meal and my nap, you shall lay the rest before me, every last bit of it!" he warns the Irish prisoner.

Peter sleeps fitfully after another heavy lunch. A fly has followed him into the stuffy, closed-shuttered bedroom. Its hungry purr bats against the netting by his head. He wakes several times, swatting and thrashing.

He leaves his nightshirt on after his ablutions, there being none but slaves and the condemned to assess his appearance; and orders the old woman Little-Something, when she brings the prisoner to the interrogation chair, to wash his fast-deteriorating lace-cuffed shirt. Tucking the nightshirt's tails into his breeches and donning his waistcoat, he adjusts the writing implements with a niggle of guilt. He is after all a doctor: the Daley woman is rotting away before his very nose. Yet sweaty and irritated, he hasn't bothered to treat her festering stripes for a day and a half. From the Governor's talk he has discerned that there's no life ahead of her beyond this testimony. The niggle seems to say it's needlessly cruel, through sudden inattentiveness, to let her know that too. A slyer side of him whispers, and maybe foreknowledge of her death sentence would shut her up. He needs her testimony. I really should make time to tend to the infection, he tells himself. It must itch and burn like holy hell! The pale-and-scarlet mottle of her cheek tells him that her fever's rising swiftly.

This tangled guilt makes him frown at her. "The Holy War?" he prompts, clearing the phlegm from his throat.

Almost woozily Cot Quashey mutters, "Sure, what can make war holy? What is it that drives a man, a woman, to go to war with bare hands against cannonballs and muskets? But first . . . many things came to pass. I lost my first son. In the last month I welled up with fluids. Though they took me from the fields when I fainted and put the leeches on me, I swole more and more; until one day I fell to the ground in a fit which brought on my travail. It was a long, hard couching. A dead infant cannot help you. And twice during my pains the seizures came again, which made things worse. Mama Chiva squeezed him out of me still in his sac, and Jiba passed him out the door to his father, who buried him in the woods immediately, beneath tree roots. I do not know the place: we weren't to speak of it.

"Jack Vaughton was informed. Through Quashey he sent me oranges and wild figs, a bit of rum, some eggs. Mama Chiva said he seemed exasperated, yet he told Quashey to buck up, for a year from thence we'd surely see another pickaninny from myself and one from Jiba too. Of course Vaughton did not know that they were kin: he told Mama Chiva he looked for a special line from Quashey and Jiba, herself stout and strong as a young man, and far from frail of sentiment.

"I did not recover for the field quickly, but the fits ceased when the babe was out of me. At first they sent me 'lolly to stew up for the pot gang at my fireside, but the heat caused me to faint. So then they brought me sewing, and I learned I could recall my father's way

of mending simple harnesses. With Quashey's influence I did not
return to the field until the full time for purification was completed
after that useless childbirth. One evening they came again, Quashey
and the other two women, and mumbled and sang. Then I was
bathed by Mama Chiva, a new mat was placed, a fish and wild plan-
tains boiled on the hob, and he visited me again when the moon
rose. My Quashey."

The very scratch of his quill across the parchment works on
Coote's nerves. It is the same sound as a faint branch scraping distant shutters in a restless wind. The sweetness of the camphor the
slaves have burned during his rest is cloying, too. "*Your* Quashey,
then," he says sarcastically.

"One night after I'd returned to fieldwork, a night on which he did
not visit me, I heard my husband exit the large hut where he slept
on the evenings meant for Jiba. There was a log outside, and he sat
there and began to weep with long, youthful sobs. First Mama
Chiva, then his sister, came out to him. There was murmuring, then
a quiet and weird chanted song. They stilled, went off to sleep, I
did the same. But the next night he was due to come to me and he
did not, nor the next.

"I would see him in the yard; sometimes he laid scavenged carcasses beside my door and went away. And at this time they had
made no steps toward The Unity with me: I was the outsider, those
three of one mind. I never heard them fight, although their language had explosive sounds and passionate wavings of the hand.
But they were quick to laugh—a rare enough thing among we
slaves. When I asked Mama Chiva, in shame and anger, why he no
longer came to me, she muttered that I needed my strength. But
later, when I asked her why he'd sobbed and sobbed like a grieving
Irishman that night, she told me of his heart-fast wife, the one the
slavers had stolen away in Africa, along with their four wee'ns. It

seemed Quashey had borne this quietly during his years at the Glebe, by dragging his mind away from every memory of them. But our dead baby they had handed him and who he'd buried . . . it wore the look of one of its lost, far-off brothers, and then the grief roared over him. It became all he could do to rise at dawn with the bland face the overseers and gentry had grown used to. Faith in the Jihad: that was what returned him to mildness and balance as he steered the small sloop up the river, or shoed an ox, or listened to his orders with a cheerful mein. For the Jihad was not ready by a long ways, since it was not only to be the private kind.

"I asked Chiva if he had, from grief, gone off women. Was that why he never came to me? 'No,' she replied, pulling the dirty red veil close to her cheek in the grizzled shadow, 'but you look like *them,* you smell like *them.* He was . . . terrified . . . to see a dead thing which should have been his own, his son, emerge from . . . one of *them.* Don't worry, Daughter, it will pass . . . he is learning that no matter how much like the ghost masters you look, your lot in life is his, is mine . . .'"

"When Vaughton began to question trading Jiba for a woman from upriver who had bred, seeing that no issue had come from her in the three years of their residence at Glebe, Quashey returned to me again. Oh I was angry! I was shamed and hurt. I wanted to be beautiful, or gay, or whatever was the quality of that African wife who'd held his heart. For I hated that these black folk spoke and laughed with heart when they were together; but all three became solemn and dull around me. And I so lonely. So hungry for his smooth and silent back, and the times when his hands clutched like blind things at my shoulders, our breaths rasping in the darkness. The fluid human warmth of him as he melted into sweat. One night I sent my tongue tip out like a spy, I found his sweat although I could not see it in that windowless hovel; I drank it, and it tasted like my own tears. 'Twas after that the fondness for him began to grow in me so fast."

"Please . . ." mumbles Peter Coote, faintly.

Cot Quashey's voice gathers into clarity.

"All during this time . . . well over a year from when I was given to Quashey, I spent very little time with the other wives, Sargeant Jiba and Mama Chiva, except as our paths crossed upon the day of rest, or our few festivals, or the odd evening when Chiva was sent to pull me to their cook fire for a bite of fresh fish netted from the sloop. On days of rest we all fell into the tasks we did the best. Mine was the weaving of new mats, the mending of the old, and I also found that I could cope well enough with the weaving of cane trash into our thatch roofs. I did this several times, Quashey hoisting me upon his shoulders to the housetop, where I crawled onto the bracing poles, testing for rotten straw. I wove new bundles of ratoon to replace it. No matter how tightly I would tie it, though, the first fierce gale and rain would drip onto our clay floors again. Thatching was hard work, dirty too. Cuts from cane trash often fester, and once I was stung on the leg by a brown spider. My whole leg swelled and purpled for a fortnight. But Mama had the cure, she wrapped some leaves that smelled like mildewed cloves in mud, and packed them round my calf and also on my forehead. To balance out the poison was what she said. She was the real curer among us, and the midwife to any who asked for her. Some of the tribes—the Ibo in particular—were afraid of her, and would never suffer her touch no matter how bad off they were. They said she did Obeah, but I tell you she did not. Born in Brazil, she had been reared a Catholic by her Dutch master—the one who fathered thirteen children from her. Later, she told me how she'd come to add many things to flavor the same faith I once knew. Well, not to flavor it, but to give the saints weapons and shields they had not needed on their own tame ground. She knew the Virgin, Saint Anne, and Saint Martha, though she told me once that these had yet to become warriors on Barbados, to earn the name of Mothers.

"But her mumbling and motions, the wailing dedication of animals she slit open for feasts, these were things she took from Quashey's Muslim ways. For though by the time I met her Mama Chiva was a sagging mound of rags, root-dyed hair, and flashing scrimshaw teeth, she was still keen to know what people thought in different places, and she found something of use on every path."

"The one called Sargeant Jiba, did she receive that appellation for her part in her brother's tyranny?" asks Coote.

"No. She was called that for her part in fighting the raiders back in their own place, a place where women ought to fight as hard as men when they were needed. Like Mary Dove. When they brought Jiba here, someone translated her title into English. She was a woman like a thunderbolt. You should have seen her on a Sunday, jabbing her digging stick deep into the soil of the garden, making a contest of how far she could fling the unearthed stones. She also did most of the heavy tasks: she carried loads and water, for she loved the feel of her muscles straining to their utmost. She was also sent with messages, for she liked to run. Though she was in the first-gang crew opposite mine, I always heard that she was tireless in the field: as I have told you, due to this Jack Vaughton waited with great interest for her and Quashey to produce a child. Ha! He is waiting still.

"There came a time," Cot Quashey relates, "when I was in the family way again. This time Mama Chiva gave me stews of leaves, and they shortened field hours according to my thickening, sending me to draggle after the little ones of the pot gang as these roved the fields and yards each afternoon searching for the grass and worms and things they call the 'hog's meat.' As before, my husband left off his connubial duty when I was with child: but this time he himself called in almost every night, sometimes with Chiva, and he would bring me fowl and roots to grow the babe. Somehow, this time, I bore the bloom of health. There were no seizures. When my time came I felt the first cramp at sundown, and by sunrise held my darling lad, Bin Quashey—'son of Quashey,' though he was written in the book of increase as Ben—cradled under my chin. How small and perfect was wee Ben. Even slave children are born with silken flesh and petal mouths, and eyes remote and molten as an angel's from the stars."

"This would have been in the year 1669?"

"No, it was in the week of Christmas, '68. So that I strapped my swaddled son to my chest and set out for the fields in a new year, and felt myself entering a most wonderful period of health. Yes, from that moment of his birth began the happiest epoch of my life."

His tone as wan as his long face, Peter Coote asks, "Why, pray tell, does his Eminence the Governor need to know about your great happiness in order to understand this Jihad that you speak of?"

Outside in the garden a surly rain begins to spatter sun-packed clay. A sighing shakes the blossoms on the grapefruit trees. "Shameless," whispers the prisoner. "Happiness is shameless; and a Jihad is the only sort of war which bears no shame. Yes . . . yes. But you and the one you serve, you shall hear of my happiness because my fall from it, through common failings such as jealousy, brought about a shameful debacle. Ah, is this not the course of every history?"

"History?" snorts Coote. "What makes you think your ilk can speak for history, the history that changes nations, worlds?"

"No doubt, sir, you've forgotten that I went to school. 'Twas in the town of Galway, overrun by the steaming ponies and marching metal of the Sassenach . . . and some nuns took great pains that we should learn the history of how our nation used to be, and how it came to fall to Strongbow, and how it still remains, at heart. But that's another tale . . ."

A tale you will not live to tell, thinks Coote, poised with his pen and waiting.

Cot Quashey continues with the story of the circumstances of her years with the rebel leader Quashey. "Most of the language between us, beyond the simplest commands, took place with our hands and eyes. His eyes had nothing but benign tolerance to say to me before I bore my Ben. So what a joyful thing it was to see them fill with speech once our son was born, and he took the baby from my arms at the end of our labors every night. God! I see him, I see him! Jouncing the limpness of Ben's peaceful limbs on his own purple-tattooed arms until the baby coos and drools. He brought me victuals he had caught or filched each evening, till my milk became as rich as a fine lady's nursemaid's. Our child grew in strength and wit, with eyes that gleamed in curiosity, and great fat thighs which kicked and pedaled at the air. I made the two orange cloths my husband had given me into a little robe for Ben. As his father carried him in state to his first plantation feast, I heard Quashey humming in his serious two-note way. And it was I who walked at his side—though to the public mind I was only his third wife. His soft slanty eyes that night shimmered at me with a prideful smile as I danced in the circle, and I gave over the rum ladle early. Quashey and his look, Ben and his sweet suckle, the new kindness of Mama Chiva and Sargeant Jiba—in spite of unremitting toil and little else, these melted my troubles for a time.

"Ah, the tenderness with which he came to look on me as I sat nussing Ben by the cook fire in my hut. Sometimes he called us in to him in the big cabin where he had his sleeping bench, and we lay by his side, the child squawking softly as he wagged his father's finger in his lovely little fist. Quashey would speak to him in a low rumbling croon, then grasp him tightly and squash him to his breast, rubbing their cheeks together. How startled Ben looked during his father's fits of passion for him: his little eyes would roll to me, brow furrowed, seeking reassurance. His sire and myself, how we would laugh! Then sometimes Quashey'd stretch his arm and pull me into their embrace, and rub his cheek against my own as well, in the light of the cook fire. He had a tight thick beard. It felt like sun-dried moss. The first word my Ben crowed in triumph was

''Bu,' which means Abu, or father in the common tongue of those Africans. Though when he was a baby, he called us both that. 'Bububu!' he crowed!

"But although Quashey came to me each third night, I was giving suck and so did not conceive. By this time my son had been crawling for a time, and had begun to pull himself up to my neck, standing and bouncing in my lap. And while Quashey's eyes showed pleasure with me and he taught me words of the Muslim tongue as he conversed with little Ben, when he lay with me his concern was ever with the child, and he was quiet, quick, and more remote when he made his husband's duty upon me. Then one evening I came up from the fields to find smoke blowing from the empty hut, the fourth wife's hut, beside my own. It was Afebwa."

Of course, the Irishwoman tells Peter Coote, the bondspeople knew that Jack Vaughton and Robert Rigley had gone to Bridgeport with the cart for several days, to inspect a fresh load of Africans that had arrived. "There were many rumors as to where the new boat sailed from. Whydah? The marts of Egypt? When the cart returned, it seemed that there were specimens from all the lands of misery. But for the first time since their acquisition, Jiba and Quashey returned home for their evening meal to hear scolding shouted by a female mouth in their own mother tongue. A half-dozen Coromantee had been captured, and at the Glebe as well as island-wide, the Coromantee were the darling chattel of yourselves."

"Until the uprising of '75, you mean . . . ," Coote corrects angrily.

The program of increase at the Glebe had not impressed Lord Cleypole's London accountants, who'd sent back a plan to breed more hands, who in turn would ship more sugar to an earlier market every year, which would then command a higher price. Vaughton chose Afebwa right there at the docks for Quashey, Jiba having borne no fruit and himself eager to breed a strain of pure, strong, Coromantee Bajan-born field hands. "Mama Chiva stood in the yard supervising the pot-gang children when the cart came ricketing up the track: Afebwa was handed over to her. From Chiva I learned that in those days, when the overseers relied as happily on Quashey as if he were a willing convert to slavery, Vaughton still sought to please him whenever possible. Our husband, he told Chiva, would be well content with a girl who understood his native speech. Chiva herself knew the Muslim words which were the common lingo between many Africans; but Afebwa knew the language of his very village. And sure enough: as he and his sister, who was working in the fields at the upriver spread, loped up from the landing that night, the new wife crouched at the door of her hut, weeping. He walked over. All of us kept silence as he stared down at her bowed back. Then she muttered something, sobbing. He squatted, eyes growing round and large. She repeated. They began to discourse rapidly. And already that first evening she was brought into the larger cabin, where he and Jiba spoke to her most kindly and comforted her wails while we others cooked. He even took my son and put him on her knee, coaxing wee Ben until he smiled at her.

"Afebwa. As with myself, and Chiva first of all, my Quashey made a ceremony, chanting his prayers, which we all had to attend in peace and welcome with the growing boy kinsman and three new fieldhands who had come with Afebwa from the Coromantee lands. These were her own clansmen. I had to kneel there, head bowed, while they did their hocus-pocus and she became his bride. He painted the same sign above her small hut's door that crowned the entry to each cabin in his compound.

"Had Mama Chiva felt this way when I had come to share his nights? Had even Jiba felt this ire toward me, knowing she must share her brother's time and food with an alien bitch? I seethed. Ben drank my rancor through his milk, and cried, colicky, throughout the night. That first night. When my Quashey stayed with her. And afterward everything changed."

Coote croons, without raising his eyes, "I think not everything. The record shows that you bore him a daughter in '73."

"Oh, that is true, in '73 my Betty came, Lord love her. And before her I bore one more stillborn son, and there was one miscarriage . . ."

"Which this Phoebe, Afebwa, the one you're speaking of . . . I can't recall that she bore any young."

"No. That is correct. Afebwa knew a weed whose cousin grows in Africa, and brewed that every month between her courses. Though Quashey wanted to have sons with her, she said that she would mother them only in freedom, after the Jihad." But, insists the prisoner, her husband was delighted with his new wife. Though he remained fair, according to his Book, to his other two true wives, he went in to his new tribeswoman on both her own night and the night falsely reserved for Jiba, "which had been his night of rest." According to Cot Quashey, the new Coromantee men were put out on the ground nearby so that Quashey could train them, setting his mark of industriousness upon them. "As time went by they built their huts but remained frequent visitors to the compound where I abode, drinking grass tea out of calabashes as Afebwa served them. And often they all found things to laugh about together. Cudjoe was the name of the one Quashey liked best: they had a sort of fist-fight contest now and then.

"But Quashey was not cruel: although he liked to bring his young son Ben into this company, he did not deprive me. My son learned to walk at my own side before he was turned over to a granny in the daytime, then put into the pot gang when he was a graceful lad of four.

"And now that it is over, I think my Quashey was a good husband to us all."

Coote lifts his eyes. He studies her; the repulsion, marvel, and curiosity he feels is something akin to viewing a deformed newborn calf or lamb in the straw of the livestock sheds when he was young himself.

"While Mama Chiva was too old by this time to bear children,"

Cot Quashey muses aloud, "she was the one among us perhaps most loved by Quashey as his consort. I say that because until the end he took solemn council with her, and they made their wailing prayers together now and then. But most of all I think this because in her presence he was his most . . . chiefly . . . self. I think he loved her for calling out that part of him which he was born to, but which Barbados gave no notice to.

"The parts of himself he brought to us others, even Afebwa, were younger, more excitable, less full. He was watchful for his sister Jiba, chiding her gently for her words and ways in situations when he might ignore the rest of us. Many's the time I knew him to wag his finger, reminding her of what line she had sprung from, and her duties as a woman. Or so Chiva translated. It was himself who took the offers of the Coromantee slave she wed, and he who convinced Vaughton not to sell her off the Glebe but to try her powers of fertility with this new man for one season. With hands, and face, and Mama Chiva's skills at translating, he confided to Vaughton that while Jiba was a willing wife, he himself could not desire her as he could we others. We laughed about that later on, for Quashey avoided telling lies by coming around the overseer this way.

"As for myself, the Quashey who held my dear Ben in his arms, taught him Coromantee words, and placed his own knit woolen cap upon that wobbling, drooling head to keep it warm—he was the tenderest, wisest father. If he looked upon me with eyes which were reserved, they also said I was of worth. I was the precious wife who again bore him the hope of children in this place across hell's waters. Before me, he had been a walking, working ghost; an ox, not a bull; a thing for the master. Now, through me, his son's arms opened wide in greeting every night, and he heard the glad cry 'Father'!

"But alas, it was Afebwa whose waist drew the brief touch of those calloused hands I so desired, a smothered smile across the pit as he sat feasting with the men. And she drew laughter—even giggles—during his double visits to her. I heard them, and I hated her. But she did nothing to harm me, if I tell the truth. She was silent and indifferent to me, and did not try to woo my Ben away as Jiba did, insisting that this was his auntie's right. It was myself who could not accept her. I began to spit where Afebwa had passed. When my husband ate with me I'd 'tchh' my lips, and with resentful hands and eyes insinuate that only Afebwa's food could please him.

"At first he tried to laugh all this away, puzzled and bemused. He gave me dogs' claws for a necklace, and a length of yellow calico from his stored goods. Solemnly he came to visit me and through Chiva told me that all his wives had his regard, but that I was special, for as he said, 'Heaven lies under a mother's feet.' When these things did not placate me, he sent Mama Chiva to tell me in her broken speech about my duties as a wife, and my need to learn gentleness and patience with the married lot. The shouting that I gave her sent her rushing out, and made Ben cry; this anger I felt made me falsely strong, and it was not much time until the thing which Dinah saw had come again, clinging to my moments like an unseen vine. Waiting for its chance to prick.

"Afebwa got the bloody flux. Certain herbs soaked in the urine of a little boy are good for that. I took the leaves which Mama Chiva brought me, but instead of collecting Ben's pure water, I processed them in the urine of a sow. Still, Afebwa recovered, wormy and thin enough to merit discharge from her gang and join the stock tenders until harvest time. Ah, I wasn't right in the head those days, those nights. Even, at times, I spoke to my dear son with venom, although I never struck him. Then Quashey held a meeting of us all."

"These were the meetings which led to treason?" murmurs Coote, dipping his pen afresh.

"You would say so, sir. Though at that time Quashey's intent was that they, the Africans, should study their faith, remembering it completely, to pass on to their young . . ."

"What year would that have been?"

"Why, my son Bin Quashey was scarcely four . . . it would have been before sugaring in '73. Ah, what a lovely lad was he . . . famous among the bondspeople for his thick brown curls and snapping eyes, his love of the dance when I piped him a tune outside our little cabin . . ."

"The meetings! The meetings!"

"Well yes . . . my husband began to call meetings in the evenings. The people brought their loblolly and dried herring rations to share when they met. It was all the Coromantee men on Glebe—six of them plus Quashey—and sometimes the two they'd sent to the new holdings up the river where he sailed the sloop each day would clamber along the riverbanks and enter the light of the fire late, like shades. Afterward—by the second year—more began to join in. These were Coromantee from the neighboring plantations. Also there were women: Chiva, Jiba, and Afebwa, but also there were other 'Mantee women at the Glebe from the shipment that the thorn in my bed, Afebwa, came from."

"And what transpired?"

"At first the Coromantee came together to eat. From time to time there were the wailing sessions 'mongst the men, which meant that they were praying, stretching and bowing as they did. The women sat together on one side of the fire, mumbling and sometimes breaking into high-pitched songs or laughter. I was the only one there with a child: how proud I used to be when Ben bent his little legs and whirled and bounced to the women's choir. But otherwise, they left me sitting on my own. I never learned their language: in fact 'twas Mama Chiva who explained to me they took pains not to share it. For already they had seen that they could mind their tone and speak about anything in front of the masters and overseers with no fear of being understood. You might say, then, that their way of speech—being set up nothing like yours nor mine—worked like a code. And they were loath that anyone outside their clan should know much of what they were thinking, or how they saw the world. But when the 'Mantee wanted to come across to other Africans they had the Arab speech of their Prophet among most of them, as we have Latin. As for me . . . I was suffered in their presence as Quashey's woman and as Ben's mother. They ignored me, just as you do not see your maids or menservants from day to day, sir, although they stand beside you."

Except for Lucy that is true, he thinks. I cannot hold their names.

"Mama Chiva it was who told me that they came for company, and to pray, and because in their own place men of like generation formed a society which was as tight in duty and loving bonds as are blood-kin ties. And truly Quashey liked to have his son on the men's side of the fire during these meetings, moving from knee to knee, playing with this 'uncle' and that. But I misliked it. I saw my little lad barely at all, working as I did from dark to dark down in the fields. I was often too far from him, or too knackered, to visit him at midday break. I misliked hearing his baby voice whisper their thick words through the darkness, myself once again excluded. However, these meetings did not happen every night. My Ben and I looked to the nights when we had his father to ourselves, though often enough I could not control my resentments and drove Quashey away without one caress between us. More than once when he left he carried Ben in his purple tattooed arms till I calmed down.

"You would not call him comely, Quashey, but once I came to know him I came to look for nighttime in his eye, the fullness of his mouth and how he pursed it when he was thinking hard and humming. His hands were small, his fingers short, the insides like old ivory in color and tough as brogues, but very warm and very capable. When he spoke, he sculptured what he told of from the air with those strong hands. And when he laughed he tipped his chin back to the sun and rumbled mirth from the belly upward. His arms, as I have told you, were tattooed in patterns of raised purplish welts that formed bands like bracelets of ivy over his muscles. But his shoulders and his back were smooth and supple, his wide chest bare of any hair . . ."

Peter Coote glares at her. "We need not hear the anatomy of your Negra, biddy," he grates. "Move quickly please, to the center of rebellion."

"Ah, how quickly, how quickly we moved toward rebellion," echoes the Irishwoman. He marks the sweat upon her brow, the palsy in her hands which twist her shawl. The reek of her! Truly: he cannot bear much more of this!

"You must remember, sir, that I made you a bargain. I said that I'd reveal what you were seeking, but that in the end you must meet my needs. These matters, as I know them, do not fall together as you might prefer. Perhaps the rising was not a plot of savage Africans and Christian traitors, foiled by finer British minds and weapons, as you now see it. Perhaps it was the lifted weapon of a Holy War, raised by a god who teaches freedom as a duty. But it was foiled from the inside by small infections such as grief and jealousy and vengefulness.

"At any rate, after I nussed my son several of my teeth went bad. In fear of the blacksmith and his forceps I waited much too long to have them pulled, and by the time my husband forced me down into the smithy yard one Sunday, my whole jaw was infected. In spite of all the rum they gave me, Jiba later scoffed that my shrieked curses could be heard to the top of Slave Hill. The able smith held me between his knees, my husband grasped my hands, and the five rotten stumps were yanked out of my head.

"But there were abscesses, you see. The pus spread in a red line down my neck and up into my ear. For many days I wandered in fever, and when I woke there on my cabin pallet the pain had me demented. I was laid up for three weeks, from which I lost all hearing in my right ear here"—she tugs it with a slow and bony finger— "and the poison spread to two other teeth, which then had to be pulled. Jack Vaughton said, as he watched the rum administered again, 'What does she need them teeth for with soft rations? It is best to take them all and get it over with.' But my husband, walking him outside the hut, interceded, and I got to keep these I have left.

"The thing was that during my illness, Afebwa watched my son by night. Yes, they moved his pallet in there next to hers while I was wandering with fever and with pain, and in those few short weeks she enticed him, as she had his father, to run in through her door with merriment and boyish secrets, looking for her every day. How I would scream for him, once I heard his babble coming from her shanty. So that he came back to our yard—my yard, for truly the whole compound was his—with downcast eyes and sullen mein. Still, he was such a soft lad, easy to get around you might say: I would tootle him a tune or tell him a mighty tale, or give him aught important-seeming to do, and soon he would be making faces of delight and laughing up at me. My Ben . . .

"I went back to the fields, then to the sugar house when the season came upon us, and that year the yield was wonderfully high. You should have seen the overseers standing there on the rise by the master's house, watching the carts tote off strapped barrels of muscavado, casks of rum, the precious load of clay pots my husband had curved and stoppered in the yard, full of fine bleached sugar for sale to noble households across the sea. We heard the healthy creak of harness, clop of hooves, groan of shifting wagon beds, rattle of strapped cargo, as they rounded the road's bend and headed down into the St. George Valley, which wound across the island to Bridgetown and the waiting ships. How gay was that day, the colors round us clear, a fresh breeze to the morning in spite of the storm season almost upon us. All the bondsfolk were given the rest of the day off, except for primary workers like the livestock rangers. The fields were bare, but for the scruffiest of cane trash to be picked up another day. It was a Friday. On the Sunday there was to be a feast. We needed that feast, I tell you now.

"The season had gone on almost a full extra month. That is; seven days a week, sometimes eighteen hours a day, we worked at loading, grinding, boiling; stirring, straining, drying; packing and brewing; whilst cutting, baling, loading, and carrying in more cane. Too tired: many got too tired, too hot, too hungry. There were deaths. One man crushed to death down at the mill; six failed hearts; a pregnant woman felled by steam in the rum vat, she and the child suffocated by the fumes. And there were horrid burns that led to death and two amputations, and withered limbs. Oh God: we were done in! So on that Friday, when we had slept, the Coromantees came to share their rations. And one had trapped a sort of rodent, with meat like a rabbit, but very large, very fine. We roasted that, letting the fat drop down into the kettle of loblolly, and we sprawled around the yard dipping our fingers into our calabashes and sucking them clean. Ben raced around the circle, standing with his belly out, his knobby little arms behind his back, waiting until each adult held out his calabash to share. Then Quashey suggested that the next day, Saturday, we walk downriver to a place he'd seen from the sloop, and have a picknick. Like yourselves might have, sir, on a fine day in the early summertime.

"Early the next morning he got permission from the overseers to walk along the riverbank with his wives, that they might bathe in privacy and wash the clothes. The other Coromantee were to join us if they wished to take the risk: as you know, any unauthorized movement into the forest could be taken as an attempt to escape, punishable by flogging. But it was not possible for Quashey to *ask* that any but his women be authorized to go together downriver. You know well that the overseers suspected the conjoining of many slaves, and for what purpose. D'ye see? Alerted, they might also become vigilant about our gatherings several nights a week. Best not to draw their interest, Quashey and the others all decided.

"So we of Quashey's household arose and walked along, single file, through the thick soft leaves and red-belled bushes which lined the riverbank. How the water winked at us that day, as it swirled and plashed on its unquestioned way. Quashey went first, our Ben upon his shoulders like the Christ Child on Saint Christopher's. He was pointing and calling out questions in his father's tongue which I heard Quashey answer in his patient way. Jiba was next, singing to herself and carrying a small fishnet from Quashey's sloop over her smooth shoulders. Then I came, for I had squeezed closer to himself than Afebwa. I was carrying one of Quashey's broken sugar pots containing coals from my house fire. We were going to catch our meal from the river. Afebwa, behind me, had picked up Jiba's melody and they were singing in a sort of round or counterpart as we waded through the bush. The birds had quieted to listen. At the end of our small band came Mama Chiva, peering on each side for herbs and simples. It was a Saturday at the waxing of the moon. Saturday is a good day to gather plants, while those taken on Sunday have no cure in them at all.

"What I remember best about that walk was the generous sigh of breeze: how it tossed the boughs above us so that the cool shawl of shade would part to let a spot of sun warm my back and chest, then close again to pleasant coolness.

"Quashey led us down a brackened bank to a site that first looked like a rubbled strand. Fronting the water was a sweep of fine blond sand. But on each side lay tall mounds which, I saw later, were thousands of thousands of thousands of shells, bleached by the sun. There were pinky clamshells and purple-black mussels, and oysters' fans as wide as Quashey's hand. But the shells were mostly in shards, except a few we dug out from the cool inside of the pile to examine late that afternoon.

"It was the simplest of days. Jiba strode into the brown current up to her thighs, swooping the net around her, while Mama Chiva searched the forest's edge for a digging stick. I went with her, collecting twigs and dead branches, and back on the beach I dug a pit and placed the coals for my small fire. There were Afebwa and little

Ben, holding hands and splashing in stumbling circles at the water's edge. 'It's cold! It's cold, Mammy,' he called out to me. 'Then come and help me build the fire,' I invited him. But he would not leave Afebwa and the teasing river, not even when he tripped on a stone and plunged in. Laughing, his father hauled him out and carried him under one arm, like a loaf. He took our darling son around the next bend where they bathed and frolicked and called out to each other in African, their clothes drying on the rocks.

"Jiba had netted three fat fish and Chiva dug up a pile of shells and crabs. Afebwa was squatting in the loincloth we wore beneath our clothing in our monthlies, at the water's edge, slapping her petticoat on a slick green stone, then kneading the fabric between her two fists. Slowly, I looked at her. How her back bunched and rolled over her skinny wing bones as she worked. She'd had a yellowy cast to her skin ever since the bloody flux, and there were scars on her buttocks. I thought of her face—it was dimpled, but still spotted each month with the blemishes of childhood. There came a wince of pity in my heart . . . a pity for her youth, my narrow jealousy, our human lot. And right after that surge of pity followed peace. For that day at least, my hate for her was gone.

"You would have to know the rareness of the day! My man and child calling out to each other in glee, we women working slowly on the beach. Afebwa took Mama Chiva's overskirt, her red veil and vest, and began to scrub these too, as Mama, droopy and naked, slid an obsidian knife between the clenched lips of the shells and Jiba and I gutted fish. The sun drew the river up into a shimmering ray. All human discord was stilled; beyond the human, birds zipped by scolding, bees buzzed, and there was a lovely light tinkle, as of wind chimes made of glass or shell.

"When the sun was rolling down from the heights of heaven, my son began to shriek. I halted my work. We were roasting the fish and mollusks by then. I prickled with fear: but this was a scream of mock terror, he was playing at something. They came back through the bushes, my man, our child, in their sun-stiff clothes, and told a wild story in Arabic. 'Bin Quashey has seen a crocodile,' Mama Chiva explained, 'but he and his father have scared it away!'

"We reclined there on that beach, nibbling soft sweet flesh from leaf platters. And as my son curled against my side sucking on poached winkles, that tinkling sound came again, sudden and louder. Mama Chiva's face went alert and quiet, and Quashey looked over his shoulders quizzically. But I felt great peace, for I knew what that music was. We were sitting in a midden of the old ones, where since ancient times they had come to catch and cook their prey. It was in quality somewhat like that midden on the banks of the Shannon, where my parents took me each ripe-apple autumn when I was a tiny child. The air was thick with spirits that once had been human, and with their happy industry. So through Mama Chiva I said to Quashey and them all, 'Ye need not be afeared, we have such places in the land I come from. The old ones can bless us, even though we are not of their blood. At least while the sun is shining down. I know this in my bones.'

"I cannot say why, but from that afternoon my husband's eyes began to shine upon me, looking far beneath my red, parched skin to something else. Looking into my eyes as I in his; both of us seeking to find a clearing ampler than we found up on Slave Hill, or in the cane fields, or when we looked upon our own lives back in time.

"In the weeks to come, Quashey questioned me through Mama Chiva. How that delighted me! I told him of my ancestors; of how they never left the land they loved, but hovered above the ground in stones and underground in tunneled halls, the even-older ones living inside the mountains except at special times.

"His words in turn rumbled to Chiva, who explained that Coromantee ancestors also walked with them, and were a part of their community, and hovered bodiless above their lands. Oh yes! I cried. And told them about Samhain, when the dead, the living, and those from different planes all shared the earth. But, Chiva conveyed, the

Coromantee were worried that being stolen so far away from their own lands and streams, their special stars, trees that were whole kingdoms on their own, their ancestors could no longer find them till they were dead and buried and journeyed home again. Yes, they were terribly afraid that their ancestors could no longer guide them in this new condition, this new place.

"'Ah husband,' I told him, 'I cannot see my mother's face; only her rough hands reaching, reaching toward me. It is the same with my saints, they whose wells we used to dance about; who blessed our hearths each morning. I remember, I said, many holy charms and tales: but the heart has gone away from them. My saints can no longer find me.' Quashey nodded then, and straightened. His ancestors might not sniff them out, he said; but his God could find them anywhere if they would call on him in the right way.

"Through Chiva I told him how I, all alone in my practice, had lost the way to my God's side. My childhood prayers, said all alone, were useless as milk teeth at a bone. Those old words seemed drowned out by the ringing heat of this inverted Eden, this . . . Barbados. Only that day, in the midden of the old ones who had fled away before the slavers' ships; there I felt the holy confidence I'd known as a small child. I struggled for the words: it is, I said, as if these days of hell are only a small corner part of some world that will ever be preserved, and we must put our confidence in that. 'Yes! Yes!' cried Quashey: 'this is why my own clan has to meet, remembering the good ways we were taught, trying to practice them together. Someday'—he spread his arms on high— 'there will come a different dawn.'

"But on the strand that afternoon, during our first talk about such things, the tinkling picked up again although there was no wind. Down on the shore, Afebwa strewed a pile of fish guts into the water and began to sway and dance to that faint music. I let her. To dance to fey music is the beginning of the end. Still, I let her. But when Ben made to join her, I grabbed him to my side and bade him rest and take a nap. His little head lay on my hip, my hand wandering his hot, dry curls as his eyes drooped, then slept.

"Before the sun went low we started back. We dawdled in the dappled wood. Ben once again rode on his father's shoulder down the path, I right behind. Quashey's body sent waves of feeling back to me. My breasts felt heavy, full of rich song, like the nests of river orioles in the jungle trees above. The air lay charged between us, though we spoke not.

"At the compound Afebwa and Jiba leaned against each other whispering. Mama Chiva stirred the fire in the large hut's pit and sent them off for water. Soon the bland smell of loblolly rolled on smoke across the yard. Things seemed as they had been. But Quashey came to my hut that night, his eyes searching, searching. He gave me words, translated, from the Coromantee tongue, words he was teaching Ben. Only a few, but I wore them like a necklace for the rest of his life, with the rare others that he gave me. We sat up late, a pool of patience dark and shimmering between us, until our son lay sprawled in sleep upon his mat, lips and legs apart—tall infant that he was. Then we went to my pallet, and looking each into the other's eyes as if we stared into a double well of clear, sweet, healthful water, we made my baby girl."

Coote shifts his back to right, to left, and cracks his tired neck. The tedium of it! "The meetings, biddy!"

"By the time my Betty came, in '73, more people were attending. I cannot tell you what they said, for, as I've told, I never learnt the language. And once himself took an interest in me I took the meets for an annoyance. No longer did I care to fit in with these folk, or be accepted. I wanted all the visitors to go away so I could have my husband to myself. I wanted to forget the fields, the hunger, wet, drought, what have you, with my head held to his, like a mango to the mouth of the hungry.

"Jiba left us in the time after the storms, and married the 'Mantee who had asked for her hand."

"The one called Cudjoe?"

"Yes."

"The same Cudjoe who was Quashey's first lieutenant during the uprising?"

"The same. And she proved fertile before planting time, which made the overseers pleased as they prepared their report of increase and accounts for England. So now I had only the wife Afebwa to divide me from my man. For Mama Chiva, while still he visited her and took her council every third night, had become a go-between for us. When my belly swelled, keeping him off me in consideration for the child, he brought her to my cabin at night that she might translate our words.

"How we delighted in all we found in common, we two people separated so by tongue, by race, by nation, creed, and history! Beneath the skin of differentness, we held so many of the same things to examine in the twin lights of belief and trust. There were the ancestors, who still dwelt among us and whose intercession we implored, although you think of these as ghosts. There was the high place of music, song, and dance among our peoples. I mean how both our peoples know that music calls—calls the spirit of things, the angels and the faeries, the sprites of earth and sky, and animals. We knew that there are spirits everywhere, in the land, the stones—truly, the air is full of them, and animals have magic too, though maybe crocodiles and snakes for Coromantee folk, whilst hares and cows and wise fish for myself.

"For each of us, coming to any crossroad is different than it would be for you; and the magic properties of certain trees, though you would not want these in your renowned gardens, are legendary. Each knew exactly what the other meant about the disorientation of this place: of how we must be buried East if we were to face the kingdoms of our ancestors. Yet if we were home we would be buried facing West. For Quashey and I both knew that West has a different character than East, no matter what East faces: something

beyond directions. Truly, the dead go home to the West. But oddly
the most . . . invigorating . . . discovery between us was the history
of war amongst our peoples: of how neither buckled or succumbed, but against polished sword and harquebus fought with
bare knuckles for our freedoms and our lands.

"Ours was a late and lovely courtship, coming when already we
shared two children between us. It was a courting of growing
friends, through eye and handclasp, shared smile, knowing sigh.
And rather than watch my man across the fire in heated speech I
could not understand with some Coromantee, I was fain to have
him woo me more. Fain to feel his chapped lips graze my forehead
as we tumbled into sleep, and his hand seek mine in dreams. No, I
can tell you nothing of those early meetings except the tone was
changing to an urgency, and shadowy faces I had never seen before
were stepping to the fire to clasp hands in odd patterns with
Quashey, their harsh whispers keeping us awake till all hours when
we needed our sleep for the fields."

Coote takes note that the child registered as Betty was born in
the last days of 1673. The mother had been given eight days in bed,
a jar of rum to bring on the milk, and several pieces of fruit. A
chicken had been given to the compound to provide eggs, but had
been stolen and cooked by another slave, later flogged for stealing a
hen from his overseers' fowl yard. Betty's father had been given two
pieces of silver, one for each child he had produced.

Then in early '74 the child Bin Quashey sickened. The sickness
began with a pain in both legs. He lost his breathing powers. The
prisoner becomes agitated as she describes this, saying, "Certain I
was that he had the *drohuil* laid upon him. And I was sure that
Afebwa, who'd no child of her own, who encouraged my Ben's visits every day, had coveted him so much that she had laid the evil eye
upon him.

"And still I am not sure that she was innocent, though I know
now she was unwitting of her harm. But Quashey would not hear

of it. I went out, I collected medicines, and Mama Chiva stayed up tireless nights making poultices of them. But Ben grew frailer, frailer, all in a matter of days, until he could not catch his breath unless propped up in somebody's lap. Quashey raised his beard to the moon and wailed his prayers, while I went collecting *lus-more* leaves in morning dew to brew into a tea. Finally, when all hope seemed gone Quashey agreed: he took Afebwa by the hair and pushed her into my small overheated hut. He made her spit. The Coromantee do not give their fluids away, so he was forced to slap her. But I had seen her dance to the music at the midden, and she longed so for my son's company . . . and sure, the only way to cure the evil eye is that they who cast it spit upon their victims to break the spell." Cot Quashey's breath is coming ragged now, though she is only whispering.

"But it was too late. He died. Bin Quashey died. How vividly I see my baby Betty, lying in the crook of my arm and peering startled round the shadows of the hut as we wailed for him. There came forty days of mourning. My son's thin body folded into the soft clay, facing East for Ireland's West and for his canoe journey from Guinea to that other paradise. Once I tried to beat Afebwa with a hoe handle as the two gangs trudged up Ibo hill after fieldwork. I was constrained; but no one punished me.

"At night I sat alone with my new daughter. Mama Chiva sat by me. He did not come to me during my mourning: it was his mourning too, he did not go to anyone. But when the forty days were done the precious thread he and I'd been weaving had turned gray, bedraggled, lifeless. It was cut. All had unraveled, and we could not go back."

VI

The final interrogation begins quite late the following morning. First came the great flurry and clatter of a coach and four on the cobblestones outside Speightstown Gaol. The interrogation room has been rearranged by the time the prisoner is brought in to be seated. Now the Apothecary's cherry escritoire, instead of sitting with its back to the window, faces the bright garden from across the room. There's a wide space between Coote's desk and the prisoner's chair, set under the wide-flung windows. Their shutters are tied back so the sea breeze might carry off the odor of her wounds. A red velvet chair of state has been unloaded from the roof of the coach and placed in the dim recesses behind Coote's station. There sits a man with pouting chest and belly above thin legs crossed at the white-stockinged ankles. He lolls in utter silence, a dull ray here and there penetrating the shadows to highlight the lustrous nap of velvet on his chair. The same rays shoot thin cylinders of radiance over his sky-blue satin suit and limn the left edge of his curly nut-brown wig. Over his face he holds a full-length mask of dark blue velvet, made for such occasions and padded with camphored herbs against the pestilence and reek of foul places.

Coote's voice, as he begins, is somewhat faltering. At the same time he is resolute and stern in his demeanor. "This is the joyful day when you will come to the point, biddy," he declares. "The

Coromantee uprising of 1675, the execution of the blackguards who fomented it, and how you came to join their cause. Posthumously. Which ended you here, your life in peril, for your disloyalty to your rightful government of fellow Christians." Rapidly he strokes these words for all posterity.

The Irishwoman clears her voice. Her voice slides and slips, as if upon her own sweat. "Sir, I'm so woozy," she croaks. This time Coote bids Lucy bring her tea with rum. She must not fail me now, he thinks, not with His Eminence seated behind me, and Arlington or someplace like it shining in my future. I won't have her fainting away. In the corner, the satin-suited man squints at the prisoner as she drinks the mug which Lucy proffers. He coughs and pulls a pomander from his reticule to hold before the nose holes of his mask.

"Although my life has had many endings and new starts, my tale yesterday brought me to the end of the scant joy I knew in it. My son, Bin Quashey, had his nose plugged up with the clay of his grave. And in the days that followed, though we continued to work from dark to dark, and the cane flowers continued to bloom, and my tiny daughter continued to suckle and coo and become both more lively and more bonny, death's pall lay upon everything. As if even inside the sun-fed grass there hid a core of ... As if ... lurid ... the days like moving through the worst seasickness, our squeamishness not of the belly but the heart.

"I blamed Afebwa, with her yearning toward my lad which drew the evil eye upon him. For it lives everywhere. The only haunt whose like can't be found the whole world over is the Ban Sí: otherwise ... the sprites and faeries shape change everywhere. But my husband Quashey blamed many other things. He blamed how far he was from his clan's lands—so far that his ancestors could not smell the blood of their own small kinsman, and guard him. Bit by bit he came to blame how far he himself had come from what he had learned were the right ways. He chastised himself for getting a little drunk on days of rest instead of praying, and for trying to find his greatest pleasure in his women and his son, instead of living for the *tawhid*—the Unity of all who knew his God. Bitter he was, indeed. One family lost in Africa. Now, another slipping away in Barbados.

"On the surface he and I held the same picture of death: children die because they're sweet and pure; very often people envy that; so God, who loves them best, brings them home to his happier gardens. We knew our young lad was in Heaven: what had he wrought on earth but sparks of glee and love in the hearts of all in misery around him? But in truth, rather than feeling happy that Ben was free of a life of toil and punishment ahead, I myself felt further from grace and kindness, love and holiness, than I had ever felt before. And Quashey, while he'd been schooled to accept all death as the will of God, and therefore destiny, with Ben's death began to doubt that his death was destiny. Like a fist uncurling after sleep he began to unfold into a driving purpose to *fight* for the freedom to know and live one's full god-given destiny.

"In the Jihad many die, but that is different. In the Holy War you stand forward and put yourself in God's hand as a weapon for the fight. That is better than a life wasted for want of food, and care, and healthy living, and respect. I once asked my husband if he was not afraid to fight against so well-equipped and organized a foe, but through Mama Chiva he answered with a smile that those who die in Jihad will go to Zhenna."

"And where is this Zhenna?"

"It is a sort of garden, the garden of perfection which humans were evicted from with Adam and Eve's mistake. The place, the way the Creator had it in mind for people to live till they grew greedy, and preferred to take, rather than to receive . . .

"Right from the funeral feast the Coromantee meetings in our compound took on a different fervor. All the bondspeople of the Glebe roared and feasted wee Ben on his way, whilst I drank myself into such a stupor that some Fon woman took my Betty off me and gave her suck. A few times I roused myself, croaking out lone

shrieks of the *olagon*. But then, as I lay sprawled there in the soil beside the grave, the wet nurse handed my loose-limbed sleeping baby
over to sober Afebwa, and I rose up off the ground in one motion.
I publicly accused her, and pulled my one remaining child into my
arms so roughly that I stumbled back against the crowd, the baby
waking, flailing, sobbing with such fear that Quashey himself
guided me all the way back to my hut.

"Mama Chiva stayed that night with me. When I awoke, crawling over my skirts for a ladle of water from the calabash, then out
the doorway to vomit it up, they were still there. The men; Coromantee and others too, sitting in a weary red-eyed circle under the
palm panoply while Mama Chiva stirred the morning 'lolly. There
were new faces among them. More came later.

"These men came from the big houses along the St. John's River,
all the way up to St. Andrew's and St. Lucy's Parish, and from a
house called Brighton in St. Michael's on the road to Bridgetown.
Not all at once. One would bring another, and another link was
added to the chain. Yet their faces, their lives, seemed somehow in-
terchangeable when I saw them in my time of mourning, dragging
along with Betty strapped to me. I moved past them from the field
on the way to my own hut, to nuss her and to sleep, then to the field
again. All was in mist. The men around the fire, the messengers
coming to find Quashey late at night to lead him to some midway
point out in the wood where men from upriver or down were waiting to add their force to his. At times he was with me when they
came to speak with him in gravelly mutters. Protected, I suppose
they felt; for I had never learned their African tongue. Once, I remember, we heard a soft scuffling down the path while my husband
lay upon me, both of us trying to take some silent comfort from
our simple animal closeness. But when the visitor called out their
common greeting, my Quashey halted, raised upon his quivering
arms, and controlling his breath called out low that same greeting.
Then, brushing his hand over my wet forehead and his mouth over

our daughter's sleeping cheek, he sprang to his legs, wrapped on his loincloth, and took his warmth from us again. So that, when Mama Chiva came to tell me of Jihad, the Holy War, I felt rancor, ill will, and contempt toward all of them who meant to steal my family"—here the prisoner begins to weep brief gritty tears—"the only family I would ever have, from me."

The observer in the satin suit shifts on his chaise, and says, "Ahem," theatrically.

In tones both anxious and exasperated, Coote exhorts her: "Pray do not wander with your fever so, Cot Daley. Finish now with what you know of the treachery of '75, then go and have a rest while we take our meal."

"There came a time when Mama Chiva came to me, as I have said. And she was sent by Quashey. At this time I lay upon my pallet once again, for I had conceived almost at once after the period of mourning but had lost the embryo, with much of my own blood, after scarce three months of pregnancy. Suckling is meant to keep a woman from catching while her strength is needed elsewhere; but suckling Betty was like feeding a feather, and . . . well, there I was. So while I lay upon my pallet, wordless, weak, and white, my husband in his compassion decided. He decided to see me not as one of *them*, that's to say one of *ye*, sir; but as one of *his own kind.* For my health was ruint in trying to bring forth and maintain his children, and he felt that through them I had become flesh of his flesh, blood of his blood. Because of his decision, which Jiba, Cudjoe, but not Afebwa stood against, Mama Chiva began to explain things to me. From her lips I first heard that those who joined with Quashey were building an *umma.*"

"A what!" demands Peter Coote.

"The *umma* is the brotherhood of those who band together under the eye of God—a brotherhood which also invites women warriors for Jihad. And this Jihad, the Holy War for God, begins with a lengthy period of self-purification. So that before a Holy War against the slavers, the Spirits of Night, could begin, each rebel had the task of warring with himself for self-control, bringing himself to the obedience of God, who would protect him unto triumph. My husband, Mama Chiva said, would call upon Betty and me, and would be asking for my help and patience as our cause developed. But he would remove himself from my bed—and the beds, Chiva hastened to assure me—of his other wives. As much as possible, he would try to consume even less of the special rations we were given, though because Betty depended upon my milk he would still bring me fish and little wild animals when he could net them. But he implored me to purify myself as well, letting go all of my jealousy of Afebwa, and to give over letting my loneliness and longing for him turn to spite. Oh! Here I cast my eyes down in mortification, shame, and the very raging spite he spoke about. For those three were my alchemy, in bondage. Quashey could see to the quick of me. He knew my battles without my being able to say them.

"In the days to come other faces arrived at the midnight fires," said the prisoner. "Africans who spoke with a Scots burr; two Irishmen who spoke Arabic words. I was at one hasty hushed gathering in the woods when the *umma* met an African Maroon who'd sailed all the way from Montserrat and told of won uprisings on that little island. The Maroon from Montserrat lived in a mountain fastness with his wives and children, and a dozen other men and women: this was their *umma*. And Chiva translated what he told the hesitant among us. Smiling kindly, nodding wisely, listening to objections first, he quoth from the holy Book they shared, urging, 'Fight in the cause of God those who fight you . . . let there be no hostility except to those who practice oppression.' We are both taught this—Muslims or Irish—that the cause of oppression is against the cause of God. For God's cause is the cause of equality, of the commonage, of work together. Whether we knew it in the lands we'd come from or not, in this new garden where we find ourselves now growing—tangled, twisted, but still growing—in this garden we must plant the equally created seeds of God."

Cot Quashey says, "Among us at that meeting there were also white-faced men who came to see about joining their cause to Quashey's. And some Africans demanded of the Maroon man from Montserrat whether these Christians should not be kept out from the Holy War, not being Muslims. But our visitor, looking at the paling sky, said as he rose to leave, 'Doesn't the Exalted One say . . . "ah, what will convey unto thee what the Ascent is! It is to free a slave!" My friends,' he told us, 'those words don't pick out this slave, that slave, just my family. No! They mean that all of slavery is a condition against holiness! And all of us who fight it—for another, for our families, within ourselves—whether we follow this way or that, we begin to rise to God.'

"We watched him lift his little anchor and slide the carved log boat into the glassy water. As he saluted us from its prow and rowed away, my wee dote Betty jogged upon my hip, and crowed and waved to him.

"We made it back to our loblolly, then to the fields with the other hands. The overseers, they knew nothing. And though that day seemed long for want of sleep, it flew fast on wings of inspiration. I never saw that man again, though Quashey and Cudjoe met up with him in the parish of St. Lucy just before the end.

"Shortly thereafter, Quashey sent Mama Chiva to me. They wanted me to come into the woods one Sunday morn, to meet with men from the European islands who did not speak the African. Mama Chiva came with me, my Betty tied around my back kicking me with her strengthening feet. But every step we took, my son Ben haunted me. I was not with the living, but with him that wondrous picknick Sunday when, single file, I followed him upon his father's rolling shoulders through the singing wood.

"Now, on this mockingly lovely day, Chiva led me to a path I had not walked before. It wound inland from the river and the coast. We came upon the men seated on the ground at the base of a natural circle of tall cottonwood trees."

"And what did you interpret to them, and from them?" comes the one rheumy question from the blue-masked man in the chair of state behind Coote.

"They were Englishmen, though indentured. I mistrusted them greatly, though they had brought weapons which they gave us as a gesture of goodwill. I told Chiva what they said, but it wasn't much. They mostly murmured into one anothers' ears."

"They *gifted* the Coromantee with weapons, you say? No payment was involved?"

"Sure, what payment had we to offer?" The prisoner smiles dully, rubbing sweat from her cheek with a fist. Mosquitoes and flies whine and hover over the sick banquet beneath her shawl. The Governor suddenly slumps in his chair, bends a bit forward, tugs a crystal vial from inside his waist, and pulls the cap off his smelling salts. He takes one vast gulping breath; and another.

"No, I suppose they wanted to wait and see: if the 'Mantee enjoyed success, and took these lands from the hands of Darkness, they would expect to join forces, or at least hope to call on support for their own plots and frays.

"That day turned a corner for me. I saw the seriousness of the thing. For although those British strangers who met us in the forest added no numbers to Quashey's soldiery, in one of the high trees I first saw the arsenal. Our men had built a tree house high up in the branches, and Cudjoe and another were busy sorting inventory out that day."

"What did you see?"

"There was the rake that had gone missing on Vaughton, and there the three cane knives that had been misplaced. I saw hoes whittled to sharp narrow points, and several poles of hardwood with spikes retrieved from the floor of the smithy, bent through them for gouges. There were also cudgels with spikes hammered in all around them, like pikes or maces they were. The British rebels, as I've told ye, had brought along pistols: two pistols, and a small deer horn stuffed with shot.

"How odd that morning was: my baby girl creeping over the soft dry forest bed, men coming to and fro, climbing up and down, Mama Chiva smoking her little white clay pipe and gazing into the future. And I, the fool, was only grateful that Afebwa was nowhere to be seen so I could feel my husband's tired strength, smell his worry, hear the hum that at times accompanied his thoughts, all by myself. At that time, the plan was for the overthrow to take place almost a year from thence. The children of the Prophet were not to start a war, you see, during three months of the year . . ."

"Which months? Name them!" interrupts Coote, eager to gain strategic knowledge. But she answers, "I do not know. For their months spin round, and are never the same from one year to the next. At any rate, who can say if we'd be seated in this arrangement today if they had kept to their plans." Coote's masked guest inhales with a hissing sound like a waking snake. "But four months later came the hurricane of '75, and overnight the Jihad was begun. For as you know, sirs, this cyclone came in February. You yourselves would call it a freak storm. It ripped the seedlings from their tender moorings, the roofs from the sugary; it gouged the windows and doors from the big house like the eyes from one's foe. Whole herds of cattle were dashed against buildings and trees and I saw, Lord save us, a four-year-old pickaninny shooting through the air like an arrow, his eyes wide in conscious terror! The slave cabins were demolished into piles of rubble. But though the whipped river dashed the sloop onto the muddy shore where it mired, the boat was saved. Quashey hurried ourselves, his small family—then the rest of the *umma* of the Glebe—into the fringe of the forest. Most of the slaves took refuge there, moaning and calling throughout the night. But it proved the safest place, for the young trees at the fringe were supple, not stiff: dense-seeded like grass blades, with little room to fall and without much weight to bring them crashing to the ground. Yes, we at the forest's edge were drenched, and scratched, a broken limb here and there, but again we survived to do the overseers' work once the watery sun had reappeared.

"When the wan-faced overseers came to gather us in midmorning, our small encampment had already cast their sticks and decided. The Coromantee saw the unseasonable cyclone as a miracle from God. A cover of pandemonium, in which hammers and axes and cane knives were gathered up and relayed to the forest, as if by swirling winds. That the sloop was saved, said Quashey, was as in the age of Noah. It was meant to take us to a new and righteous place. Mama Chiva related all this, stirring loblolly from the overseers' own stock of corn. But as soon as we had eaten, bedraggled and exhausted as we were, Vaughton was circling on his buttercolored horse, urging us to a million tasks.

"Afebwa was with the other first-gang group: they went into the fields, assessing all the damage, digging ditches, on their knees in cold mud, pressing drainage stones then frail seedling roots back into rows whene'er they could. But I and the other first-gang crew, plus the second-gang youth, were divided up in squads. Some lads crawled up upon the roofbeams of the big house, others nailed canvas tightly over windows to keep the cold and vermin out. Others headed off to pasture, crying, 'Suui, Bossy,' for the swine and kine and other stock that may have huddled in the bushes, escaping death. The smith was in his smithy, scratching his head and wondering at all the metal that had blown away. The group that I was in were piling stones left from the walls of the slave huts, and hacking sturdy branches for temporary beams to hold up palm-leaf roofs. Betty had caught cold.

"At this time I had been at the Glebe for almost eighteen years, and many had been there even longer. Yet all of us—new bondspeople or old—found ourselves starting over. Yes, once again we were put out upon the ground.

"What a melee," exclaims the prisoner, squinting down the hallway as if she sees it there. "People were running by with barrows, with loads upon their shoulders, with a cauldron of corn grits for the field-workers. They were boiling river water; hauling sacks of feed, racing against the coming of the dark. By afternoon the sun shone blankly once again. Yet the air had cooled. The wind was very brisk, and we were soaked and resoaked in the ooze. At eventide a barrel of dried mackerel was passed out by the drivers, plus a drop of rum. I had found an iron pot rolled into a ditch which looked enough like Quashey's to claim it. That was all of home we had, except the clothing on our backs, the rusted old tin whistle in my pocket, and Mama Chiva—well she had her well-kept secret.

"By nightfall, as we took our food upon the same spot where five cabins had stood yesterday, close by the grave where our Ben's bones lay sleeping in the mould, shelter was already growing up around us. I had stuck four sapling poles into the ground and laid palm fronds across them. We sat on palm fronds too to stay out of the mud, and wondered how we'd keep the baby warm all night. But our questions were soon answered:

"Jack Vaughton came riding up to us with a lantern. 'Finish your victuals, then we must continue building if it takes all night.' He meant to see the warehouse and the storehouses, but most especially the big house, roofed temporary-like that night. More than anything he wanted to report 'no damage' inside the polished mansion halls to Cleypole's man. My Betty coughed and coughed as he was speaking. He told us he had sent the cart to Bridgetown to get blankets for ourselves from our master's merchants there. Raising his voice, his arms in anti-Christly benediction over us, he cried, 'They'll be bringing food and clothing, pots and medicines, in two short days! Hold on, people! The Glebe will go on! Hold on! The Glebe will prosper once again!' He seemed to be confused: as if we, too, cared passionately that the rich furnishings, the tapestries and curtains and carved mahogany presses in the big house, should be perfectly preserved.

"As the overseers and drivers met, and milled, and planned, then came to round us up for all-night tasks, my Quashey slipped past on his way to another family of the *umma*. His leaf of fish unfinished in his hand, he talked in undertones to Chiva, then Afebwa. Then feeling Betty's forehead he spoke to me three of his rare English words. 'Tonight,' he said. 'We mus', tonight.'

"Vaughton was waiting for him. He unlocked the toolshed and parceled out spades, so that Quashey and some laborers might unground the sloop. First thing on the morrow Vaughton wanted the upriver holding inspected."

Cot Quashey's tale sets the scene. Bondspeople, exhausted, rushing pell-mell this way and that as the dusky chill goes black. Pounding and hammering to the light of pine-pitch torches. Wild calls from confused directions. Wilder silences. The baby Betty crying: kicking to get down, stumbling on her one-year legs. Crying to be picked up again. Crashes. A round song, sung in African, intersected by the close-by squeal of a stepped-on rat.

"I was sorting through the grain: barrowing out corn that the rain had soaked, before it mildewed and infected the whole storehouse. Up above me two Ibo were plaiting a thick roof of fronds. Mama Chiva came into the corn shed with my husband at her side. The sloop was in the river again, moored to a sturdy tree. She was carrying a trowel in one hand, a caved-in wooden box in the other. Quashey spoke to her, taking the box hastily, and she translated to me. At this time Betty was sleeping on some sacks. In a low voice after Quashey spoke, she said, 'Sister, he needs your help.' From Quashey's waistband he withdrew three sheets of creased vellum, a stolen quill, and a tiny vial of ink. He held these out to me and waited. Chiva said, 'The time has come to make our Holy War.' I swear, I thought my bowels would let loose right then from the fearfulness of it. How many Coromantee? How many masters, overseers, redshanked militiamen? I must have shook my head.

"'Listen to me, Cot Quashey,' Mama Chiva whispered while the palm trash and pollen fell upon our heads from the roofers hammering up above. 'This is his plan. I have dug up my pieces of eight from my time with the Dutchman. Quashey needs them now for pistols, all over the island. Contacts have been made: we know where to buy them in St. Lucy, and over in Bridgetown. The thing is, we must strike at once. We don't know how things stand at the other houses, but here we are tonight, half of our overseers off the place, the horses and the cart away in Bridgetown. Who's to send for help?'

"Our husband, she explained—it was a term I did not mind from her—his sister and her husband, the other wife, the entire *umma*, had cast their sticks: they had agreed. All the way from Bridgetown, up the east coast of the island to the northern tip, we would mutiny. The overseers would die. Militiamen would die. In the big town, in their beds with fine Irish linen sheets and lacey coverlets, merchants and senators would die.

"Meanwhile Quashey would make ready the plantation sloop to go to sea. I was terrified. Mary Dove! Arlington! Sold away, away, away! I looked at my one child and could not see how we could win this fight. Saw only many costs of losing it . . ."

"At least you'd sense in that," Coote states firmly, dipping his hasty quill and smearing damp script as he does so. A new dark streak on his cuff, he scatters sand over the paper like seed to birds, then rushes on.

"My husband pushed the writing implements toward me. His shapely eyes burned in the night. He asked myself, his wife, who could read and write the English tongue, to write three passes. One for Cudjoe to run through the forest with, so that he might buy the pistols to give to the warriors of St. Lucy before the new day dawned. They'd often snuck on Sundays or late at night into the woods near Glebe for meetings without incident: but Cudjoe would have to pass two large plantations, and strange barking dogs. In case he was halted, the pass would help ensure that he, and the waiting pistols, would arrive. 'Sign the passes with Jack Vaughton's name,' Mama Chiva instructed me.

"The other two passes were to send Afebwa and the English pistols to a man from Brighton House, who'd then run all the way to Bridgetown with those guns and Chiva's money for more artillery. The last was for a man from St. Lucy's to hightail it far inland, and to meet a third arms trader. Commandants were waiting to attack plantations, once their warriors were given weapons.

"I have stated I was horrified. My face felt numb. I sat upon a feed sack and picked up my child, but she was Ben, no she was Moya, no it was myself; it was 1651, it was 1681—the year I was to go free. But gaunt and starved and beaten, my term renewed, I would never now be free to go. I saw the Spirits of the Night batting me around like a wolf bats a rabbit; but no, that was my Betty they were batting, my Betty who I vaguely hoped to buy into freedom after myself. 'No,' I told my husband. 'Betty . . . Betty has a cold . . .' I undid my bodice and swirled her sweaty hair with my palm, pressing her to the safety of my pounding chest.

"He had no time for my carry-on with a rebellion to bring off that night. But for a moment he squatted before us on the loose grain of the shed which shone like gold in the lantern light. 'Mother of my children, I will bring the sloop before morning,' Mama Chiva recited. 'We are going to the Maroon man, to the isle of Montserrat. Sister Jiba and I met with him last fortnight, and he gave me a star map. By tomorrow the sea will calm. There are caves to hide in. Others of our *umma* must fight to take the capital. But we will go to a clean, kind, pious land where they will welcome us, the Maroons and a band of people like yourself, led by a man named Bat Fish . . .'

"Then I began to scream. Chiva had to slap me hard. Quashey lowered his eyes, pulled Betty's rags around her shoulders tightly, and said, 'Who knows if your fears are founded? For as the Prophet says, Heaven is found under a mother's feet,' then strode off into the night to carry on Jihad. Mama Chiva pulled me to the river. Black it was, ice cold, strong-currented. She held my Betty as she pushed me in. She let me float until the cold circles flowing round me calmed me. While I was carrying on this way, then putting on my one change of garments with Mama Chiva's help, my husband sent Afebwa toward Brighton House and Cudjoe speeding toward St. Lucy's. You know that Cudjoe was found face down in the slough, with not a penny on him. But Afebwa was picked up outside Brighton, cornered by a pack of hunting hounds, no pass upon her. She did not spill. Ah no, the one I did not know was my own courageous sister till it was too late—she said not a word. It was someone there who recognized her, stripped her down, and found two cold bright pistols in her loin covering, that sounded the militia cry. If she'd been carrying a pass, who knows? Who knows . . . ?

"It took the militia a longer time than usual to arrive from Bridgetown. The road had been successfully blocked by the sideways cart and murdered horses of our overseer Rigley. Meanwhile, back at Glebe, they ran with pitch torches streaking the black night to the houses of the overseers. And as you know, sir, Jack Vaughton never lived to see the dawn."

The smells of crisping fish compete with the prisoner's odor. The noon sun is thin and white. In the garden the fruit trees hunch, wilted and pale. But Coote hears the slaves scraping chairs into position. There will be a luncheon on the verandah for the Governor.

Suddenly, with a grunt of pure disgust, the masked dignitary stands up from his chair. He says no word, but flicks his hand impatiently at the prisoner. Holding the protective mask a bit away from his face with a liver-spotted hand, he murmurs to Coote in passing, "What a tiresome morning! Too little, too late. Dispose of this, *demain*." Lucy, who stands grilling fish as he enters the swept garden, sees a haggard ghoul slumped inside the clothing of a bonny pink-cheeked prince. She flips a brown-crusted fillet with a long fork.

VII

He lies pressed face first into the pillow, aware of spittle pooled beneath the corner of his mouth as Lucy wakes him. "Suh," she says as neutrally as if she spoke the words "floor" or "dish," then waits, hands cupping each elbow folded across her waist as he settles his focus on her. How many times has she spoken before he woke? How many minutes stood there in the darkened doorway looking at the thin balding hair without its powdered demi-wig, his nightshirt rutched and twisted over thin thighs bitten red by the mosquitoes whining all around? In his cups he has forgotten to lower the fine netting over his couch. He can smell himself. "Suh," she speaks again, "suh," as flat and regular as the ticking of the clock on the mantle in his mother's small reception room on rainy afternoons when . . .

"What it it?" he asks, growling the phlegm away and clutching at the oversheet.

"The pris'nuh in her chair."

"What? I did not call her . . ."

"Cot Quashey waitin'."

"The damnable cheek . . . !"

But he enters the interrogation room dressed to the surcoat. The silver buttons on his waistcoat gleam as in a painting of Dutch burghers. The old slavewoman polished them most carefully before

his dinner with the Governor. He will have them cut off and transferred to a new waistcoat, perhaps a ruby brocade lined with silver
sateen. His mood brinks between peevish and mildly harassed.
What does the old cow want with him? There is no point to further
questioning. Colonel Stede has spoken: "Dispose of her" upon the
morrow. During their excellent luncheon in the garden it was as if
she never had existed; or had been a low mist pierced and burned
entirely away by the ruling of the sun. Nothing. She is nothing.
Not even worth discussing.

The Governor had been delightful, chatting about this episode
from his past, that ball, a fine tailor about to come out from England, an opportunity to invest in an import operation shipping
barreled herring from the northern colonies. When Peter expressed
a tentative enthusiasm on behalf of his merchant group in Bristol,
the Governor, who was dabbing at his lip with a fine lawn lace-
edged handkerchief, moved the handkerchief to Peter's frowsy cuff.
Continuing the daubing motion, he smiled. "Well yes, but you're
here and they're there, and what they do not know . . ." A warm
glow had suffused Peter Coote's chest at this camaraderie.

There had been a fine torte made with island oranges, and the
Governor's gift of butter kegged in Ulster had still been sweet as
the grass the Irish cows munched up with blunt patient teeth. The
old slave Daniel had come forward time and time again with a
pitcher of punch made of cool well water, fresh mint leaves crushed
to paste with sugar, and the finest amber rum. But now . . . now his
tongue lies thick, his feet squeeze swollen into cracked black leather
pumps . . .

"What do you want with me?" he demands.

Before him sits the perspiring prisoner, Cot Daley, Cot Quashey,
the disposable one, the waste/the wasted. The shutters are closed as
they were left when the morning interrogation was dismissed. Only
a thin lip of light plays from the ceiling to the windowsill, for they
have not been latched. In the dark, then, the shape of the Irish-

woman. Behind him he can feel Lucy standing. He himself stands impatiently beside his desk. *"What?"*

There comes no spoken reply. Lucy, who sometimes sings and hums, is silent as well. He feels wrapped, smothered, caught inside their silence.

"Biddy," he coaxes. "You are not well. You have been given the afternoon to rest, rest is often the only cure for an infection once washes and tinctures have failed."

From the sepia lump that is the prisoner a wavery voice begins to speak. "I am Cot Quashey, born Cot Daley in the city of Galway in the nation of Eirean around the year 16 and 40; and my tale must be full told."

"What is the point . . ."

"It was in '75 when my husband, Quaco Quashey, led, with his brother and sister Coromantees of the island *umma*, plus many stragglers from nations like mine and your own, sir, a great uprising."

"A failed uprising!"

". . . Failed," she seems to echo. At the end of her completed testimony he fills in the words he misses now, before he concedes and sits, in weary desperation, curiosity, pique, ambition, to record her tale one final time.

"They failed only at the moment. But first the sun had to fail to rise another day. An imposter, that is what mounted in the sky. I stayed there in the corn shed with my child, the workmen calling and thumping in their thatching work above. I hid inside their noise, then when they too ran with torches to the overseers' houses I hid behind the piled sacks with Betty to my heart. I came out only when the militia galloped into the yard, swords slashing. When, at the end, they had rounded those of us remaining into the drive that circled the portico of the big house and reviewed us, they counted us the loyal ones. The ones not to be punished, but to be rewarded like pet dogs with a dry corner, no kick, a bone. But oh, the torment in my head. For Quashey, Jiba, Cudjoe, Mama Chiva, many others . . . they were gone. Before us the militia dragged, in chains, a dozen beaten men whom they would march to Bridgetown. And the pale ratty Lieutenant, wielding his musket like a scourge, shouted how Afebwa and others they had passed down the line were waiting to be tied onto Glebe's criminal coffle.

"I knew him to be dead. But it was as if my dear son Ben were there, running ghostly up and down crying out 'Abu! Pappy!' and I grew faint with guilt and shame that I had not protected his father, or at least stuck with him and the others who had finally accepted me, me and Betty. At that time I was certain that they all were dead. But as you know, as I myself learned later, Quashey had taken those I named upon the sloop, and like Noah was sailing through deep waters, with the plan to pick up members of the *umma* who had revolted in the northern parishes, that they might head across the channel to that island. That place which they call Montserrat, under Our Lady's protection; peopled by Muslims and rebels from Eirean and Brazil and who knows where? All marooned together. With powdered lords like ye, sir, to try to hold them all in check."

"My records show that Quashey was picked up with these others at Cuckhold's Bay, while taking on more traitors," sighs Peter Coote as he flips the split tail of his surcoat up, scrapes his chair back, and finally sits down.

"Yes. That is as far to freedom as they got in mortal life. Never did I see his face again, or Chiva smiling at me with her ivory man o' war grin. Jiba they never took, for she dived overboard to Guinea; and for years I, drowning in remorse, felt that is what I best had done in '51, from the deck of the *Falconer*. But I have come to feel different, and I will tell you why, sir."

Coote keeps dunking his plume, then scraping and blotting it as he stares toward her shape. The entire front of her is in shadow. The direction of her eyes cannot be seen, though the bright filament of afternoon which leaks through the unlatched shutters casts a ruddy nimbus over the graduated mound of her shawled head and slumping shoulders.

"He was not executed until '76, after that great folderol of fear meant to bring all bondsfolk to their knees forever in Barbados, and to clear the conscience of Christian folk of any doubts about the need for harshest cruelty on the plantations. They dragged him here and there as an example, before . . . But I felt my Quashey's death that morning, when the militia stood us on the steps of the Glebe and shouted in our faces with threats and questions. I tell you, the land itself expressed some great and solemn shift. For there was a hollow silence under everything. In spite of threats and weaponry, the clanking of the slaves' chains as they began to shuffle down the road, the barked orders of the soldiers left in charge to restore order until fresh overseers could be appointed, Rigley scrambling in panic from the jungle where he'd run when his cart was overtaken . . . in spite of all this commotion, a finished silence underlay all. A pallor one could hear, a very . . . abandonment . . . of life from its center; a center which is the focused and unnoticed core that holds together that which is still pulsing. Why can I still not say this? It was as if the stones and grasses, the buildings and the waving trees; as if everything under the sun lay in an empty vault, calm only because life itself had been extinguished. The last breath of something burning with life's orange flame had been exhaled. Further . . . further . . . losing shape, then visibility . . . spreading out smaller than dust motes toward the cold cold stars."

The prisoner relates that she'd not been compelled to attend the final executions in Bridgetown; nor had she been to town during the months when the heads of Chiva, Quashey, Afebwa, Cudjoe, and their band hung along the town wall on iron spikes. Yes, she knew that six were beheaded, eleven hanged, many others burned at stake. She had remained at the Glebe raising her daughter Betty until New Year's, 1680, when her indenture had at last been up. But at the end, because the child was chattel of Lord Cleypole for life (the father having been an African), the Irishwoman had not wished to leave. Had pleaded to stay, a paid servant on the place, to remain with her daughter.

Permission had been refused. Her own record, as well as the record of the Irish as troublemakers in general, had gone against her, in spite of the fact that she knew sewing and harness making as well as sugarhouse and fieldwork. She was ejected twice from hiding places in the woods nearby. Flogged the second time she was captured, though only eight stripes, then driven from the parish by two redshanked militia with gleaming bayonets.

She became a huckster in the parish of St. George. "And," she tells Coote defiantly, "I began my trade with three clay pots of rum, stolen by the slaves of Glebe, for which I smuggled them a wild piglet. The piglet was for a ceremony of Bantu bondsfolk from a land where I hear tell there are elephants and tigers; these folk eat bacon, while Quashey and the *umma* sort of folk do not. Perhaps you know that wild pig runs as freely through the hills here as it does on Ben Bulben. The Portuguese it was who brought the hogs, before the British came. But something that they saw here, felt here, when the last people of the middens were still packing their canoes and rowing off, made them sail away, never to return. The Portuguese were in a hurry. They did not collect their swine. At any rate, I kept one pot of poteen for myself. I drank it for the pain, you see, at night when the market was over and the hell of loneliness tormented me."

"Which slaves would those be, biddy? The Bantu thieves? Name them!" Coote commands, pulling a new page toward himself.

"Ah, gone and buried now. So soon gone and buried. Disremembered. I made mats too, and once I got some coin to clink together in my pocket, I began to be the middle-wench. Cheating everybody, you might say. Or helping everybody, from the other point of view."

"Where was your domicile?"

"I who had been put out upon the ground was familiar with the ground, sir. I could post some poles and spread mat walls and a brush floor in a few hours, wherever I needed to be for the trade. I made my food, I took my drink, I early got hold of a dagger which I strapped to my waist, as those who tried to rob a drunken harpy in her stupor soon found out. I shifted here and there . . ."

Coote rubs his head, impatient, then demands cool water from Lucy, who stands behind him still. "What I want to know is how came you from St. John's to St. George's, then from there to St. Lucy's Parish, where you were apprehended by the troops."

"I wandered everywhere," she tells. "Awake, I crossed this island with my feet. But in a sort of dreaming, I also rambled back to Ireland. Or Montserrat. Then it might be Guinea, and I was in the place where he had come from. Quashey. Except that darling Mama Chiva was there with him. And little Ben. Afebwa too. I would come upon them in a pleasant village, going about their chores, my son walking at his father's heel or tugging at his elbow to show him aught. There were many huts, like up on Slave Hill, and the people spoke a foreign tongue; but when I came among them I was welcome. Not like at a reunion, mind, but like a person who has never been away and whose welcome is taken for granted. I mean that no one made a fuss of me, nor did my husband speak my name or greet me: but the friendliness that sparked within his eyes when he gazed in peace on me before returning to his task! I was loath to leave this family: to spread a mat, unroll my wares, begin the oily bartering of goods.

"Yes, I lived everywhere. In this world, and in a better world, and in the world where their second souls have gone. Happy. Happy were they, including that brave and humble queen Afebwa, who now indeed must watch my darling Ben until I join him once again. If only I can find the canoe they left for me . . .

"And in the marketplace, where I earned what kept me crawling around in this flesh, I heard many things. We are a great gaggle of races at the market, sir. All those who'd signed on from the European islands for seven years, with promise of free land at the end of it—there has been no land for them. But you'd know that. Though some say there's still land being passed to and fro among the wily: enough to make hearts quicken and keep false hopes, like paper notes, in circulation . . . And so the voluntary indentured, freed, found themselves homeless: selling fish, selling stolen forks and blue ribands and filched medicaments to keep their bellies full.

"Then there were others, like myself here, who had not enlisted, but were stolen away, to be put out into destitution. Refused paid service, left to shift or starve in our mock freedom. Many other market folk, however, were the children of those lonely-hearted planters and merchants of Bridgetown: those who had made by-blow increase with African girls—girls of beauty, girls of grace, girls you can feel a kind of royalty rising from, sir, like our Lucy there. These—the largest clan at market—were freed mixed-blooded blacks, or mixed-blooded whites. Many of these see themselves the true heirs of this island. And everyone knew who I was—that I belonged to Quashey's clan here in Barbados. So they reckoned there was a place for me too at that inheritance. So they said."

"Who? Give me names," he almost entreats.

"Arra, how would I know, an old sot like myself, wandering from marketplace to marketplace and sleeping under bushes? It was the story, not the teller, that concerned me. Then, about two years ago, among this polyglot of races, I began to hear tales of the rising of '75. They were talking about things I had not seen: things I'd cowered in a shed with my girl Betty to keep from crediting. They spoke of fires, spread by the after-winds of a hurricane; of angry spirits rising up; of cattle and horses let loose from barns, eyes rolling yellow in the glint of flame as they ran free. They spoke about a slave girl, Phoebe, who ran through the forest with an arsenal tucked beneath her petticoat, and how her panting can still be heard in the woods between the capital and Brighton plantation, as she runs, runs, runs, relaying us to freedom. These murmured rumors stirred my soul to put down the rum jar and take out for the crossroads, looking—well, they spoke, sir, of places up the country by the coast where even in broad daylight there appeared the leader . . .

"Some said they saw him, tattooed bracelets on his arms as he plunged from forest into water, or from strand to bush. But others saw nothing. The thing was, they all heard, sir. They heard a sort of hum or buzzing, but in patches like, so no tune could be discerned. It was not a clear song, not even notes to cobble together. But it was Quashey's, of that I am certain. His eyes and thoughts are loose still, or loose again, still on the Jihad for freedom. His body's bones were thrown in a zigzag heap after they stuck his head upon a spike. But his spirit—can you imagine it, how one morning with the sun it lifted like humble steam from the deserted corpus, ascending, rising up for freedom?"

Coote speaks, his tone inflexible as metal: "Woman. Will you tell me once and for all how and why you came to transport weapons for the traitors we have hanged?"

"I will," says she, simply. Coote finds his writing hand begin to shake.

"A year ago I received word at the market that wee Betty had been sold away to a ship's captain, trading in tobacco. Like my Moya, Betty was taken to be reared for some officer's concubine. Things are heating up, sir, is what I hear. All throughout the colonies, they say, there are objections on the part of bondspeople of every sort. The more objections, the more officers required, is what they say. The more officers away from their powdered wives and pampered children, the more of our own lively young they look for to wind in satin and lay on beds under damask canopies, where spiders nest all winter long, and birds fly through the open casements to eat them up come summer. My husband's last words to me told me how to do my part. 'Heaven lies under a mother's feet,' he said.

"Aye, I know 'twill be long after my own Betty's teeth have fallen from growing her own young—for that's the fate of women, sir—before enough objections will rise up to make a wall of sound. Still. The more I sat at the market among those whisperings and whimpers, jokes and taunts, complaints and blame, hatred and scandal, apparitions and histories and plans, the more I weaned myself off of the rum. Because I began to hear patterns—no, a patchwork—not of meaning so much as surges of feelings, callings, desires, that make up our lives. Patchwork patterns of a freedom I, and perhaps you, have never known."

"What are you on about?" Coote sputters sternly.

"Freedom *to* and freedom *from*, sir. Freedom *from* being another person's thing to gain the sour rations of survival, rather than rising up to our full statures and filling them, every inch, scab, gland, and hair. This is the freedom Quashey and them died living, in his Jihad." Coote sees the sweat run down her skinny neck: she raves. "Bishop's in thrall to Archbishop, Duke to his King . . ."

He averts his eyes. She is very ill. Her mind is rambling the darkest tunnels where the human mind ought never go.

"Biddy . . . madam . . . this is not necessary . . ."

But she continues, panting.

"I wandered and wandered, listening with younger ears, as if I had the ears of Moya and of Betty, my living daughters, who in a better time would have shared hearth and understanding with their Mam. I listened to the sweat of people who from pot gang to field accident to a cold pallet were valued slightly above beasts only because they could hold the instruments of harvest between their fingers and obey complex instructions, while beasts could not. I saw people lulled, like myself, into sullen confusion by a few jars of rum, a bright bit of clothing, a promise not to sell their best-loved kinfolk away. And I saw people who'd been refused all of these, as punishment."

"Who? Who did you carry the guns for?" A curl of warm wind blows the stink of her toward him. He is shouting.

In a bell-like voice she answers, "Paudi Iasc."

"You idiot!" he grates. "Stop your rambling and make some sense. I don't want the name of some redshank clapped into the Arlington stocks thirty years ago! Tell me who you carried those bloody guns from and to!"

A definite pride rings from her voice. "I have told you. 'Twas Paudi Iasc himself. Returning that silky morning in his log boat, the Maroon told the one he called Bat Fish about the wife of Quaco, a woman who had his same 'fish-colored' hair. And one day, even before the leaders of the Jihad were executed, a message came to me. From the headlands of St. Lucy, the parish across the waters to Montserrat—to Bridgetown, where they were taken from me, I carried what arms and maps I could. First a black man was my connection, then an old granny; but the last sir, was one like yourself."

"English!"

"No, sir, or yes, but when I say like yourself, I mean a gentleman, sir. The sort you'd think would be happy with the way Barbados is run as is. But who can say? There are those here who are greedy, sir. Then again there are those born with the spleen of conscience and a heart for brotherhood, no matter what their class. The Quakers up in St. Lucy are like that. I met some. They seem to stand fair and tall, though they could stand like silk-swathed puppets. Others do . . . In the end, sir, I think there are two kinds of folk. People who look up, wanting to see themselves in their high-placed betters; and people who find the best of themselves upon the midden of the humble poor."

There's a pause; she is seeking something through scarves of fever.

"If you've the strength to philosophize, biddy, you've the strength to tell me: Where can we find Paud Iasc? Tell me, and I swear it shall go easier with you . . ."

"Freedom *from*. And freedom *to* follow the cold milling stars in new directions, or to lose the self in the red moon of the hearth, a child's life burning like a small safe flame in the next room . . ."

A knock sounds tentatively upon the outer door. Then another. "Lucy. Answer that," says Peter Coote.

She complies. She returns, leading the wiry Scots lad the Governor sent those several weeks ago with a parchment inviting Peter Coote to become his man at Speightstown Gaol. The door, held open to admit the youth, admits as well the purpled weal of evening. On the freshening breeze comes a faint sound like small fine bones, clacking together, as if chimes were hanging in a tree in the fruit garden.

Eyes on the ground, the lad calls loudly, "Sir. The Gov'nor has sent me."

Coote holds forth his hand expectantly, but there is no scroll.

"His Excellency's spoken with the widow, sir. Them shirts ye ordered. They been paid for by the Gov'nor. You need only fetch them first thing in the morning . . ."

Another fragile gust of sound, as if strung shells were blowing backward, inhaled into one another. "Another way," the prisoner mumbles, "to see it is that they're all our ancestors. Quashey had his own, and I have mine, you with your family crest and this lad from the crofts, those who piled up the midden on the St. John's River—of course everybody comes from his own clan. But in some other way, all the ancestors are ours, and we are theirs—they pick us out and call on us. Yes, if you asked me why I carried pistols in with my papayas, 'tis because Afebwa is as much my ancestor as any Daley. And I have come to know that I too will become everyone's ancestor. So I must choose the right road for the progeny I've mothered: I have chosen where to set my mother's-feet. That this inverted paradise, sir, might become someday that garden-heaven, where people are at peace and plenty. Free, to discover their very destinies."

Rising, Peter Coote says, "Thank His Excellence for me," and searches for a small coin.

But in his rote and piping voice the young man goes on, "You are to come for tea upriver at the mansion once you've got the shirts, says the Gov'nor, sir. After you have disposed of the old project. There is a new matter for you to start upon, says he. That is all, sir." The lad ducks back through the door into the dusk. Bare feet slap down the road. The tinkling has stopped.

"Lucy, get the prisoner out of here. Make her a posset, get her an extra covering. The night is cool, and in her fever she has lost her senses. But I . . . I am *done* with her."

In the garden the stiff young fruit trees spread their blanket of lacy shadow. Shutting the door after the messenger sucks the last mote of light from the office. "Send Daniel. I need a lamp," says the Apothecary. When one comes he will take down the journal where his mercantile hypothesis rests, and write the confused and disillusioned computations this investigation has led him to. Eventually he will grow tangled, melancholy, frustrated. He will never consider changing the hypothesis.

EPILOGUE

He sees them, though he makes as if he hasn't. They are parallel to each other, the rowboat still tied to the pier, and Peter Coote, as he sets out down the walkway from his lodgings to fetch the crisp new linen shirts. Questioning is over. What a fine fresh day! Free of darkened corners, rotten smells, tainting tales, the solemn discipline of duty; a duty the Governor is rewarding as well done! In the pocket of his surcoat he fingers the sketch he's made for a new ruby suit of clothes. The widow can take measurements, at any rate. Perhaps the Governor will know a source for ordering the sort of fabric he envisions. Keeping his head down, smiling as much as public dignity allows on this fine morning, Coote notes the dog-daisies popping up along the edges of his path. He floats a glance discretely to the side.

They have already handed her into the boat; Lucy, Daniel, the old black woman who's gone frail but is a superb cook. Cot Quashey stands patiently, hunched beneath her great black shawl. The jovial boatswain is settling her on a plank across the stern. He wears no black mask this morning; but the six fingers on each hand as he draws the prisoner down are the fingers of the Bridgetown executioner. He who whipped the prisoner only weeks before, while Coote stood by fastidiously, waiting to claim her once she had fainted in the straw.

Of course the prisoner has recognized the executioner too. She knows that she will never see Jamaica's shores or carry on her huckstering for a few more years. Coote pulls his eyes ahead, placing each newly polished slipper carefully, to avoid the feces of dogs and pigs and humans along the path. He does not see the old couple bending to place calabashes in the slow bilge at the prisoner's feet. The sea winks and sloshes a pure Prussian blue against red wooden planks. Now Lucy hands down a white clay pipe—a *duidín*—into the prisoner's lap. If any words are exchanged, they're soft enough for the calm roll of the sea to wash them all away. Coote only hears the oars squeak in their locks, then their groan and splash as the lethal boatsman rows the vessel forward, away from the three Africans standing silent on the pier.

Several minutes later, just after he has raised his hat in greeting to the deacon of All Saints Church, he hears an amateurish piping. Thin; sour; rusty. His head swivels round in curiosity and disconcerted apprehension.

All the gold and blue of the morning rests on Lucy; kisses the fruity roundness of her cheeks, outlines her turbaned head, halos her kerchiefed shoulders and her high posterior as she follows the old and withered couple along the quay, blowing life's fragile breath into a dented rusty Irish whistle. Lucy, who after the old bachelor Coote's death at his small plantation, The Downs, at the turn of the next century, will take the hidden/forgotten bundle of a manuscript from its mouldy leather wrappings at the bottom of a broken trunk and pass it to his only son, who is also her own. This son, a freedman from the age of twenty-one, will make enquiries. Until he finds where Betty has been sold in the northern colonies. Rather, he finds her owner. He has to wait twenty-three months, but finally, per his mother's wishes, is put in touch with a low deckhand to whom he pays a stolen ring from the house of Coote. He sends the testimony. And he hears God laughing. But that's another tale: a tale not recorded here.

AFTERWORD

The majority of indentured Irish brought to Barbados between 1630 and 1660 received no contract, but were sold upon the open market. Indentured labor was cheaper than slave labor, hence adoption of the former. In January 1637, fifty-six servants from the ship *Abraham* were sold on the open market at destination's end for £7 per head. But during Cromwell's heyday until the mid-1650s, Irish were sold to merchant captains for as low as £3–£5 per head, plus feeding for the voyage. However, by the mid-'60s prices had increased to £10–£14 per head. By 1690, the average price on the open market for an indentured servant from Europe had reached £18. Slave labor became cheaper. By 1660, a typical African slave was going for £23 for *life* (rather than 7–10 years), while any offspring born to an African belonged to its "master" in perpetuity.

Thus economics played a large role in the switchover from Irish indentured labor on Barbados, to African slavery. But there was another reason. By 1640 Scots had begun to be favored over Irish as indentured Euro-labor. The Scot was considered industrious and biddable—not subversive or seditious, as was the Irishman or Irishwoman. (Perhaps the most famous example of a recalcitrant Irishman in bondage is that of Cornelius Bryan, who was flogged 120 strokes in January 1656 for stating, as he ate meat from a tray, that "if there was so much English blood in the tray as there was meat he would [also] eat it.") By 1660 Scots in Barbados were typically brought in for shorter indentures of four to six years. And by 1690, *only* indentured Scots were to be hired by plantations as militiamen. To serve as militia was a coveted job, for indentured servants were granted remission of half their remaining service time if they fought "manfully" against "the enemy" (rebels and Maroons).

The story of Cot Daley spins itself out of a historic happening: the islandwide Coromantee revolt of 1675. In spite of increasing the militia, another "uprising of slaves in conjunction with white servants was foiled" in 1686. In that year, Governor Stede informed his Parliament that Creole slaves and some of the "Irish nation" had aligned against English interests. Still, another mixed revolt was exposed in 1688, when Bajan parliamentarians passed the "Act for the Good Governing of Negros." This Act also left the Irish on the island entirely disarmed. Yet in spite of executions, legal action, and overturned coups, in 1692 another foiled slave revolt took place in St. Michael's Parish.

While Irish people ceased to be forcibly imported to the sugar islands in favor of their African cousins, their descendants, the "redshanks," help form the poorest stratum of society in Barbados to this day.

NOTES TO THE PREFACE

1. Hillary Beckles, *White Servitude and Black Slavery in Barbados, 1627–1715* (Knoxville: University of Tennessee Press, 1989), p. 38.
2. Peter Beresford Ellis, *Hell or Connaught* (New York: St. Martin's Press, 1975), pp. 153–54.
3. Ibid., p. 149.
4. Beckles, *White Servitude*, p. 71.
5. J. S. Hander, *The Unappropriated People* (Baltimore: Johns Hopkins Press, 1974), p. 203.
6. Beckles, *White Servitude*, p. 71.
7. Hillary Beckles, *A History of Barbados* (Cambridge: Cambridge University Press, 1990).
8. Ellis, *Hell or Connaught*, p. 161.
9. Ibid., p. 151.
10. Beckles, *White Servitude*, p. 71.

GLOSSARY

arra: an Irish interjection, like "well . . . ," that introduces an idea

aught: something/nothing

boherin: a small rural road (lit. "cow path")

bonham: an infant pig

brack: a bread/cake with raisins or currants in it

by-blow: a child resulting from casual sexual relations

chimbley pot: vernacular pronunciation of chimney pot in rural areas

coffle: a caravan of slaves, usually manacled together

commonage: a shared agricultural area in Ireland

dast: a country form of "dare"

drohuil: the evil eye, a curse that results from admiration or envy

duidín: traditional white-clay Irish peasant pipe

foolscap: writing paper used in seventeenth-century England

gewgaw: a bright, glittering treasure in the knickknack realm

glowworm: lightning bug

gob: mouth, throat

hibber-jibber: babbling hyperactivity, madly disorganized

High Brazil: an island said to be visible from the West coast of Kerry on the clearest of days: the island St. Brendan went in search of

hog's meat: what swine eat (including grasses, plants, grubs, as well as slop) in Barbados

hoorson: a curse: son of a whore

housheen: a little cottage or cabin

iasc: fish

Jihad: Holy War, whether internal or external, through the word or the sword

kine: cattle

loblolly: West Indian slave rations of boiled cornmeal

lus-more: a field herb, related to mullein

Mam: the Irish vernacular for one's mother: Mom/Mama

navvies: sailors

nuss: vernacular for nursing a child

og: young

olagon: the wailing tradition of Irishwomen, after a death

oncet: Irish vernacular for "once"

ould: Irish vernacular for "old"

phuca/puca: a ghost

poteen: traditional Irish homebrew

redshanks: European-Barbajians, so called due to the effect of the sun on their skin

Samhain: the late autumn day of the dead, All Souls' Day

Sassenach: Irish word for the British

Sí/siogue: the fey people; the ancient inhabitants of Ireland who now live in the earth, the old forts, and the mountains

smallclothes: undergarments

spailpin: a wandering farm laborer

tawhid: an Islamic community

Tir na nOg: "Land of the forever young"; home of the sí, where life is beautiful and happy forever

trepan: to procure slaves through ensnarement or entrapment, for example, by the clandestine administering of drugs or alcohol, or by sexual seduction

umma: the brother- and sisterhood of all who are practicing Muslims

wee'n: North West/North Irish word for a child, like Scots "bairn"

Zhenna: the Muslim heaven, the beautiful garden from which Adam and Eve were expelled